*Truth may seem, but cannot be:*
*Beauty brag, but 'tis not she;*
*Truth and beauty buried be.*

*To this urn let those repair*
*That are either true or fair;*
*For these dead birds sigh a prayer.*

***Bacon***

Never had an eclipse produced such a wonderful display of optical instruments.

*Frontispiece*

THE

# CLIPPER OF THE CLOUDS

BY

JULES VERNE

AUTHOR OF "THE LOTTERY TICKET," "FIVE WEEKS IN A BALLOON," "ROUND THE WORLD IN EIGHTY DAYS," ETC., ETC.

ILLUSTRATED

London

SAMPSON LOW, MARSTON, SEARLE, & RIVINGTON

St. Dunstan's House

FETTER LANE, FLEET STREET, E.C.

1887

# CONTENTS.


CHAPTER I.

PAGE

Mysterious sounds . . . . . . . . . . . . 1

CHAPTER II.

Agreement impossible . . . . . . . . . . . 13

CHAPTER III.

A visitor is announced . . . . . . . . . . . 20

CHAPTER IV.

In which a new character appears . . . . . . . 27

CHAPTER V.

Another disappearance . . . . . . . . . . . 39

CHAPTER VI.

The president and secretary suspend hostilities . . . . . 48

CHAPTER VII.

On board the Albatross . . . . . . . . . . 60

CHAPTER VIII.

The balloonists refuse to be convinced . . . . . . 71

CHAPTER IX.

Across the prairie . . . . . . . . . . . . 83

CHAPTER X.

Westward—but whither? . . . . . . . . . . 90

CHAPTER XI.

The wide Pacific . . . . . . . . . . . . 98

CHAPTER XII.

PAGE

Through the Himalayas . . . . . . . . . . 109

CHAPTER XIII.

Over the Caspian . . . . . . . . . . . 116

CHAPTER XIV.

The aeronef at full speed . . . . . . . . . 131

CHAPTER XV.

A skirmish in Dahomey . . . . . . . . . 141

CHAPTER XVI.

Over the Atlantic . . . . . . . . . . . 157

CHAPTER XVII.

The shipwrecked crew . . . . . . . . . . 169

CHAPTER XVIII.

Over the volcano . . . . . . . . . . . 176

CHAPTER XIX.

Anchored at last . . . . . . . . . . . 187

CHAPTER XX.

The wreck of the Albatross . . . . . . . . 200

CHAPTER XXI.

The Institute again . . . . . . . . . . 208

CHAPTER XXII.

The Goahead is launched . . . . . . . . . 220

CHAPTER XXIII.

The grand collapse . . . . . . . . . . 228

# LIST OF ILLUSTRATIONS.

PAGE

Never had an eclipse produced such a wonderful display of optical instruments . . . . . . . *Frontispiece*
Both of them were old enough to know better . . . . . 1
The meeting was much embarrassed . . . . . . . 18
The third, which ended in a frightful fall . . . . . . 23
"My name is Robur" . . . . . . . . . . 27
"You are not Americans" . . . . . . . . . 38
They had reached the centre of a wide clump of trees . . 44
They were carried off across the clearing . . . . . . 46
"It is unbreakable glass" . . . . . . . . . 58
And what did they see? . . . . . . . . . . 59
The Clipper of the Clouds . . . . . . . . . 64
Above the deck rose thirty-seven vertical axes . . . . . 66
A meal would commit them to nothing . . . . . . 74
Tom Turner . . . . . . . . . . . . 76
The Falls of Niagara . . . . . . . . . . 81
It was really extraordinary . . . . . . . . . 94
It was a train on the Pacific Railway . . . . . . . 95
With a blow of the hatchet the mate severed the line . . . . 104
"This town is Tokio, the capital of Japan" . . . . . 108
Avoiding the Lung Mountains . . . . . . . . 112
Gliding like a ship between enormous reefs . . . . . . 113
They tried to throw off those who held them . . . . . 118
An hour's work sufficed to fill up the larders . . . . . 125

PAGE

Frycollin, of course, had a bath . . . . . . . . . 130
Away from the others . . . . . . . . . . . 138
The lamps of the Albatross were turned on . . . . . . 138
Flocks of elephants and buffaloes . . . . . . . 149
The little gun shot forth its shrapnel . . . . . . . 155
Exploded like so many small shells . . . . . . . 156
A volcanic eruption had projected this cloud into the air . . 160
Enveloped in the eddy of an enormous waterspout . . . 162
Here was work for the cook . . . . . . . . . 168
"Who are you?" . . . . . . . . . . . . 174
While they were busy in the bow . . . . . . . . 191
Uncle Prudent lighted the end . . . . . . . . 196
"Down you go" . . . . . . . . . . . . 198
In a few seconds the cable was cut . . . . . . . 199
The Albatross dropped into the abyss . . . . . . . 207
The grass looked to be pressed down . . . . . . . 210
They worshipped them, we ought rather to say . . . . . 217
Let go!" shouted Uncle Prudent . . . . . . . 224
He was going to save her crew . . . . . . . . 232

Both of them were old enough to know better.

# THE CLIPPER OF THE CLOUDS.

## CHAPTER I.

### MYSTERIOUS SOUNDS.

"BANG! Bang!"

The pistol-shots were almost simultaneous. A cow peacefully grazing fifty yards away received one of the bullets in her back. She had nothing to do with the quarrel all the same.

Neither of the adversaries was hit.

Who were these two gentlemen? We do not know, although this would be an excellent opportunity to hand down their names to posterity. All we can say is that the elder was an Englishman and the younger an American, and both of them were old enough to know better.

So far as recording in what locality the inoffensive ruminant had just tasted her last tuft of herbage, nothing can be easier. It was on the left bank of the Niagara, not far from the suspension bridge which joins the American to the Canadian bank three miles from the falls.

The Englishman stepped up to the American.

"I contend, nevertheless, that it was 'Rule Britannia!'"

"And I say it was 'Yankee Doodle!'" replied the other.

The dispute was about to begin again when one of the seconds—doubtless in the interests of the milk trade—interposed.

"Suppose we say it was 'Rule Doodle' and 'Yankee Britannia,' and adjourn to breakfast?"

This compromise between the national airs of Great Britain and the United States was adopted to the general satisfaction. The Americans and Englishmen walked up the left bank of the Niagara on their way to Goat Island, the neutral ground between the falls. Let us leave them in the presence of the boiled eggs and traditional ham, and floods enough of tea to make the cataract jealous, and trouble ourselves no more about them. It is extremely unlikely that we shall again meet with them in this story.

Which was right; the Englishman or the American? It is not easy to say. Anyhow the duel shows how great was the excitement, not only in the new but also in the old world, with regard to an inexplicable phenomenon which for a month or more had driven everybody to distraction.

Never had the sky been so much looked at since the appearance of man on the terrestrial globe. The night before an aërial trumpet had blared its brazen notes through space immediately over that part of Canada between Lake Ontario and Lake Erie. Some people had heard those notes as "Yankee Doodle," others had heard them as "Rule Britannia," and hence the quarrel between the Anglo-Saxons, which ended with the breakfast on Goat Island. Perhaps it was neither one nor the other of these patriotic tunes, but what was undoubted by all was that these extraordinary sounds had seemed to descend from the sky to the earth.

What could it be? Was it some exuberant aeronaut rejoicing on that sonorous instrument of which the Renommée makes such obstreperous use?

No! There was no balloon and there were no aeronauts. Some strange phenomenon had occurred in the higher zones of the atmosphere, a phenomenon of which neither the nature nor the cause could be explained. To-day it appeared over America; forty-eight hours afterwards it was over Europe; a week later it was in Asia over the Celestial Empire.

Hence in every country of the world—empire, kingdom, or republic—there was anxiety which it was important to allay. If you hear in your house strange and inexplicable noises, do you not at once endeavour to discover the cause? And if your search is in vain, do you not leave your house and take up your quarters in another? Yes, of course you do! But in this case the house was the terrestrial globe! There are no means of leaving that house for the moon, or Mars, or Venus, or Jupiter, or any other planet of the solar system. And so of necessity we have to find out what it is that takes place, not in the infinite void, but within the atmospherical zones. In fact, if there is no air there is no noise, and as there was a noise—that famous trumpet to wit—the phenomenon must occur in the air, the density of which invariably diminishes, and which does not extend for more than six miles around our spheroid.

Naturally the newspapers took up the question in their thousands, and treated it in every form, throwing on it both light and darkness, recording many things about it true or false, alarming and tranquillizing their readers—as the sale required—and almost driving ordinary people mad. At one blow party politics dropped unheeded—and the affairs of the world went on none the worse for it.

But what could this thing be?

There was not an observatory that was not applied to. If an observatory could not give a satisfactory answer, what was the use of observatories? If astronomers, who doubled and tripled the stars a hundred thousand million miles away, could not explain a phenomenon occurring only a few miles off, what was the use of astronomers?

How many eye-glasses, spectacles, field-glasses, sea-glasses, binoculars, monoculars, reflectors and refractors were pointed at the sky during the clear summer nights it would be impossible to say. There were hundreds of thousands of them at the least. Ten times, twenty times as many as the stars that can be seen by the naked eye on the celestial sphere. Never had an eclipse, observed simultaneously over half the globe, produced such a wonderful display of optical instruments.

The observatories gave their answers, but the answers were very unsatisfactory. Each offered an opinion, but each opinion differed from the others, and therefore during the last weeks of April and the early weeks of May, there arose an intestine war in the scientific world.

The observatory at Paris was very guarded in what it said. In the mathematical section they had not thought the statement worth noticing; in the meridional section they knew nothing about it; in the physical observatory they had not come across it; in the geodetic section they had had no observation; in the meteorological section there had been no record; in the calculating-room they had had nothing to deal with. At any rate this confession was a frank one, and the same frankness characterized the replies from the observatory of Montsouris and the magnetic station in the park of St. Maur. The same repect for the truth distinguished the Bureau des Longitudes.

The provinces were slightly more affirmative. Perhaps in the night of the fifth and morning of the sixth of May there had appeared a flash of light of electrical origin which lasted about twenty seconds. At the Pic du Midi this light appeared between nine and ten in the evening. At the Meteorological Observatory on the Puy de Dome the light had been observed between one and two o'clock in the morning; at Mont Ventoux in Provence it had been seen between two and three o'clock; at Nice it had been noticed between three and four o'clock; while at the Semnoz Alps between Annecy, Le Bourget, and Le Léman, it had been detected just as the zenith was paling with the dawn.

Now it evidently would not do to disregard these observations altogether. There could be no doubt that a light had been observed at different places, in succession, at intervals, during some hours. Hence, whether it had been produced from many centres in the terrestrial atmosphere, or from one centre, it was plain that the light must have travelled at a speed of over one hundred and twenty miles an hour.

But had there been anything abnormal in the air during the day?

Nothing of the sort.

Had the trumpet been heard in the aerial domain?

No note of a trumpet had been detected between sunrise and sundown.

In the United Kingdom there was much perplexity. The observatories were not in agreement. Greenwich would not consent to the proposition of Oxford. They were agreed on one point, however, and that was—

"It was nothing at all!"

But, said one,

"It was an optical illusion!"

While the other contended that

"It was an acoustical illusion!"

And so they disputed. Something, however, was, it will be seen, common to both.

"It was an illusion."

Between the observatory of Berlin and the observatory of Vienna the discussion threatened to end in international complications; but Russia, in the person of the director of the observatory at Pulkowa, showed that both were right. It all depended on the point of view from which they attacked the phenomenon, which, though impossible in theory, was possible in practice.

In Switzerland, at the observatory of Sautis in the canton of Appenzell, at the Righi, at the Gäbris, in the passes of the St. Gothard, at the St. Bernard, at the Julier, at the Simplon, at Zurich, at Somblick in the Tyrolean Alps, there was a very strong disinclination to say anything about what nobody could prove—and that was nothing but reasonable.

But in Italy, at the meteorological stations on Vesuvius, on Etna in the old Casa Inglesi, at Monte Cavo, the observers made no hesitation in admitting the materiality of the phenomenon, particularly as they had seen it by day in the form of a small cloud of vapour, and by night in that of a shooting star. But of what it was they knew nothing.

Scientists began at last to tire of the mystery, while they continued to disagree about it, and even to frighten the lowly and the ignorant, who, thanks to one of the wisest laws of nature, have formed, form, and will form the immense majority of the world's inhabitants. Astronomers and meteorologists would soon have dropped the subject altogether had not, on the night of the 26th and 27th, the observatory of Kautokeino at Finmark, in Norway, and during the night of the 28th and 29th that of Isfjord at Spitzbergen—Norwegian one and Swedish the other—found themselves agreed in recording that in the centre of an aurora borealis there had appeared a sort of huge bird, an aerial monster, whose structure they were unable to determine, but who, there was no doubt, was showering off from his body certain corpuscles which exploded like bombs.

In Europe not a doubt was thrown on this observation of the stations in Finmark and Spitzbergen. But what appeared the most phenomenal about it was that the Swedes and Norwegians could find themselves in agreement on any subject whatever.

There was a laugh at the asserted discovery in all the observatories of South America, in Brazil, Peru, and La Plata, and in those of Australia at Sydney, Adelaide, and Melbourne; and Australian laughter is very catching.

To sum up, only one chief of a meteorological station ventured on a decided answer to this question, notwithstanding the sarcasms that his solution provoked. This was a Chinaman, the director of the observatory at Zi-Ka-Wey which rises in the centre of a vast plateau less than thirty miles from the sea, having an immense horizon and wonderfully pure atmosphere.

"It is possible," said he, "that the object was an aviform apparatus—a flying machine!"

What nonsense!

But if the controversy was keen in the old world, we can imagine what it was like in that portion of the new of which the United States occupy so vast an area.

A Yankee, we know, does not waste time on the road. He takes the street that leads him straight to his end. And the observatories of the American Federation did not hesitate to do their best. If they did not hurl their objectives at each other's heads, it was because they would have had to put them back just when they most wanted to use them. In this much-disputed question the observatories of Washington in the district of Columbia, and Cambridge in Massachusetts, found themselves opposed by those of Dartmouth College in Connecticut, and Ann Arbor in Michigan. The subject of their dispute was not the nature of the body observed, but the precise moment of its observation. All of them claimed to have seen it the same night, the same hour, the same minute, the same second, although the trajectory of the mysterious voyager took it but a moderate height above the horizon. Now from Massachusetts to Michigan, from Connecticut to Columbia, the distance is too great for this double observation, made at the same moment, to be considered possible.

Dudley at Albany, in the State of New York, and West Point, the Military Academy, showed that their colleagues were wrong by an elaborate calculation of the right ascension and declination of the aforesaid body.

But later on it was discovered that the observers had

been deceived in the body, and that what they had seen was an aerolite. This aerolite could not be the object in question, for how could an aerolite blow a trumpet?

It was in vain that they tried to get rid of this trumpet as an acoustical illusion. The ears were no more deceived than the eyes. Something had assuredly been seen, and something had assuredly been heard. In the night of the 12th and 13th of May—a very dark night—the observers at Yale College, in the Sheffield Science School, had been able to take down a few bars of a musical phrase in D major, common time, which gave note for note, rhythm for rhythm, the chorus of the Chant du Départ.

"Good," said the Yankee wags. "There is a French band well up in the air."

"But to joke is not to answer." Thus said the observatory at Boston, founded by the Atlantic Iron Works Society, whose opinions in matters of astronomy and meteorology began to have much weight in the world of science.

Then there intervened the observatory at Cincinnati, founded in 1870, on Mount Lookout, thanks to the generosity of Mr. Kilgour, and known for its micrometrical measurements of double stars. Its director declared with the utmost good faith that there had certainly been something, that a travelling body had shown itself at very short periods at different points in the atmosphere, but what were the nature of this body, its dimensions, its speed, and its trajectory, it was impossible to say.

It was then that a journal whose publicity is immense—

the *New York Herald*—received the anonymous contribution hereunder.

"There will be in the recollection of most people the rivalry which existed a few years ago between the two heirs of the Begum of Ragginahra, the French doctor Sarrasin, in the city of Franceville, and the German engineer Schultze, in the city of Stahlstadt, both in the south of Oregon in the United States.

"It will not have been forgotten that, with the object of destroying Franceville, Herr Schultze launched a formidable engine, intended to beat down the town and annihilate it at a single blow.

"Still less will it be forgotten that this engine, whose initial velocity as it left the mouth of the monster cannon had been erroneously calculated, had flown off at a speed exceeding by sixteen times that of ordinary projectiles—or about four hundred and fifty miles an hour—that it did not fall to the ground, and that it passed into an aerolitic stage, so as to circle for ever round our globe.

"Why should not this be the body in question?"

Very ingenious, Mr. Correspondent of the *New York Herald!* But how about the trumpet? There was no trumpet in Herr Schultze's projectile!

So all the explanations explained nothing, and all the observers had observed in vain. There remained only the suggestion offered by the director of Zi-Ka-Wey. But the opinion of a Chinaman! . . . .

The discussion continued, and there was no sign of

agreement. Then came a short period of rest. Some days elapsed without any object, aerolite or otherwise, being descried, and without any trumpet notes being heard in the atmosphere. The body then had fallen on some part of the globe where it had been difficult to trace it; in the sea, perhaps! Had it sunk in the depths of the Atlantic, the Pacific, or the Indian Ocean? What was to be said in this matter?

But then, between the 2nd and 9th of June, there came a new series of facts which could not possibly be explained by the unaided existence of a cosmic phenomenon.

In a week the Hamburgers at the top of St. Michael's Tower, the Turks on the highest minaret of St. Sophia, the Rouennais at the end of the metal spire of their cathedral, the Strasburgers at the summit of their minster, the Americans on the head of the Liberty statue at the entrance of the Hudson and on the Washington monument at Boston, the Chinese at the spike of the temple of the Four Hundred Genii at Canton, the Hindoos on the sixteenth terrace of the pyramid of the temple at Tanjore, the San Pietrini at the cross of St. Peter's at Rome, the English at the cross of St. Paul's in London, the Egyptians at the apex of the Great Pyramid of Ghizeh, the Parisians at the lightning conductor of the iron tower of the Exposition of 1889, a thousand feet high, all of them beheld a flag floating from some one of these inaccessible points.

And the flag was black, dotted with stars, and it bore a golden sun in its centre.

## CHAPTER II.

### AGREEMENT IMPOSSIBLE.

"AND the first who says the contrary—"

"Indeed! But we will say the contrary so long as there is a place to say it in!"

"And in spite of your threats—"

"Mind what you are saying, Bat Fynn!"

"Mind what you are saying, Uncle Prudent!"

"I maintain that the screw ought to be behind!"

"And so do we! And so do we!" replied half a hundred voices confounded in one.

"No! It ought to be in front!" shouted Phil Evans.

"In front!" roared fifty other voices, with a vigour in no whit less remarkable.

"We shall never agree!"

"Never! Never!"

"Then what is the use of a dispute?"

"It is not a dispute! It is a discussion!"

One would not have thought so to listen to the taunts, objurgations, and vociferations which filled the lecture-room for a good quarter of an hour.

The room was one of the largest in the Weldon Institute,

the well-known club in Walnut Street, Philadelphia, Pennsylvania, U.S.A.

The evening before there had been an election of a lamplighter, occasioning many public manifestations, noisy meetings, and even interchanges of blows, resulting in an effervescence which had not yet subsided, and which would account for some of the excitement just exhibited by the members of the Weldon Institute. For this was merely a meeting of balloonists, discussing the burning question of the direction of balloons.

It took place in a town of the United States whose development has been more rapid than that of New York, Chicago, Cincinnati, or San Francisco, a city which is neither a port nor a mining centre for coal or petroleum, nor an agglomeration of manufactories, nor a terminus of radiating railways; a town larger than Manchester, Edinburgh, Liverpool, Vienna, Petersburg, or Dublin; a town possessing a park in which the seven parks of the English capital could all be packed together; a town containing over a million people; the fourth or fifth town of the world after London, Paris, and New York.

Philadelphia is almost a city of marble, with its palatial houses and its unrivalled public establishments. The most important of the colleges of the New World is the Girard College, and it is at Philadelphia. The largest iron bridge on the globe is that across the Schuylkill, and that is at Philadelphia. The finest temple of the Freemasons is the Masonic Temple at Philadelphia. And the largest club of experts in aerial navigation is at Philadelphia, and if we had visited it on this evening of the 12th of June we might have found something to interest us.

In this great saloon there were struggling, pushing, gesticulating, shouting, arguing, disputing, a hundred balloonists, all with their hats on, under the authority of a president, assisted by a secretary and treasurer. They were not engineers by profession, but simply amateurs of all that appertained to aerostatics, and they were amateurs in a fury, and especially foes of those who would oppose to aerostats "apparatuses heavier than the air," flying machines, aerial ships, or what not. That these people might one day discover the method of guiding balloons is possible. There could be no doubt that their president had considerable difficulty in guiding them.

This president, well known in Philadelphia, was the famous Uncle Prudent, Prudent being his family name. There is nothing surprising in America in the qualificative uncle, for you can there be uncle without having either nephew or niece. There they speak of uncle as in other places they speak of father, though the father may have had no children.

Uncle Prudent was a personage of consideration, and in spite of his name was well known for his audacity. He was very rich, and that is no drawback even in the United States; and how could it be otherwise when he owned the greater part of the shares in Niagara Falls? A society of engineers had just been founded at Buffalo for working the cataract. It seemed to be an excellent speculation. The seven thousand five hundred cubic metres that Niagara passes over in a second would produce seven millions of horse-power. This enormous power, distributed amongst all the workshops within a radius of three hundred miles, would return an annual income of three hundred million dollars, of which the greater part would find its way into the pocket of Uncle Prudent. He was a bachelor, he lived quietly, and for his only servant had his valet Frycollin, who was hardly worthy of being the servant of so audacious a master.

Uncle Prudent was rich, and therefore he had friends, as was natural; but he also had enemies, although he was president of the club—among others all those who envied his position. Amongst his bitterest foes we may mention the secretary of the Weldon Institute.

This was Phil Evans, who was also very rich, being the manager of the Wheelem Watch Company, an important manufactory, which makes every day five hundred movements equal in every respect to the best Swiss workmanship. Phil Evans would have passed for one of the happiest men in the world, and even in the United States, if it had not been for Uncle Prudent. Like him he was in his forty-sixth year; like him of invariable health; like him of undoubted boldness. They were two men made to thoroughly understand each other, but they did not, for both were of extreme violence of character. Uncle Prudent was furiously hot; Phil Evans was abnormally cool.

And why had not Phil Evans been elected president of the club? The votes were exactly divided between Uncle Prudent and him. Twenty times there had been a scrutiny, and twenty times the majority had not declared for either one or the other. The position was embarrassing, and it might have lasted for the lifetime of the candidates.

One of the members of the club then proposed a way out of the difficulty. This was Jem Chip, the treasurer of the Weldon Institute. Chip was a confirmed vegetarian, a proscriber of all animal nourishment, of all fermented liquors, half a Mussulman, half a Brahman. On this occasion Jem Chip was supported by another member of the club, William T. Forbes, the manager of a large factory where they made glucose by treating rags with sulphuric acid. A man of good standing was this William T. Forbes, the father of two charming girls—Miss Dorothy, called Doll, and Miss Martha, called Mat, who gave the tone to the best society in Philadelphia.

It followed, then, on the proposition of Jem Chip, supported by William T. Forbes and others, that it was decided to elect the president "on the centre point."

This mode of election can be applied in all cases when it is desired to elect the most worthy; and a number of Americans of high intelligence are already thinking of employing it in the nomination of the President of the Republic of the United States.

On two boards of perfect whiteness a black line is traced. The length of each of these lines is mathematically the same, for they have been determined with as much accuracy as the base of the first triangle in a trigonometrical survey. That done, the two boards were erected on the same day in the centre of the conference room, and the two candidates, each armed with a fine needle, marched towards the board that had fallen to his lot. The man who planted his needle nearest the centre of the line would be proclaimed President of the Weldon Institute.

The operation must be done at once—no guide marks or trial shots allowed; nothing but sureness of eye. The man must have a compass in his eye, as the saying goes; that was all.

Uncle Prudent stuck in his needle at the same moment as Phil Evans did his. Then there began the measurement to discover which of the two competitors had most nearly approached the centre.

Wonderful! Such had been the precision of the shots that the measures gave no appreciable difference. If they were not exactly in the mathematical centre of the line, the distance between the needles was so small as to be invisible to the naked eye.

The meeting was much embarrassed.

Fortunately one of the members, Truck Milnor, insisted that the measurements should be remade by means of a rule graduated by the micrometrical machine of M. Perreaux, which can divide a millimetre into fifteen hundred parts. This rule, dividing the fifteen-hundredths

The meeting was much embarrassed.

Page 18

of a millimetre with a diamond splinter, was brought to bear on the lines, and on reading the divisions through a microscope the following were the results:—

Uncle Prudent had approached the centre within less than six fifteen-hundredths of a millimetre. Phil Evans was within nine fifteen-hundredths.

And that is why Phil Evans was only secretary of the the Weldon Institute, whereas Uncle Prudent was president. A difference of three fifteen-hundredths of a millimetre! And on account of it Phil Evans vowed against Uncle Prudent one of those hatreds which are none the less fierce for being latent.

## CHAPTER III.

### A VISITOR IS ANNOUNCED.

THE many experiments made during this last quarter of the nineteenth century have given considerable impetus to the question of guidable balloons. The cars furnished with propellers attached in 1852 to the aerostats of the elongated form introduced by Henry Giffard, the machines of Dupuy de Lome in 1872, of the Tissandier brothers in 1883, and of Captains Krebs and Renard in 1884, yielded many important results. But if these machines, moving in a medium heavier than themselves, manœuvring under the propulsion of a screw, working at an angle to the direction of the wind, and even against the wind, to return to their point of departure, had been really "guidable," they had only succeeded under very favourable conditions. In large covered halls their success was perfect. In a calm atmosphere they did very well. In a light wind of five or six yards a second they still moved. But nothing practical had been obtained. Against a miller's wind—nine yards a second—the machines had remained almost stationary. Against a fresh breeze—eleven yards a second—they would have advanced backwards. In a storm—twenty-seven to thirty-three yards a second—they would have been blown about like a feather. In a hurricane—sixty yards a second—they would have run the risk of being dashed to pieces. And in one of those cyclones which exceed a hundred yards a second not a fragment of them would have been left. It remained, then, even after the striking experiments of Captains Krebs and Renard, that though guidable aerostats had gained a little speed, they could not be kept going in a moderate breeze. Hence the impossibility of making practical use of this mode of aerial locomotion.

With regard to the means employed to give the aerostat its motion a great deal of progress had been made. For the steam-engines of Henry Giffard, and the muscular force of Dupuy de Lome, electric motors had gradually been substituted. The batteries of bichromate of potassium of the Tissandier brothers had given a speed of four yards a second. The dynamo-electric machines of Captains Krebs and Renard had developed a force of twelve-horse power and yielded a speed of six and a half yards per second.

With regard to this motor, engineers and electricians had been approaching more and more to that desideratum which is known as a steam-horse in a watch-case. Gradually the results of the pile of which Captains Krebs and Renard had kept the secret had been surpassed, and aeronants had become able to avail themselves of motors whose lightness increased at the same time as their power.

In this there was much to encourage those who believed in the utilization of guidable balloons. But yet how many good people there are who refuse to admit the possibility of such a thing! If the aerostat finds support in the air it belongs to the medium in which it moves; under such conditions, how can its mass, which offers so much resistance to the currents of the atmosphere, make its way against the wind?

In this struggle of the inventors after a light and powerful motor, the Americans had most nearly attained what they sought. A dynamo-electric apparatus, in which a new pile was employed the composition of which was still a mystery, had been bought from its inventor, a Boston chemist up to then unknown. Calculations made with the greatest care, diagrams drawn with the utmost exactitude, showed that by means of this apparatus driving a screw of given dimensions a displacement could be obtained of from twenty to twenty-two yards a second.

Now this was magnificent!

"And it is not dear," said Uncle Prudent, as he handed to the inventor in return for his formal receipt the last instalment of the hundred thousand paper dollars he had paid for his invention.

Immediately the Weldon Institute set to work. When there comes along a project of practical utility the money

The third, which ended in a frightful fall

Page 23

leaps nimbly enough from American pockets. The funds flowed in even without its being necessary to form a syndicate. Three hundred thousand dollars came into the club's account at the first appeal. The work began under the superintendence of the most celebrated aeronaut of the United States, Harry W. Tinder, immortalized by three of his ascents out of a thousand, one in which he rose to a height of twelve thousand yards, higher than Gay Lussac, Coxwell, Sivet, Crocé-Spinelli, Tissandier, Glaisher; another in which he had crossed America from New York to San Francisco, exceeding by many hundred leagues the journeys of Nadar, Godard, and others, to say nothing of that of John Wise, who accomplished eleven hundred and fifty miles from St. Louis to Jefferson county; the third, which ended in a frightful fall from fifteen hundred feet at the cost of a slight sprain in the right thumb, while the less fortunate Pilâtre de Rozier fell only seven hundred feet, and yet killed himself on the spot!

At the time this story begins the Weldon Institute had got their work well in hand. In the Turner yard at Philadelphia there reposed an enormous aerostat, whose strength had been tried by highly compressed air. It well merited the name of the monster balloon.

How large was Nadar's Géant? Six thousand cubic metres. How large was John Wise's balloon? Twenty thousand cubic metres. How large was the Giffard balloon at the 1878 Exhibition? Twenty-five thousand cubic metres. Compare these three aerostats with the aerial machine of the Weldon Institute, whose volume amounted to forty thousand cubic metres, and you will understand why Uncle Prudent and his colleagues were so justifiably proud of it.

This balloon not being destined for the exploration of the higher strata of the atmosphere, was not called the Excelsior, a name which is rather too much held in honour among the citizens of America. No! It was called, simply, the Go-ahead, and all it had to do was to justify its name by going ahead obediently to the wishes of its commander.

The dynamo-electric machine, according to the patent purchased by the Weldon Institute, was nearly ready. In less than six weeks the Go-ahead would start for its first cruise through space.

But, as we have seen, all the mechanical difficulties had not been overcome. Many evenings had been devoted to discussing, not the form of its screw nor its dimensions, but whether it ought to be put behind, as the Tissandier brothers had done, or before as Captains Krebs and Renard had done. It is unnecessary to add that the partisans of the two systems had almost come to blows. The group of "Beforists" were equalled in number by the group of "Behindists." Uncle Prudent, who ought to have given the casting vote—Uncle Prudent, brought up doubtless in the school of Professor Buridan—could not bring himself to decide.

Hence the impossibility of getting the screw into place. The dispute might last for some time, unless the Government interfered. But in the United States the Government meddles with private affairs as little as it possibly can. And it is right.

Things were in this state at this meeting on the 13th of June, which threatened to end in a riot—insults exchanged, fisticuffs succeeding the insults, cane thrashings succeeding the fisticuffs, revolver shots succeeding the cane thrashings—when at thirty-seven minutes past eight there occurred a diversion.

The porter of the Weldon Institute coolly and calmly, like a policeman amid the storm of the meeting, approached the presidential desk. On it he placed a card. He awaited the orders that Uncle Prudent found it convenient to give.

Uncle Prudent turned on the steam whistle, which did duty for the presidential bell, for even the Kremlin clock would have struck in vain! But the tumult slackened not.

Then the president removed his hat. Thanks to this extreme measure a semi-silence was obtained.

"A communication!" said Uncle Prudent, after taking a huge pinch from the snuff-box which never left him.

"Speak up!" answered eighty-nine voices, accidentally in agreement on this one point.

"A stranger, my dear colleagues, asks to be admitted to the meeting."

"Never!" replied every voice.

"He desires to prove to us, it would appear," continued Uncle Prudent, "that to believe in guiding balloons is to believe in the absurdest of Utopias!"

"Let him in! Let him in!"

"What is the name of this singular personage?" asked secretary Phil Evans.

"Robur," replied Uncle Prudent.

"Robur! Robur! Robur!" yelled the assembly. And the welcome accorded so quickly to the curious name was chiefly due to the Weldon Institute hoping to vent its exasperation on the head of him who bore it!

"My name is Robur!"

Page 27.

## CHAPTER IV.

### IN WHICH A NEW CHARACTER APPEARS.

"CITIZENS of the United States! My name is Robur. I am worthy of the name! I am forty years old, although I look but thirty, and I have a constitution of iron, a healthy vigour that nothing can shake, a muscular strength that few can equal, and a digestion that would be thought first-class even in an ostrich!"

They were listening! Yes! The riot was quelled at once by the totally unexpected fashion of the speech. Was this fellow a madman or a hoaxer? Whoever he was, he kept his audience in hand. There was not a whisper in the meeting in which but a few minutes ago the storm was in full fury.

And Robur looked the man he said he was. Of middle height and geometric breadth, his figure was a regular trapezium with the greatest of its parallel sides formed by the line of his shoulders. On this line attached by a robust neck there rose an enormous spheroidal head. The head of what animal did it resemble from the point of view of passional analogy? The head of a bull; but a bull with an intelligent face. Eyes which at the least opposition would glow like coals of fire; and above them a permanent contraction of the superciliary muscle, an invariable sign of extreme energy. Short hair, slightly woolly, with metallic reflections; large chest rising and falling like a smith's bellows; arms, hands, legs, feet, all worthy of the trunk. No moustaches, no whiskers, but a large American goatee, revealing the attachments of the jaw whose masseter muscles were evidently of formidable strength. It has been calculated—what has not been calculated?—that the pressure of the jaw of an ordinary crocodile can reach four hundred atmospheres, while that of a hound can only amount to one hundred. From this the following curious ormula has been deduced:—If a kilogram of dog produces eight kilograms of masseteric force, a kilogram of crocodile could produce twelve. Now, a kilogram of the aforesaid Robur would not produce less than ten, so that he came between the dog and the crocodile.

From what country did this remarkable specimen come? It was difficult to say. One thing was noticeable, and that was that he expressed himself fluently in English without a trace of the drawling twang that distinguishes the Yankees of New England.

He continued:—

"And now, honourable citizens, for my mental faculties. You see before you an engineer whose nerves are in no way inferior to his muscles. I have no fear of anything or anybody. I have a strength of will that has never had to yield. When I have decided on a thing all America, all the world, may strive in vain to keep me from it. When I have an idea I allow no one to share it, and I do not permit any contradiction. I insist on these details, honourable citizens, because it is necessary you should quite understand me. Perhaps you think I am talking too much about myself? It does not matter if you do! And now consider a little before you interrupt me, as I have come to tell you something that you may not be particularly pleased to hear."

A sound as of the surf on the beach began to rise along the first rows of seats—a sign that the sea would not be long in getting stormy again.

"Speak, stranger!" said Uncle Prudent, who had some difficulty in restraining himself.

And Robur spoke as follows, without troubling himself any more about his audience.

"Yes! I know it well! After a century of experiments that have led to nothing, and trials giving no result, there still exist ill-balanced minds who believe in guiding balloons. They imagine that a motor of some sort, electric or otherwise, might be applied to their pretentious skin bags which are at the mercy of every current in the atmosphere. They persuade themselves that they can be masters of an aerostat as they can be masters of a ship on the surface of the sea. Because a few inventors in calm or nearly calm weather have succeeded in working on an angle with the wind, or even beating to windward in a gentle breeze they think that the steering of aerial apparatus lighter than the air is a practicable matter. Well, now, look here! You hundred, who believe in the realization of your dreams, are throwing your thousands of dollars not into water but into space! You are fighting the impossible!"

Strange it was that at this affirmation the members of the Weldon Institute did not move. Had they become as deaf as they were patient? Or were they reserving themselves to see how far this audacious contradicter would dare to go?

Robur continued :—

"What? A balloon! When to obtain the raising of a couple of pounds you require a cubic yard of gas. A balloon pretending to resist the wind by aid of its mechanism, when the pressure of a light breeze on a vessel's sails is not less than that of four hundred horse-power; when in the accident at the Tay Bridge you saw the storm produce a pressure of eight and a half hundredweight on a square yard. A balloon, when on such a system nature has never constructed anything flying, whether furnished with wings like birds, or membranes like certain fish, or certain mammalia—"

"Mammalia?" exclaimed one of the members of the club.

"Yes! Mammalia! The bat, which flies, if I am not mistaken! Is the gentleman unaware that this flyer is a mammal? Did he ever see an omelette made of bat's eggs?"

And the interrupter reserved himself for future interruption, and Robur resumed :—

"But does that mean that man is to give up the conquest of the air, and the transformation of the domestic and political manners of the old world, by the use of this admirable means of locomotion? By no means. As he has become master of the seas with the ship, by the oar, the sail, the wheel, and the screw, so shall he become master of atmospherical space by apparatus heavier than the air —for it must be heavier to be stronger than the air!"

And then the assembly exploded. What a broadside of yells escaped from all these mouths, aimed at Robur like the muzzles of so many guns! Was not this hurling a declaration of war into the very camp of the balloonists? Was not this the stirring up of strife between "the lighter" and "the heavier" than air?

Robur did not even frown. With folded arms he waited bravely till silence was obtained.

By a gesture Uncle Prudent ordered the firing to cease.

"Yes," continued Robur, "the future is for the flying-machine. The air affords a solid fulcrum. If you will give a column of air an ascensional movement of forty-five metres a second, a man can support himself on the top of it if the soles of his boots have a superficies of only the eighth of a square metre. And if the speed be increased to ninety metres, he can walk on it with naked feet. Or if, by means of a screw, you drive a mass of air at this speed, you get the same result."

What Robur said had been said before by all the partisans of aviation, whose work slowly but surely is leading on to the solution of the problem. To Ponton d'Amécourt, La Landelle, Nadar, De Luzy, De Louvrié, Liais, Beleguir, Moreau, the brothers Richard, Babinet, Jobert, Du Temple, Salives, Penaud, De Villeneuve, Gauchot and Tatin, Michel Loup, Edison, Planavergne, and so many others, belongs the honour of having brought forward ideas of such simplicity. Abandoned and resumed times without number, they are sure some day to triumph. To the enemies of aviation, who urge that the bird only sustains himself by warming the air he strikes, their answer is ready. Have they not proved that an eagle weighing five kilograms would have to fill fifty cubic metres with his warm fluid merely to sustain himself in space?

This is what Robur demonstrated with undeniable logic amid the uproar that arose on all sides. And in conclusion these are the words he hurled in the faces of the balloonists:—

"With your aerostats you can do nothing—you will arrive at nothing—you dare do nothing! The boldest of your aeronauts, John Wise, although he has made an aerial voyage of twelve hundred miles above the American continent, has had to give up his project of crossing the Atlantic! And you have not advanced a step—not one step—towards your end."

"Sir," said the president, who in vain endeavoured to keep himself cool, "you forget what was said by our immortal Franklin at the first appearance of the fire balloon, 'It is but a child, but it will grow!' It was but a child, and it has grown."

"No, Mr. President it has not grown! It has got fatter —and that is not the same thing!"

This was a direct attack on the Weldon Institute, which had decreed, helped, and paid for the making of a monster balloon. And so propositions of the following kind began to fly about the room:—

"Turn him out!"

"Throw him off the platform!"

"Prove that he is heavier than the air!"

And many others.

But these were only words, not means to an end.

Robur remained impassible, and continued, "There is no progress for your aerostats, my citizen balloonists; progress is for flying machines. The bird flies, and he is not a balloon, he is a piece of mechanism!"

"Yes, he flies!" exclaimed the fiery Bat. T. Fynn; "but he flies against all the laws of mechanics."

"Indeed!" said Robur, shrugging his shoulders.

And, resuming, "Since we have begun the study of the flight of large and small birds one simple idea has prevailed—to imitate nature, which never makes mistakes. Between the albatross, which gives hardly ten beats of the wing per minute, between the pelican, which gives seventy—"

"Seventy-one," said the voice of a scoffer.

"And the bee, which gives one hundred and ninety-two per second—"

"One hundred and ninety-three!" said the facetious individual.

"And the common house-fly, which gives three hundred and thirty—"

"And a half!"

"And the mosquito, which give millions—"

"No, milliards!"

But Robur, the interrupted, interrupted not his demonstration.

"Between these different rates—" he continued.

"There is a difference," said a voice.

"There is a possibility of finding a practical solution. When De Lucy showed that the stag-beetle, an insect weighing only two grammes, could lift a weight of four hundred grammes, or two hundred times its own weight, the problem of aviation was solved. Besides, it has been shown that the wing surface decreases in proportion to the increase of the size and weight of the animal. Hence we can look forward to such contrivances—"

"Which would never fly!" said secretary Phil Evans.

"Which have flown, and which will fly," said Robur, without being in the least disconcerted, "and which we can call streophores, helicopters, orthopters—or, in imitation of the word 'nef,' which comes from 'navis,' call them from 'avis,' 'efs'—by means of which man will become the master of space. The helix—"

"Ah, the helix!" replied Phil Evans. "But the bird has no helix; that we know!"

"So," said Robur; "but Penaud has shown that in reality the bird makes a helix, and its flight is helicopteral. And the motor of the future is the screw—"

"From such a maladee
Saint Helix keep us free!"

sung out one of the members, who had accidentally hit upon the air from Herold's "Zampa."

And they all took up the chorus:—

"From such a maladee
Saint Helix keep us free!"

with such intonations and variations as would have made the French composer groan in his grave.

As the last notes died away in a frightful discord Uncle Prudent took advantage of the momentary calm to say,—

"Stranger, up to now we let you speak without interruption."

It seemed that for the president of the Weldon Institute shouts, yells, and catcalls were not interruptions, but only an exchange of arguments.

"But I may remind you, all the same, that the theory of aviation is condemned beforehand, and rejected by the majority of American and foreign engineers. It is a system which was the cause of the death of the Flying Saracen at Constantinople, of the monk Volador at Lisbon, of De

Letur in 1852, of De Groof in 1864, besides the victims I forget since the mythological Icarus—"

"A system," replied Robur, "no more to be condemned than that whose martyrology contains the names of Pilâtre de Rozier at Calais, of Blanchard at Paris, of Donaldson and Grimwood in Lake Michigan, of Sivel and of Crocé-Spinelli of Eloy, and so many others whom it takes good care to forget."

This was a counter-thrust with a vengeance.

"Besides," continued Robur, "with your balloons as good as you can make them you will never obtain any speed worth mentioning. It would take you ten years to go round the world—and a flying-machine could do it in a week!"

Here arose a new tempest of protests and denials, which lasted for three long minutes. And then Phil Evans took up the word.

"Mr. Aviator," he said, "you who talk so much of the benefits of aviation, have you ever aviated?"

"I have."

"And made the conquest of the air?"

"Not unlikely."

"Hooray for Robur the Conqueror!" shouted an ironical voice.

"Well, yes! Robur the Conqueror! I accept the name and I will bear it, for I have a right to it."

"We beg to doubt it!" said Jem Chip.

"Gentlemen," said Robur, and his brows knit, "when I

have just seriously stated a serious thing I do not permit any one to reply to me by a flat denial, and I shall be glad to know the name of the interrupter."

"My name is Chip, and I am a vegetarian."

"Citizen Chip," said Robur, "I knew that vegetarians had longer alimentary canals than other men—a good foot longer at the least. That is quite long enough; and so do not compel me to make yours any longer by beginning at your ears and—"

"Throw him out."

"Into the street with him!"

"Limb him!"

"Lynch him!"

"Helix him!"

The rage of the balloonists burst forth at last.

They rushed at the platform Robur disappeared amid a sheaf of hands that were thrown about as if caught in a storm. In vain the steam-whistle screamed its fanfares on to the assembly. Philadelphia might well think that a fire was devouring one of its quarters and that all the water of the Schuylkill could not put it out.

Suddenly there was a recoil in the tumult. Robur had put his hands into his pockets and now held them out at the front ranks of the infuriated mob.

In each hand was one of those American institutions known as revolvers, which the mere pressure of the fingers is enough to fire—pocket mitrailleuses in fact.

And taking advantage not only of the recoil of his assailants but also of the silence which accompanied it:

"Decidedly," said he, "it was not Amerigo that discovered the New World, it was Cabot! You are not Americans, citizen balloonists! You are only Cabo—"

Four or five pistol shots cracked out, fired into space. They hurt nobody. Amid the smoke the engineer vanished; and when it had thinned away there was no trace of him. Robur the Conqueror had flown, as if some apparatus of aviation had borne him into the air.

"You are not Americans."

Page 38.

## CHAPTER V.

### ANOTHER DISAPPEARANCE.

THIS was not the first occasion on which, at the end of their stormy discussions, the members of the Weldon Institute had filled Walnut Street and its neighbourhood with their tumult. Several times had the inhabitants complained of the noisy way in which the proceedings ended, and more than once had the policemen had to interfere to clear the thoroughfare for the passers-by, who for the most part were supremely indifferent on this question of aerial navigation. But never before had the tumult attained such proportions, never had the complaints been better founded, never had the intervention of the police been more necessary.

But there was some excuse for the members of the Weldon Institute. They had been attacked in their own house. To these enthusiasts for "lighter than air" a no less enthusiast for "heavier than air" had said things absolutely abhorrent. And at the moment they were about to treat him as he deserved he had disappeared.

And so they cried aloud for vengeance. To leave such

insults unpunished was impossible to all with American blood in their veins. Had not the sons of Amerigo been called the sons of Cabot? Was not that an insult as unpardonable as it happened to be just—historically?

The members of the club in several groups rushed down Walnut Street, then into the adjoining streets, and then all over the neighbourhood. They woke up the householders; they compelled them to search their houses, prepared to indemnify them later on for the outrage on their privacy. Vain were all their trouble and searching. Robur was nowhere to be found; there was no trace of him. He might have gone off in the Goahead, the balloon of the Institute, for all they could tell. After an hour's hunt the members had to give in and separate, not before they had agreed to extend their search over the whole territory of the twin Americas that form the new continent.

By eleven o'clock quiet had been restored in the neighbourhood of Walnut Street. Philadelphia was able to sink again into that sound sleep which is the privilege of non-manufacturing towns. The different members of the club parted to seek their respective houses. To mention the most distinguished amongst them, William T. Forbes sought his large sugar establishment, where Miss Doll and Miss Mat had prepared for him his evening tea, sweetened with his own glucose. Truck Milnor took the road to his factory in the distant suburb, where the engines worked day and night. Treasurer Jem Chip, publicly accused of possessing an alimentary canal twelve inches longer than that of other men, returned to the vegetable soup that was waiting for him.

Two of the most important balloonists—two only—did not seem to think of returning so soon to their domicile. They availed themselves of the opportunity to discuss the question with more than usual acrimony. These were the irreconcilables, Uncle Prudent and Phil Evans, the president and secretary of the Weldon Institute.

At the door of the club the valet Frycollin waited for Uncle Prudent, his master, and at last he went after him, though he cared but little for the subject which had set the two colleagues at loggerheads.

It is only by an euphemism that the verb "discuss" can be used to express the way in which the duet between the president and secretary was being performed. As a matter of fact they were in full wrangle with an energy born of their old rivalry.

"No, sir, no," said Phil Evans. "If I had had the honour of being president of the Weldon Institute, there never, no, never, would have been such a scandal."

"And what would you have done, if you had had the honour?" demanded Uncle Prudent.

"I would have stopped the insulter before he had opened his mouth."

"It seems to me it would have been impossible to stop him until he had opened his mouth."

"Not in America, sir; not in America."

And exchanging such observations, increasing in bitterness as they went, they walked on through the streets farther and farther from their homes, until they reached a part of the city whence they had to go a long way round to get back.

Frycollin followed, by no means at ease to see his master plunging into such deserted spots. He did not like deserted spots, particularly after midnight. In fact the darkness was profound and the moon was only a thin crescent just beginning its monthly life.

Frycollin kept a look-out to the left and right of him to see if he was followed. And he fancied he could see five or six hulking fellows dogging his footsteps.

Instinctively he drew nearer to his master, but not for the world would he have dared to break in on the conversation of which the fragments reached him.

In short it so chanced that the president and secretary of the Weldon Institute found themselves on the road to Fairmont Park. In the full heat of their dispute they crossed the Schuylkill river by the famous iron bridge. They met only a few belated wayfarers, and pressed on across a wide open tract where the immense prairie was broken every now and then by the patches of thick woodland which make the park different to any other in the world.

There Frycollin's terror became acute, particularly as he saw the five or six shadows gliding after him across the Schuylkill bridge. The pupils of his eyes broadened out to the circumference of his iris, and his limbs seemed to diminish as if endowed with the contractility peculiar to the mollusca and certain of the articulata; for Frycollin, the valet, was an egregious coward.

He was a pure South Carolina negro, with the head of a fool and the carcase of an imbecile. Being only one-and-twenty, he had never been a slave, not even by birth, but that made no difference to him. Grinning and greedy and idle, and a magnificent poltroon, he had been the servant of Uncle Prudent for about three years. Over and over again had his master threatened to kick him out, but had kept him on for fear of doing worse. With a master ever ready to venture on the most audacious enterprises, Frycollin's cowardice had brought him many arduous trials. But he had some compensation. Very little had been said about his gluttony, and still less about his laziness.

Ah, Valet Frycollin, if you could only have read the future! Why, oh why, Frycollin, did you not remain at Boston with the Sneffels, and not have given them up when they talked of going to Switzerland? Was not that a much more suitable place for you than this of Uncle Prudent's, where danger was daily welcomed?

But here he was, and his master had become used to his faults. He had one advantage, and that was a consideration. Although he was a negro by birth he did not speak like a negro, and nothing is so irritating as that hateful jargon in which all the pronouns are possessive and all the verbs infinitive.

Let it be understood, then, that Frycollin was a thorough coward.

And now it was midnight, and the pale crescent of the moon began to sink in the west behind the trees in the park. The rays streaming fitfully through the branches made the shadows darker than ever.

Frycollin looked round him anxiously.

"Brrr!" he said. "There are those fellows there all the time. Positively they are getting nearer! . . . Master Uncle!" he shouted.

It was thus he called the president of the Weldon Institute, and thus did the president desire to be called.

At the moment the dispute of the rivals had reached its maximum, and as they hurled their epithets at each other they walked faster and faster, and drew farther and farther away from the Schuylkill bridge.

They had reached the centre of a wide clump of trees, whose summits were just tipped by the parting rays of the moon. Beyond the trees was a large clearing—an oval field, a complete amphitheatre. Not a hillock was there to hinder the gallop of the horses, not a bush to stop the view of the spectators.

And if Uncle Prudent and Phil Evans had not been so deep in their dispute, and had used their eyes as they were accustomed to, they would have found the clearing was not in its usual state. Was it a flour-mill that had anchored on it during the night? It looked like it, with

They had reached the centre of a wide clump of trees.

Page 44.

its wings and sails—motionless and mysterious in the gathering gloom.

But neither the president nor the secretary of the Weldon Institute noticed the strange modification in the landscape of Fairmont Park ; and neither did Frycollin. It seemed to him that the thieves were approaching, and preparing for their attack ; and he was seized with convulsive fear, paralyzed in his limbs, with every hair he could boast on the bristle. His terror was extreme.

His knees bent under him, but he had just strength enough to exclaim for the last time,—

"Master Uncle ! Master Uncle !"

"What is the matter with you ?" asked Uncle Prudent.

Perhaps the disputants would not have been sorry to have relieved their fury at the expense of the unfortunate valet. But they had no time ; and neither even had he time to answer.

A whistle was heard. A flash of electric light shot across the clearing.

A signal, doubtless ? The moment had come for the deed of violence !

In less time than it takes to tell, six men came leaping across from under the trees, two on to Uncle Prudent, two on to Phil Evans, two on to Frycollin—there was no need for the two last, for the negro was incapable of defending himself.

The president and secretary of the Weldon Institute, although taken by surprise, would have resisted.

They had neither time nor strength to do so. In a second they were rendered speechless by a gag, blind by a bandage, thrown down, pinioned and carried bodily off across the clearing. What could they think except that they had fallen into the hands of people who intended to rob them? The people did nothing of the sort, however. They did not even touch Uncle Prudent's pockets, although, according to his custom, they were full of paper dollars.

Within a minute of the attack, without a word being passed, Uncle Prudent, Phil Evans, and Frycollin felt themselves laid gently down, not on the grass, but on a sort of plank that creaked beneath them. They were laid down side by side.

A door was shut; and the grating of a bolt in a staple told them that they were prisoners.

Then there came a continuous buzzing, a quivering, a frrrr, with the rrr unending.

And that was the only sound that broke the quiet of the night.

* * * * * * *

Great was the excitement next morning in Philadelphia! Very early was it known what had passed at the meeting of the Institute. Every one knew of the appearance of the mysterious engineer named Robur—Robur the Conqueror—and the tumult among the balloonists, and his inexplicable disappearance.

But it was quite another thing when all the town heard

They were carried bodily off across the clearing

Page 46.

that the president and secretary of the club had also disappeared during the night.

Long and keen was the search in the city and neighbour hood! Useless! The newspapers of Philadelphia, the newspapers of Pennsylvania, the newspapers of the United States reported the facts and explained them in a hundred ways, not one of which was the right one. Heavy rewards were offered, and placards were pasted up, but all to no purpose. The earth seemed to have opened and bodily swallowed the president and secretary of the Weldon Institute.

## CHAPTER VI.

### THE PRESIDENT AND SECRETARY SUSPEND HOSTILITIES.

A BANDAGE over the eyes, a gag in the mouth, a cord round the wrists, a cord round the ankles, unable to see, to speak, or to move, Uncle Prudent, Phil Evans, and Frycollin were anything but pleased with their position. Knowing not who had seized them, nor in what they had been thrown like parcels in a goods waggon, nor where they were, nor what was reserved for them—it was enough to exasperate even the most patient of the ovine race, and we know that the members of the Weldon Institute were not precisely sheep as far as patience went. With his violence of character we can easily imagine how Uncle Prudent felt.

One thing was evident, that Phil Evans and he would find it difficult to attend the club next evening.

As to Frycollin, with his eyes shut and his mouth closed ; it was impossible for him to think of anything. He was more dead than alive.

For an hour the position of the prisoners remained unchanged. No one came to visit them, or to give them that liberty of movement and speech of which they lay in such need. They were reduced to stifled sighs, to grunts emitted over and under their gags, to everything that betrayed anger kept dumb and fury imprisoned, or rather bound down. Then after many fruitless efforts they remained for some time as though lifeless. Then as the sense of sight was denied them they tried by their sense of hearing to obtain some indication of the nature of this disquieting state of things. But in vain did they seek for any other sound than an interminable and inexplicable f-r-r-r which seemed to envelop them in a quivering atmosphere.

At last something happened. Phil Evans, regaining his coolness, managed to slacken the cord which bound his wrists. Little by little the knot slipped, his fingers slipped over each other, and his hands regained their usual freedom.

A vigorous rubbing restored the circulation. A moment after he had slipped off the bandage which bound his eyes, taken the gag out of his mouth, and cut the cords round his ankles with his knife. An American who has not a bowie-knife in his pocket is no longer an American.

But if Phil Evans had regained the power of moving and speaking, that was all. His eyes were useless to him—at present at any rate. The prison was quite dark, though about six feet above him a feeble gleam of light came in through a kind of loophole.

As may be imagined, Phil Evans did not hesitate to at once set free his rival. A few cuts with the bowie settled the knots which bound him foot and hand.

Immediately Uncle Prudent rose to his knees and snatched away his bandage and his gag.

"Thanks," said he, in stifled voice.

"No!" said the other, "no thanks."

"Phil Evans?"

"Uncle Prudent?"

"Here we are no longer the president and secretary of the Weldon Institute. We are adversaries no more."

"You are right," answered Evans. "We are now only two men agreed to avenge ourselves on a third whose attempt deserves severe reprisals. And this third is—"

"Robur!"

"It is Robur!"

On this point both were absolutely in accord. On this subject there was no fear of dispute.

"And your servant?" said Evans, pointing to Frycollin, who was puffing like a grampus. "We must set him free."

"Not yet," said Uncle Prudent. "He would overwhelm us with his jeremiads, and we have something else to do than abuse each other."

"What is that, Uncle Prudent?"

"To save ourselves if possible."

"And even if it is impossible."

"You are right; even if it is impossible."

There could be no doubt that this kidnapping was due to Robur, for an ordinary thief would have relieved them of their watches, jewellery, and purses, and thrown their bodies into the Schuylkill with a good gash in their throats instead of throwing them to the bottom of— Of what? That was a serious question, which would have to be answered before attempting an escape with any chance of success.

"Phil Evans," began Uncle Prudent, "if, when we came away from our meeting, instead of indulging in amenities to which we need not recur, we had kept our eyes more open, this would not have happened. Had we remained in the streets of Philadelphia there would have been none of this. Evidently Robur foresaw what would happen at the club, and had placed some of his bandits on guard at the door. When we left Walnut Street these fellows must have watched us and followed us, and when we imprudently ventured into Fairmont Park they went in for their little game."

"Agreed," said Evans. "We were wrong not to go straight home."

"It is always wrong not to be right," said Prudent.

Here a long-drawn sigh escaped from the darkest corner of the prison.

"What is that?" asked Evans.

"Nothing! Frycollin is dreaming."

"Between the moment we were seized a few steps out into the clearing and the moment we were thrown in here only two minutes elapsed. It is thus evident that these people did not take us out of Fairmont Park."

"And if they had done so we should have felt we were being moved."

"Undoubtedly; and consequently we must be in some vehicle, perhaps one of those long prairie waggons, or some show-caravan—"

"Evidently! For if we were in a boat moored on the Schuylkill we should have noticed the movement due to the current—"

"That is so; and as we are still in the clearing, I think that now is the time to get away, and we can return later to settle with this Robur—"

"And make him pay for this attempt on the liberty of two citizens of the United States."

"And he shall pay pretty dearly!"

"But who is this man? Where does he come from? Is he English, or German, or French—"

"He is a scoundrel, that is enough!" said Uncle Prudent. "Now to work."

And then the two men, with their hands stretched out and their fingers wide apart, began to feel round the walls to find a joint or crack.

Nothing. Nothing; not even at the door. It was closely shut and it was impossible to shoot back the lock. All that could be done was to make a hole, and escape through the hole. It remained to be seen if the knives could cut into the walls.

"But whence comes this never-ending rustling?" asked Evans, who was much impressed at the continuous f-r-r-r.

"The wind, doubtless," said Uncle Prudent.

"The wind! But I thought the night was quite calm."

"So it was. But if it isn't the wind, what can it be?"

Phil Evans got out the best blade of his knife and set to work on the wall near the door. Perhaps he might make a hole which would enable him to open it from the outside should it be only bolted or should the key have been left in the lock.

He worked away for some minutes. The only result was to nip up his knife, to snip off its point, and transform what was left of the blade into a saw.

"Doesn't it cut?" asked Uncle Prudent.

"No."

"Is the wall made of sheet iron?"

"No; it gives no metallic sound when you hit it."

"Is it of ironwood?"

"No; it isn't iron and it isn't wood."

"What is it, then?"

"Impossible to say. But, anyhow, steel doesn't touch it."

Uncle Prudent, in a sudden outburst of fury, began to rave and stamp on the sonorous planks, while his hands sought to strangle an imaginary Robur.

"Be calm, Prudent, be calm! You have a try."

Uncle Prudent had a try, but the bowie-knife could do nothing against a wall which its best blades could not even scratch. The wall seemed to be made of crystal.

So it became evident that all flight was impracticable except through the door, and for a time they must resign themselves to their fate—not a very pleasant thing for the Yankee temperament, and very much to the disgust of these eminently practical men. But this conclusion was not arrived at without many objurgations and loud-sounding phrases hurled at this Robur—who, from what had been seen of him at the Weldon Institute, was not the sort of man to trouble himself much about them.

Suddenly Frycollin began to give unequivocal signs of being unwell. He began to writhe in a most lamentable fashion, either with cramp in his stomach or in his limbs; and Uncle Prudent, thinking it his duty to put an end to these gymnastics, cut the cords that bound him.

He had cause to be sorry for it. Immediately there was poured forth an interminable litany, in which the terrors of fear were mingled with the tortures of hunger. Frycollin was no worse in his brain than in his stomach, and it would have been difficult to decide to which organ the chief cause of the trouble should be assigned.

"Frycollin!" said Uncle Prudent.

"Master Uncle! Master Uncle!" answered the negro between two of his lugubrious howls.

"It is possible that we are doomed to die of hunger in this prison, but we have made up our minds not to succumb until we have availed ourselves of every means of alimentation to prolong our lives."

"To eat me?" exclaimed Frycollin.

"As is always done with a nigger under such circumstances! So you had better not make yourself too obvious—"

"Or you'll have your bones picked!" said Evans.

And as Frycollin saw he might be used to prolong two existences more precious than his own, he contented himself thenceforth with groaning on the quiet.

The time went on, and all attempts to force the door or get through the wall proved fruitless. What the wall was made of was impossible to say. It was not metal; it was not wood; it was not stone. And all the cell seemed to be made of the same stuff. When they stamped on the floor it gave a peculiar sound that Uncle Prudent found it difficult to describe; and the floor seemed to sound hollow, as if it was not resting directly on the ground of the clearing. And the inexplicable f-r-r-r-r seemed to sweep along below it. All of which was rather alarming.

"Uncle Prudent!" said Phil Evans.

"Well?"

"Do you think our prison has been moved at all?"

"Not that I know of."

"Because when we were first caught I distinctly remember the fresh fragrance of the grass and the resinous odour of the park trees. While now, when I take in a good sniff of the air, it seems as though all that had gone."

"So it has."

"Why?"

"We cannot say why unless we admit that the prison has moved; and I say again that if the prison had moved, either as a vehicle on the road or a boat on the stream, we should have felt it."

Here Frycollin gave vent to a long groan, which might have been taken for his last had he not followed it up with several more.

"I expect Robur will soon have us brought before him," said Phil Evans.

"I hope so," said Uncle Prudent. "And I shall tell him—"

"What?"

"That he began by being rude and ended in being unbearable."

Here Phil Evans noticed that day was beginning to break. A gleam, still faint, filtered through the narrow window opposite the door. It ought thus to be about four o'clock in the morning, for it is at that hour in the month of June in this latitude that the horizon of Philadelphia is tinged by the first rays of the dawn.

But when Uncle Prudent sounded his repeater—which was a masterpiece from his colleague's factory—the tiny gong only gave a quarter to three, and the watch had not stopped.

"That is strange!" said Phil Evans. "At a quarter to three it ought still to be night."

"Perhaps my watch has got slow," answered Uncle Prudent.

"A watch of the Wheelton Watch Company!" exclaimed Phil Evans.

Whatever might be the reason, there was no doubt that the day was breaking. Gradually the window became white in the deep darkness of the cell. However, if the dawn appeared sooner than the fortieth parallel permitted, it did not advance with the rapidity peculiar to lower latitudes.

This was another observation of Uncle Prudent's—a new inexplicable phenomenon.

"Couldn't we get up to the window and see where we are?"

"We might," said Uncle Prudent. "Frycollin, get up!"

The negro arose.

"Put your back against the wall," continued Prudent, "and you, Evans, get on his shoulders while I buttress him up."

"Right!" said Evans.

An instant afterwards his knees were on Frycollin's shoulders, and his eyes were level with the window. The window was not of lenticular glass like those on shipboard, but was a simple flat pane. It was small, and Phil Evans found his range of view was much limited.

"Break the glass," said Prudent, "and perhaps you will be able to see better."

Phil Evans gave it a sharp knock with the handle of his bowie-knife. It gave back a silvery sound, but it did not break.

Another and more violent blow. The same result.

"It is unbreakable glass!" said Evans.

It appeared as though the pane was made of glass toughened on the Siemens system, as after several blows it remained intact.

The light had now increased, and Phil Evans could see for some distance within the radius allowed by the frame.

"What do you see?" asked Uncle Prudent.

"Nothing."

"What? Not any trees?"

"No."

"Not even the top branches?"

"No."

"Then we are not in the clearing?"

"Neither in the clearing nor in the park."

"Don't you see any roofs of houses or monuments?" said Prudent, whose disappointment and anger were increasing rapidly.

"No."

"What! Not a flagstaff, nor a church tower, nor a chimney?"

"Nothing but space."

As he uttered the words the door opened. A man appeared on the threshold.

It was Robur.

"Honourable balloonists!" he said, in a serious voice, "you are now free to go and come as you like."

"Free!" exclaimed Uncle Prudent.

"It is unbreakable glass."

Page 58.

And what did they see?

Page 59.

"Yes—within the limits of the Albatross!"

Uncle Prudent and Phil Evans rushed out of their prison.

And what did they see?

Four thousand feet below them the face of a country they sought in vain to recognize.

## CHAPTER VII.

### ON BOARD THE ALBATROSS.

"WHEN will man cease to crawl in the depths to live in the azure and quiet of the sky?"

To this question of Camille Flammarion's the answer is easy. It will be when the progress of mechanics has enabled us to solve the problem of aviation. And in a few years—as we can foresee—a more practical utilization of electricity will do much towards that solution.

In 1783, before the Montgolfier brothers had built their fire-balloon, and Charles, the physician, had devised his first aerostat, a few adventurous spirits had dreamt of the conquest of space by mechanical means. The first inventors did not think of apparatus lighter than air; for that the science of their time did not allow them to imagine. It was to contrivances heavier than air, to flying machines in imitation of the birds, that they trusted to realize aerial locomotion.

This was exactly what had been done by that madman Icarus, the son of Dædalus, whose wings, fixed together with wax, had melted as they approached the sun.

But, without going back to mythologic times, without dwelling on Archytas of Tarentum, we find in the works of Dante of Perugia, of Leonardo da Vinci and Guidotti, the idea of machines made to move through the air. Two centuries and a half afterwards inventors began to multiply. In 1742 the Marquis de Bacqueville designed a system of wings, tried it over the Seine, and fell and broke his arm. In 1768 Paucton conceived the idea of an apparatus with two screws, suspensive and propulsive. In 1781 Meerwein, the architect of the Prince of Baden, built an orthopteric machine, and protested against the tendency of the aerostats which had just been invented. In 1784 Launoy and Bienvenu had manœuvred a helicopter worked by springs. In 1808 there were the attempts at flight by the Austrian Jacques Degen. In 1810 came the pamphlet by Deniau of Nantes, in which the principles of "heavier than air" are laid down. From 1811 to 1840 came the inventions and researches of Berblinger, Vigual, Sarti, Dubochet, and Cagniard de Latour. In 1842 we have the Englishman Henson, with his system of inclined planes and screws worked by steam. In 1845 came Cossus and his ascensional screws. In 1847 came Camille Vert and his helicopter made of birds' wings. In 1852 came Letur with his system of guidable parachutes, whose trial cost him his life; and in the same year came Michael Loup with his plan of gliding through the air on four revolving wings. In 1853 came Béléguic and his aeroplane with the traction screws, Vaussin-Chardannes with his guidable kite, and George Cauley with his flying-machines driven by gas. From 1854 to 1863 appeared Joseph Pline with several patents for aerial systems. Bréant, Carlingford, Le Bris, Du Temple, Bright, whose ascensional screws were left-handed; Smythies, Panafieu, Crosnier, &c. At length, in 1863, thanks to the efforts of Nadar, a society of "heavier than air" was founded in Paris. There the inventors could experiment with the machines, of which many were patented. Ponton d'Amécourt and his steam helicopter, La Landelle and his system of combining screws with inclined planes and parachutes, Louvrié and his aeroscaph, Esterno and his mechanical bird, Groof and his apparatus with wings worked by levers. The impetus was given, inventors invented, calculators calculated all that could render aerial locomotion practicable. Bourcart, Le Bris, Kaufmann, Smyth, Stringfellow, Prigent, Danjard, Pomès and De la Pauze, Moy, Pénaud, Jobert, Hureau de Villeneuve, Achenbach, Garapon, Duchesne, Danduran, Parisel, Dieuaide, Melkisff, Forlanini, Brearey, Tatin, Dandrieux, Edison, some with wings or screws, others with inclined planes, imagined, created, constructed, perfected, their flying machines, ready to do their work, once there came to be applied to them by some inventor a motor of adequate power and excessive lightness.

This list may be a little long, but that will be forgiven, for it is necessary to give the various steps in the ladder of aerial locomotion, on the top of which appeared Robur the conqueror. Without these attempts, these experiments of his predecessors, how could the inquirer have conceived so perfect an apparatus? And though he had but contempt for those who obstinately worked away in the direction of balloons, he held in high esteem all those partisans of "heavier than air," English, American, Italian, Austrian, French—and particularly French,—whose work had been perfected by him, and led him to design and then to build this flying engine known as the Albatross, which he was guiding through the currents of the atmosphere.

"The pigeon flies!" had exclaimed one of the most persistent adepts at aviation.

"They will crowd the air as they crowd the earth!" said one of his most excited partisans.

"From the locomotive to the aeromotive!" shouted the noisiest of all, who had turned on the trumpet of publicity to awaken the Old and New Worlds.

Nothing, in fact, is better established, by experiment and calculation, than that the air is highly resistant. A circumference of only a yard in diameter in the shape of a parachute can not only impede descent in air, but can render it isochronous. That is a fact.

It is equally well known that when the speed is great the work of the weight varies in almost inverse ratio to the square of the speed, and becomes almost insignificant.

It is also known that as the weight of a flying animal increases, the less is the proportional increase in the surface beaten by the wings in order to sustain it, although the motion of the wings becomes slower.

A flying machine must therefore be constructed to take advantage of these natural laws, to imitate the bird, "that admirable type of aerial locomotion," according to Dr. Marcy, of the Institute of France.

In short, the contrivances likely to solve the problem are of three kinds:—

1. Helicopters or spiralifers, which are simply screws with vertical axes.

2. Orthopters, machines which endeavour to reproduce the natural flight of birds.

3. Aeroplanes, which are merely inclined planes like kites, but towed or driven by horizontal screws.

Each of these systems has had and still has its partisans obstinately resolved to give way in not the slightest particular.

However, Robur, for many reasons, had rejected the two first.

The orthopter, or mechanical bird, offers certain advantages, no doubt. That the work and experiments of M. Renard in 1884 have sufficiently proved. But as has been said, it is not necessary to copy Nature servilely. Locomotives are not copied from the hare, nor are ships copied from the fish. To the first we have put wheels which are not legs; to the second we have put screws which are not fins. And they do not do so badly. Besides, what is this mechanical movement in the flight of birds, whose

The Clipper of the Clouds.

Page 64.

action is so complex? Has not Doctor Marcy suspected that the feathers open during the return of the wing so as to let the air through them? And is not that rather a difficult operation for an artificial machine?

On the other hand, aeroplanes have given many good results. Screws opposing a slanting plane to the bed of air will produce an ascensional movement, and the models experimented on have shown that the disposable weight, that is to say, the weight it is possible to deal with as distinct from that of the apparatus, increases with the square of the speed. Herein the aeroplane has the advantage over the aerostat even when the aerostat is furnished with the means of locomotion.

Nevertheless Robur had thought that the simpler his contrivance the better. And the screws—the Saint Helices that had been thrown in his teeth at the Weldon Institute—had sufficed for all the needs of his flying machine. One series could hold it suspended in the air, the other could drive it along under conditions that were marvellously adapted for speed and safety.

If the orthopter—striking like the wings of a bird—raised itself by beating the air, the helicopter raised itself by striking the air obliquely with the fins of the screw as it mounted on an inclined plane. These fins, or arms, are in reality wings, but wings disposed as a helix instead of as a paddle-wheel. The helix advances in the direction of its axis. Is the axis vertical? Then it moves vertically. Is the axis horizontal? Then it moves horizontally.

The whole of Robur's flying apparatus depended on these two movements, as will be seen from the following detailed description, which can be divided under three heads—the platform, the engines of suspension and propulsion, and the machinery.

Platform.—This was a framework a hundred feet long and twelve wide, a ship's deck, in fact with a projecting prow. Beneath was a hull solidly built, enclosing the engines, stores, and provisions of all sorts, including the water tanks. Round the deck a few light uprights supported a wire trellis that did duty for bulwarks. On the deck were three houses, whose compartments were used as cabins for the crew, or as machine-rooms. In the centre house was the machine which drove the suspensory helices, in that forward was the machine that drove the bow screw, in that aft was the machine that drove the stern screw. In the bow there were the cook's galley and the crew's quarters; in the stern were several cabins, including that of the engineer, the saloon, and above them all a glass house in which stood the helmsman, who steered the vessel by means of a powerful rudder. All these cabins were lighted by portholes filled with toughened glass, which has ten times the resistance of ordinary glass. Beneath the hull was a system of flexible springs to ease off the concussion when it became advisable to land.

Engines of suspension and propulsion.—Above the deck rose thirty-seven vertical axes, fifteen along each

Above the deck rose thirty-seven vertical axes.

Page 66.

side, and seven, more elevated, in the centre. The Albatross might be called a clipper with thirty-seven masts. But these masts instead of sails bore each two horizontal screws, not very large in spread or diameter, but driven at prodigious speed. Each of these axes had its movement independent of the rest, and each alternate one spun round in a different direction from the others, so as to avoid any tendency to gyration. Hence the screws as they rose on the vertical column of air retained their equilibrium by their horizontal resistance. Consequently the apparatus was furnished with seventy-four suspensory screws, whose three branches were connected by a metallic circle which economized their motive force. In front and behind, mounted on horizontal axes, were two propelling screws, each with four arms. These screws were of much larger diameter than the suspensory ones, but could be worked at quite their speed. In fact, the vessel combined the systems of Cossus, La Landelle, and Ponton d'Amécourt, as perfected by Robur. But it was in the choice and application of his motive force that he could claim to be an inventor.

Machinery.—Robur had not availed himself of the vapour of water or other liquids, nor compressed air and other elastic gases, nor explosive mixtures capable of producing mechanical motion. He employed electricity, that agent which one day will be soul of the industrial world. But he required no electro-motor to produce it. All he trusted to was piles and accumulators. What were the elements of these piles, and what were the acids he used, Robur only knew. And the construction of the accumulators was kept equally secret. Of what were their positive and negative plates? None can say. The engineer took good care—and not unreasonably—to keep his secret unpatented. One thing was unmistakable, and that was that the piles were of extraordinary strength; and the accumulators left those of Faure-Sellon-Volckmar very far behind in yielding currents whose ampères ran into figures up to then unknown. Thus there was obtained a power to drive the screws and communicate a suspending and propelling force in excess of all his requirements under any circumstances.

But—it is as well to repeat it—this belonged entirely to Robur. He kept it a close secret. And, if the president and secretary of the Weldon Institute did not happen to discover it, it would probably be lost to humanity.

It need not be shown that the apparatus possessed sufficient stability. Its centre of gravity proved that at once. There was no danger of its making alarming angles with the horizontal, still less of its capsizing.

And now for the metal used by Robur in the construction of his aeronef—a name which can be exactly applied to the Albatross. What was this material, so hard that the bowie-knife of Phil Evans could not scratch it, and Uncle Prudent could not explain its nature? Simply paper!

For some years this fabrication had been making considerable progress. Unsized paper, with the sheets impregnated with dextrin and starch and squeezed in hydraulic presses, will form a material as hard as steel. There are made of it pulleys, rails, and waggon-wheels, much more solid than metal wheels, and far lighter. And it was this lightness and solidity which Robur availed himself of in building his aerial locomotive. Everything —framework, hull, houses, cabins—was made of straw-paper turned hard as metal by compression, and—what was not to be despised in an apparatus flying at great heights—incombustible. The different parts of the engines and the screws were made of gelatinized fibre, which combined in sufficient degree flexibility with resistance. This material could be used in every form. It was insoluble in most gases and liquids, acids or essences, to say nothing of its insulating properties, and it proved most valuable in the electric machinery of the Albatross.

Robur, his mate Tom Turner, an engineer and two assistants, two steersmen and a cook—eight men all told —formed the crew of the aeronef, and proved ample for all the manœuvres required in aerial navigation. There were arms of the chase and of war; fishing appliances; electric lights; instruments of observation, compasses, and sextants for checking the course, thermometers for studying the temperature, different barometers, some for estimating the heights attained, others for indicating the variations of atmospheric pressure; a storm-glass for forecasting tempests; a small library; a portable printing-press; a field-piece mounted on a pivot, breech-loading, and throwing a three-inch shell; a supply of powder, bullets, dynamite cartridges; a cooking-stove, warmed by currents from the accumulators; a stock of preserves, meats, and vegetables sufficient to last for months. Such were the outfit and stores of the aeronef—in addition to the famous trumpet.

There was besides a light india-rubber boat, insubmersible, which could carry eight men on the surface of a river, a lake, or a calm sea.

But were there any parachutes in case of accident? No. Robur did not believe in accidents of that kind. The axes of the screws were independent. The stoppage of a few would not affect the motion of the others; and if only half were working, the Albatross could keep afloat in her natural element.

"And with her," said Robur to his guests—guests in spite of themselves—"I am master of the seventh part of the world, larger than Africa, Oceania, Asia, America, and Europe, this aerial Icarian sea, which millions of Icarians will one day people."

## CHAPTER VIII.

### THE BALLOONISTS REFUSE TO BE CONVINCED.

THE president of the Weldon Institute was stupefied; his companion was astonished. But neither of them would allow any of their very natural amazement to be visible.

The valet Frycollin did not conceal his terror at finding himself borne through space on such a machine, and he took no pains whatever to hide it.

The suspensory screws were rapidly spinning overhead. Fast as they were going, they would have to triple their speed if the Albatross was to ascend to higher zones. The two propellers were running very easily and driving the ship at about eleven knots an hour.

As they leaned over the rail the passengers of the Albatross could perceive a long sinuous liquid ribbon which meandered like a mere brook through a varied country amid the gleaming of many lagoons obliquely struck by the rays of the sun. The brook was a river, one of the most important in that district. Along its left bank was a chain of mountains extending out of sight.

"And will you tell us where we are?" asked Uncle Prudent, in a voice tremulous with anger.

"I have nothing to teach you," answered Robur.

"And will you tell us were we are going?" said Phil Evans.

"Through space."

"And how long will that last?"

"Until it ends."

"Are we going round the world?" asked Phil Evans, ironically.

"Further than that," said Robur.

"And if this voyage does not suit us?" asked Uncle Prudent.

"It will have to suit you."

That is a foretaste of the nature of the relations that were to obtain between the master of the Albatross and his guests, not to say his prisoners. Manifestly he wished to give them time to cool down, to admire the marvellous apparatus which was bearing them through the air, and doubtless to compliment the inventor. And so he went off to the other end of the deck, leaving them to examine the arrangement of the machinery and the management of the ship or to give their whole attention to the landscape which was unrolling beneath them.

"Uncle Prudent," said Evans, "unless I am mistaken we are flying over Central Canada. That river in the north-west is the Saint Lawrence. That town we are leaving behind is Quebec."

It was indeed the old city of Champlain, whose zinc roofs were shining like reflectors in the sun. The Albatross must thus have reached the forty-sixth degree of north latitude, and thus was explained the premature advance of the day with the abnormal prolongation of the dawn.

"Yes," said Phil Evans, "there is the town in its amphitheatre, the hill with its citadel, the Gibraltar of North America. There are the cathedrals. There is the Custom House with its dome surmounted by the British flag!"

Phil Evans had not finished before the Canadian city began to slip into the distance.

The clipper entered a zone of light clouds, which gradually shut off the view of the ground.

Robur, seeing that the president and secretary of the Weldon Institute had directed their attention to the external arrangements of the Albatross, walked up to them and said,—

"Well, gentlemen, do you believe in the possibility of aerial locomotion by machines heavier than air?"

It would have been difficult not to succumb to the evidence. But Uncle Prudent and Phil Evans did not reply.

"You are silent," continued the engineer. "Doubtless hunger makes you dumb! But if I undertook to carry you through the air, I did not think of feeding you on such a poorly nutritive fluid. Your first breakfast is waiting for you."

As Uncle Prudent and Phil Evans were feeling the pangs of hunger somewhat keenly they did not care to stand upon ceremony. A meal would commit them to nothing; and when Robur put them back on the ground they could resume full liberty of action.

And so they followed into a small dining-room in the aftermost house. There they found a well-laid table at which they could take their meals during the voyage. There were different preserves; and, among other things, was a sort of bread made of equal parts of flour and meat reduced to powder and worked together with a little lard, which boiled in water made excellent soup; and there were rashers of fried ham; and for drink there was tea.

Neither had Frycollin been forgotten. He was taken forward, and there found some strong soup made of this bread. In truth, he had to be very hungry to eat at all, for his jaws shook with fear, and almost refused to work.

"If it was to break!—if it was to break!" said the unfortunate negro.

Hence continual faintings. Only think! A fall of over four thousand feet, which would smash him to a jelly!

An hour afterwards Uncle Prudent and Phil Evans appeared on the deck. Robur was no longer there. At the stern the man at the wheel in his glass cage, his eyes fixed on the compass, followed imperturbably without hesitation the route given by the engineer.

As for the rest of the crew, breakfast probably kept

A meal would commit them to nothing.

Page 74.

them from their posts. An assistant engineer, examining the machinery, went from one house to the other.

If the speed of the ship was great the two colleagues could only estimate it imperfectly, for the Albatross had passed through the cloud zone which the sun showed some four thousand feet below.

"I can hardly believe it," said Phil Evans.

"Don't believe it!" said Uncle Prudent. And going to the bow they looked out towards the western horizon.

"Another town!" said Phil Evans.

"Do you recognize it?"

"Yes! It seems to me to be Montreal."

"Montreal? But we only left Quebec two hours ago!"

"That proves that we must be going at a speed of seventy-five miles an hour."

Such was the speed of the aeronef; and if the passengers were not inconvenienced by it, it was because they were going with the wind. In a calm such speed would have been difficult and the rate would have sunk to that of an express. In a head wind the speed would have been unbearable.

Phil Evans was not mistaken. Below the Albatross appeared Montreal, easily recognizable by the Victoria Bridge, a tubular bridge thrown over the St. Lawrence like the railway viaduct over the Venice lagoon. Soon they could distinguish the town's, wide streets, its huge shops, its palatial banks, its cathedral, recently built on the model of St. Peter's at Rome, and then Mount Royal, which commands the city and forms a magnificent park.

Luckily Phil Evans had visited the chief towns of Canada, and could recognize them without asking Robur. After Montreal they passed Ottawa, whose falls, seen from above, looked like a vast cauldron in ebullition throwing off masses of steam with grand effect.

"There is the Parliament House."

And he pointed out a sort of Nuremburg toy planted on a hill top. This toy with its polychrome architecture resembled the Houses of Parliament in London much as the Montreal cathedral resembles St. Peter's at Rome. But that was of no consequence ; there could be no doubt it was Ottawa.

Soon the city faded off towards the horizon, and formed but a luminous spot on the ground.

It was almost two hours before Robur appeared. His mate, Tom Turner, accompanied him. He said only three words. These were transmitted to the two assistant-engineers in the fore and aft engine-houses. At a sign the helmsman changed the direction of the Albatross a couple of points to the south-west ; at the same time Uncle Prudent and Phil Evans felt that a greater speed had been given to the propellers.

In fact, .the speed had been doubled, and now surpassed anything that had ever been attained by terrestrial engines. Torpedo-boats do their twenty-two knots an hour ; railway trains do their sixty miles an hour ; the ice-

Tom Turner.

Page 76.

boats on the frozen Hudson do their sixty-five miles an hour; a machine built by the Patterson company, with a cogged wheel, has done its eighty miles; and another locomotive between Trenton and Jersey has done its eighty-four.

But the Albatross, at full speed, could do her hundred and twenty miles an hour, or 176 feet per second. This speed is that of the storm which tears up trees by the roots. It is the mean speed of the carrier pigeon, and is only surpassed by the flight of the swallow (220 feet per second) and that of the swift (274 feet per second).

In a word, as Robur had said, the Albatross, by using the whole force of her screws, could make the tour of the globe in two hundred hours, or less than eight days.

Is it necessary to say so? The phenomenon whose appearance had so much puzzled the people of both worlds was the aeronef of the engineer. The trumpet which blared its startling fanfares through the air was that of the mate, Tom Turner. The flag planted on the chief monuments of Europe, Asia, America, was the flag of Robur the Conqueror and his Albatross.

And if up to then the engineer had taken many precautions against being recognized, if by preference he travelled at night, clearing the way with his electric lights, and during the day vanishing into the zones above the clouds, he seemed now to have no wish to keep his secret hidden. And if he had come to Philadelphia and presented himself at the meeting of the Weldon Institute, was it not that they might share in his prodigious discovery, and convince *ipso facto* the most incredulous? We know how he had been received, and we see what reprisals he had taken on the president and secretary of the club.

Again did Robur approach his prisoners, who affected to be in no way surprised at what they saw, of what had succeeded in spite of them. Evidently beneath the cranium of these two Anglo-Saxon heads there was a thick crust of obstinacy, which would not be easy to remove.

On his part, Robur did not seem to notice anything particular, and coolly continued the conversation which he had begun two hours before.

"Gentlemen," said he, "you ask yourselves doubtless if this apparatus, so marvellously adapted for aerial locomotion, is susceptible of receiving greater speed. It is not worth while to conquer space if we cannot devour it. I wanted the air to be a solid support to me, and it is. I saw that to struggle against the wind I must be stronger than the wind, and I am. I had no need of sails to drive me, nor oars nor wheels to push me, nor rails to give me a faster road. Air is what I wanted, that was all. Air surrounds me as it surrounds the submarine boat, and in it my propellers act like the screws of a steamer. That is how I solved the problem of aviation. That is what a balloon will never do, nor will any machine that is lighter than air."

Silence, absolute, on the part of the colleagues, which did not for a moment disconcert the engineer. He contented himself with a half smile, and continued in his interrogative style,—

"Perhaps you ask if to this power of the Albatross to move horizontally there is added an equal power of vertical movement—in a word, if, when, we visit the higher zones of the atmosphere, we can compete with an aerostat? Well, I should not advise you to enter the Go-ahead against her!"

The two colleagues shrugged their shoulders. That was probably what the engineer was waiting for.

Robur made a sign. The propelling screws immediately stopped, and after running for a mile the Albatross pulled up, motionless.

At a second gesture from Robur the suspensory helices revolved at a speed that can only be compared to that of a siren in acoustical experiments. Their f-r-r-r-r rose nearly an octave in the scale of sound, diminishing gradually in intensity as the air became more rarefied, and the machine rose vertically, like a lark singing his song in space.

"Master! Master!" shouted Frycollin. "See that it doesn't break!"

A smile of disdain was Robur's only reply. In a few minutes the Albatross had attained the height of 8700 feet, and extended the range of vision by seventy miles, the barometer having fallen 480 millimetres.

Then the Albatross descended. The diminution of the pressure in high altitudes leads to the diminution of oxygen in the air, and consequently in the blood. This has been the cause of several serious accidents which have happened to aeronauts, and Robur saw no reason to run any risk.

The Albatross thus returned to the height she seemed to prefer, and her propellers beginning again, drove her off to the south-west.

"Now, sirs, if that is what you wanted you can reply."

Then, leaning over the rail, he remained absorbed in contemplation.

When he raised his head the president and secretary of the Weldon Institute stood by his side.

"Engineer Robur," said Uncle Prudent, in vain endeavouring to control himself, "we have nothing to ask about what you seem to believe, but we wish to ask you a question which we think you would do well to answer."

"Speak."

"By what right did you attack us in Philadelphia in Fairmont Park? By what right did you shut us up in that prison? By what right have you brought us against our will on board this flying machine?"

"And by what right, Messieurs Balloonists, did you insult and threaten me in your club in such a way that I am astonished I came out of it alive?"

"To ask is not to answer," said Phil Evans, "and I repeat, by what right?"

"Do you wish to know?"

"If you please."

"Well, by the right of the strongest!"

The Falls of Niagara.

Page 81.

"That is cynical."

"But it is true."

"And for how long, citizen engineer," asked Uncle Prudent, who was nearly exploding, "for how long do you intend to exercise that right?"

"How can you?" said Robur, ironically, "how can you ask me such a question when you have only to cast down your eyes to enjoy a spectacle unparalleled in the world?"

The Albatross was then sweeping across the immense expanse of Lake Ontario. She had just crossed the country so poetically described by Cooper. Then she followed the southern shore and headed for the celebrated river which pours into it the waters of Lake Erie, breaking them to powder in its cataracts.

In an instant a majestic sound, a roar as of the tempest, mounted towards them; and, as if a humid fog had been projected into the air, the atmosphere sensibly freshened.

Below were the liquid masses. They seemed like an enormous flowing sheet of crystal amid a thousand rainbows due to refraction as it decomposed the solar rays. The sight was sublime.

Before the falls a foot-bridge, stretching like a thread, united one bank to the other. Three miles below was a suspension-bridge, across which a train was crawling from the Canadian to the American bank.

"The falls of Niagara!" exclaimed Phil Evans.

And as the exclamation escaped him, Uncle Prudent was doing all he could to admire nothing of these wonders.

A minute afterwards the Albatross had crossed the river which separates the United States from Canada, and was flying over the vast territories of the West.

## CHAPTER IX.

### ACROSS THE PRAIRIE.

IN one of the cabins of the after-house Uncle Prudent and Phil Evans had found two excellent berths, with clean linen, change of clothes, and travelling cloaks and rugs. No Atlantic liner could have offered them more comfort. If they did not sleep soundly it was that they did not wish to do so, or rather that their very real anxiety prevented them. In what adventure had they embarked? To what series of experiments had they been invited? How would the business end? and above all, what was Robur going to do with them?

Frycollin, the valet, was quartered forward in a cabin adjoining that of the cook. The neighbourhood did not displease him; he liked to rub shoulders with the great in this world. But if he finally went to sleep it was to dream of fall after fall, of projections through space, which made his sleep a horrible nightmare.

However, nothing could be quieter than this journey through the atmosphere, whose currents had grown weaker with the evening. Beyond the rustling of the blades of the screws there was not a sound, except now and then the whistle from some terrestrial locomotive, or the calling of some animal. Strange instinct! These terrestrial beings felt the aeronef glide over them, and uttered cries of terror as it passed. On the morrow, 14th June, at five o'clock, Uncle Prudent and Phil Evans were walking on the deck of the Albatross. Nothing had changed since the evening; there was a look-out forward, and the helmsman was in his glass cage.

Why was there a look-out? Was there any chance of collision with another such machine? Certainly not. Robur had not yet found imitators. The chance of encountering an aerostat gliding through the air was too remote to be regarded. In any case it would be all the worse for the aerostat—the earthen pot and the iron pot. The Albatross had nothing to fear from the collision.

But what could happen? The aeronef might find herself like a ship on a lee shore if a mountain that could not be outflanked or passed barred the way. These are the reefs of the air, and they have to be avoided as a ship avoids the reefs of the sea. The engineer, it is true, had given the course, and in doing so had taken into account the altitude necessary to clear the summits of the high lands in the district. But as the aeronef was rapidly nearing a mountainous country, it was only prudent to keep a good look-out, in case some slight deviation from the course became necessary.

Looking at the country beneath them, Uncle Prudent

and Phil Evans noticed a large lake, whose lower southern end the Albatross had just reached. They concluded, therefore, that during the night the whole length of Erie had been traversed, and that, as they were going due west, they would soon be over Lake Michigan. "There can be no doubt of it," said Phil Evans, "and that group of roofs on the horizon is Chicago."

He was right. It was indeed the city from which the seventeen railways diverge, the Queen of the West, the vast reservoir into which flow the products of Indiana, Ohio, Wisconsin, Missouri, and all the States which form the western half of the Union.

Uncle Prudent, through an excellent telescope he had found in his cabin, easily recognized the principal buildings. His colleague pointed out to him the churches and public edifices, the numerous "elevators" or mechanical granaries, and the huge Sherman Hotel, whose windows seemed like a hundred glittering points on each of its faces.

"If that is Chicago," said Uncle Prudent, "it is obvious that we are going farther west than is convenient for us if we are to return to our starting-place."

And, in fact, the Albatross was travelling in a straight line from the Pennsylvanian capital.

But if Uncle Prudent wished to ask Robur to take him eastwards he could not then do so. That morning the engineer did not leave his cabin. Either he was occupied in some work, or else he was asleep, and the two colleagues sat down to breakfast without seeing him.

The speed was the same as that during last evening. The wind being easterly the rate was not interfered with at all, and as the thermometer only fails a degree centigrade for every seventy metres of elevation the temperature was not insupportable. And so, in chatting and thinking and waiting for the engineer, Uncle Prudent and Phil Evans walked about beneath the forest of screws, whose gyratory movement gave their arms the appearance of semi-diaphanous disks.

The State of Illinois was left by its northern frontier in less than two hours and a half; and they crossed the Father of Waters, the Mississippi, whose double-decked steamboats seemed no bigger than canoes. Then the Albatross flew over Iowa after having sighted Iowa city about eleven o'clock in the morning.

A few chains of hills, "bluffs" as they are called, curved across the face of the country trending from the south to the north-west, whose moderate height necessitated no rise in the course of the aeronef. Soon the bluffs gave place to the large plains of western Iowa and Nebraska—immense prairies extending all the way to the foot of the Rocky Mountains. Here and there were many rios, affluents or minor affluents of the Missouri. On their banks were towns and villages, growing more scattered as the Albatross sped farther west.

Nothing particular happened during this day. Uncle Prudent and Phil Evans were left entirely to themselves. They hardly noticed Frycollin sprawling at full length in the bow, keeping his eyes shut so that he could see nothing. And they were not attacked by vertigo, as might have been expected. There was no guiding mark, and there was nothing to cause the vertigo, as there would have been on the top of a lofty building. The abyss has no attractive power when it is gazed at from the car of a balloon or deck of an aeronef. It is not an abyss that opens beneath the aeronaut, but an horizon that rises round him on all sides like a cup.

In a couple of hours the Albatross was over Omaha, on the Nebraska frontier—Omaha city, the real head of the Pacific Railway, that long line of rails, four thousand five hundred miles in length, stretching from New York to San Francisco. For a moment they could see the yellow waters of the Missouri, then the town, with its houses of wood and brick in the centre of a rich basin, like a buckle in the iron belt which clasps North America round the waist. Doubtless, also, as the passengers in the aeronef could observe all these details, the inhabitants of Omaha noticed the strange machine. But their astonishment at seeing it gliding overhead could be no greater than that of the president and secretary of the Weldon Institute at finding themselves on board.

Anyhow, the journals of the Union would be certain to notice the fact. It would be the explanation of the astonishing phenomenon which the whole world had been wondering over for some time.

In an hour the Albatross had left Omaha and crossed

the Platte River, whose valley is followed by the Pacific Railway in its route across the prairie. Things looked serious for Uncle Prudent and Phil Evans.

"It is serious, then, this absurd project of taking us to the Antipodes."

"And whether we like it or not!" exclaimed the other. "Robur had better take care! I am not the man to stand that sort of thing."

"Nor am I!" replied Phil Evans. "But be calm, Uncle Prudent, be calm."

"Be calm!"

"And keep your temper until it is wanted."

By five o'clock they had crossed the Black Mountains, covered with pines and cedars, and the Albatross was over the appropriately named Bad Lands of Nebraska—a chaos of ochre-coloured hills, of mountainous fragments fallen on the soil and broken in their fall. At a distance these blocks take the most fantastic shapes. Here and there amid this enormous game of knucklebones there could be traced the imaginary ruins of mediæval cities with forts and dungeons, pepper-box turrets, and machicolated towers. And in truth these Bad Lands are an immense ossuary where lie bleaching in the sun myriads of fragments of pachyderms, chelonians, and even, some would have us believe, fossil men, overwhelmed by unknown cataclysms ages and ages ago.

When evening came the whole basin of the Platte River had been crossed, and the plain extended to the extreme limits of the horizon, which rose high owing to the altitude of the Albatross.

During the night there were no more shrill whistles of locomotives or deeper notes of the river steamers to trouble the quiet of the starry firmament. Long bellowings occasionally reached the aeronef from the herds of buffalo that roamed over the prairie in search of water and pasturage. And when they ceased, the trampling of the grass under their feet produced a dull roaring similar to the rushing of a flood, and very different from the continuous f-r-r-r-r of the screws.

Then from time to time came the howl of a wolf, a fox, a wild cat, or a coyote, the *Canis latrans*, whose name is justified by his sonorous bark.

Occasionally came penetrating odours of mint, and sage, and absinthe, mingled with the more powerful fragrance of the conifers which rose floating through the night air.

At last came a menacing yell, which was not due to the coyote. It was the shout of a Redskin, which no Tenderfoot would confound with the cry of a wild beast.

## CHAPTER X.

### WESTWARD—BUT WHITHER?

THE next day, the 15th of June, about five o'clock in the morning, Phil Evans left his cabin. Perhaps he would to-day have a chance of speaking to Robur? Desirous of knowing why he had not appeared the day before, Evans addressed himself to the mate, Tom Turner.

Tom Turner was an Englishman of about forty-five, broad in the shoulders and short in the legs, a man of iron, with one of those enormous characteristic heads that Hogarth rejoiced in.

"Shall we see Mr. Robur to-day?" asked Phil Evans.

"I don't know," said Turner.

"I need not ask if he has gone out."

"Perhaps he has."

"And when will he come back?"

"When he has finished his cruise."

And Tom went into his cabin.

With this reply they had to be contented. Matters did not look promising, particularly as on reference to the compass it appeared that the Albatross was still steering south-west.

Great was the contrast between the barren tract of the Bad Lands passed over during the night and the landscape then unrolling beneath them.

The aeronef was now more than six hundred miles from Omaha, and over a country which Phil Evans could not recognize because he had never been there before. A few forts to keep the Indians in order crowned the bluffs with their geometric lines, formed oftener of palisades than walls. There were few villages and few inhabitants, the country differing widely from the auriferous lands of Colorado many leagues to the south.

In the distance a long line of mountain crests, in great confusion as yet, began to appear. They were the Rocky Mountains.

For the first time that morning Uncle Prudent and Phil Evans were sensible of a certain lowness of temperature which was not due to a change in the weather, for the sun shone in superb splendour.

"It is because of the Albatross being higher in the air," said Phil Evans.

In fact the barometer outside the central deck-house had fallen 540 millimeters, thus indicating an elevation of about 10,000 feet above the sea. The aeronef was at this altitude owing to the elevation of the ground. An hour before she had been at a height of 13,000 feet, and behind her were mountains covered with perpetual snow.

There was nothing Uncle Prudent and his companion could remember which would lead them to discover where they were. During the night the Albatross had made several stretches north and south at tremendous speed, and that was what had put them out of their reckoning.

After talking over several hypotheses more or less plausible they came to the conclusion that this country encircled with mountains must be the district declared by an Act of Congress in March, 1872, to be the National Park of the United States. A strange region it was. It well merited the name of a park—a park with mountains for hills, with lakes for ponds, with rivers for streamlets, and with geysers of marvellous power instead of fountains.

In a few minutes the Albatross glided across the Yellowstone River, leaving Mount Stevenson on the right, and coasting the large lake which bears the name of the stream. Great was the variety on the banks of this basin, ribbed as they were with obsidian and tiny crystals, reflecting the sunlight on their myriad facets. Wonderful was the arrangement of the islands on its surface; magnificent were the blue reflections of the gigantic mirror. And around the lake, one of the highest in the globe, were multitudes of pelicans, swans, gulls and geese, bernicles and divers. In places the steep banks were clothed with green trees, pines and larches, and at the foot of the escarpments there shot upwards innumerable white fumaroles, the vapour escaping from the soil as from an enormous reservoir in which the water is kept in permanent ebullition by subterranean fire.

The cook might have seized the opportunity of securing an ample supply of trout, the only fish the Yellowstone Lake contains in myriads. But the Albatross kept on at such a height that there was no chance of indulging in a catch which assuredly would have been miraculous.

In three quarters of an hour the lake was overpassed, and a little farther on the last was seen of the geyser region, which rivals the finest in Iceland. Leaning over the rail, Uncle Prudent and Phil Evans watched the liquid columns which leaped up as though to furnish the aeronef with a new element. There were the Fan, with the jets shot forth in rays, the Fortress, which seemed to be defended by waterspouts, the Faithful Friend, with her plume crowned with the rainbows, the Giant, spurting forth a vertical torrent twenty feet round and more than two hundred feet high.

Robur must evidently have been familiar with this incomparable spectacle, unique in the world, for he did not appear on deck. Was it, then, for the sole pleasure of his guests that he had brought the aeronef above the national domain? If so, he came not to receive their thanks. He did not even trouble himself during the daring passage of the Rocky Mountains, which the Albatross approached at about seven o'clock.

As we know, this orographical system stretches like

an enormous backbone throughout the length of North America, and is prolonged into the Mexican Andes. It extends for over two thousand miles, its highest point being James Peak, which attains a height of twelve thousand feet.

By increasing the speed of her wings, as a bird rising in its flight, the Albatross would clear the highest ridges of the chain, and sink again over Oregon or Utah. But the manœuvre was unnecessary. The passes allowed the barrier to be crossed without ascending for the higher ridges. There are many of these canyons, or steep valleys, more or less narrow, through which they could glide, such as Bridger Gap, through which runs the Pacific Railway into the Mormon territory, and others to the north and south of it.

It was through one of these that the Albatross headed, after slackening speed so as not to dash against the walls of the canyon. The steersman, with a sureness of hand rendered more effective by the sensitiveness of the rudder, manœuvred his craft as if she were a crack racer in a Royal Victoria match. It was really extraordinary. In spite of all the jealousy of the two enemies of "lighter than air," they could not help being surprised at the perfection of this engine of aerial locomotion.

In less than two hours and a half they were through the Rockies, and the Albatross had resumed her former speed of sixty-two miles an hour. She was steering south-

It was really extraordinary.

Page 94.

It was a train on the Pacific Railway.

Page 95.

west so as to cut across Utah diagonally as she neared the ground. She had even dropped several hundred yards when the sound of a whistle attracted the attention of Uncle Prudent and Phil Evans.

It was a train on the Pacific Railway on the road to Salt Lake City.

And then, in obedience to an order secretly given, the Albatross dropped still lower so as to chase the train, which was going at full speed. She was immediately sighted. A few heads showed themselves at the doors of the cars. Then numerous passengers crowded the gangways. Some did not hesitate to climb on the roof to get a better view of the flying machine. Cheers came floating up through the air, but no Robur appeared in answer to them.

The Albatross continued her descent, slowing her suspensory screws and moderating her speed so as not to leave the train behind. She flew about it like an enormous beetle or a gigantic bird of prey. She headed off to the right and left, and swept on in front, and hung behind, and proudly displayed her flag with the golden sun, to which the conductor of the train replied by waving the Stars and Stripes.

In vain the prisoners, in their desire to take advantage of the opportunity, endeavoured to make themselves known to those below. In vain the president of the Weldon Institute roared forth at the top of his voice,—

"I am Uncle Prudent of Philadelphia!"

And the secretary followed suit with,—

"I am Phil Evans, his colleague!"

Their shouts were lost in the thousands of cheers with which the passengers greeted the aeronef.

Three or four of the crew of the Albatross had appeared on the deck, and one of them, like sailors when passing a ship less speedy than their own, held out a rope, an ironical way of offering to tow them.

And then the Albatross resumed her original speed, and in half an hour the express was out of sight.

About one o'clock there appeared a vast disk, which reflected the solar rays as if it were an immense mirror.

"That ought to be the Mormon capital, Salt Lake City," said Uncle Prudent.

And so it was, and the disk was the roof of the Tabernacle, where ten thousand saints can worship at their ease. This vast dome, like a convex mirror, threw off the rays of the sun in all directions.

There was a great city, at the foot of the Wasatch Mountains, clothed half way with cedars and pines, on the banks of the River Jordan, through which the Utah waters enter the lake. Beneath the aeronef lay the draught-board in which so many American cities are planned. Around was a well-cultivated country, in which the flocks of sheep were countable in thousands.

But the draught-board vanished like a shadow, and the Albatross sped on her way to the south-west with a speed that was not felt, because it surpassed that of the chasing wind. Soon she was in Nevada, over the silver regions, which the Sierra separates from the golden lands of California.

"We shall certainly reach San Francisco before night," said Phil Evans.

"And then?" asked Uncle Prudent.

It was six o'clock precisely when the Sierra Nevada was crossed by the same pass as that taken by the railway. Only a hundred and eighty miles then separated them from San Francisco, the Californian capital.

At the speed the Albatross was going she would be over the dome by eight o'clock.

At this moment Robur appeared on deck. The colleagues walked up to him.

"Engineer Robur," said Uncle Prudent, "we are now on the confines of America! We think the time has come for this joke to end."

"I never joke," said Robur.

He raised his hand. The Albatross swiftly dropped towards the ground, and at the same time such speed was given her as to drive the prisoners into their cabin.

As soon as the door was shut, Uncle Prudent exclaimed,—

"I could strangle him!"

"We must try to escape!" said Phil Evans.

"Yes; cost what it may!"

A long murmur greeted their ears.

It was the beating of the surf on the seashore. It was the Pacific Ocean!

## CHAPTER XI.

### THE WIDE PACIFIC.

UNCLE PRUDENT and Phil Evans had quite made up their minds to escape. If they had not had to deal with the eight particularly vigorous men who composed the crew of the aeronef they might have tried to succeed by main force. But as they were only two—for Frycollin could only be considered as a quantity of no importance—force was not to be thought of. Hence recourse must be had to strategy as soon as the Albatross again took the ground. Such was what Phil Evans endeavoured to impress on his irascible colleague, though he was in constant fear of Prudent aggravating matters by some premature outbreak.

In any case the present was not the time to attempt anything of the sort. The aeronef was sweeping along over the North Pacific. On the following morning, that of June 16th, the coast was out of sight. And as the coast curves off from Vancouver Island up to the Aleutians—belonging to that portion of America ceded by Russia to the United States in 1867—it was highly probable that the Albatross would cross it at the end of the curve, if her course remained unchanged.

How long the night appeared to be to the two friends! How eager they were to get out of their cabins! When they came on deck in the morning the dawn had for some hours been silvering the eastern horizon. They were nearing the June solstice, the longest day of the year in the northern hemisphere, when there is hardly any night along the sixtieth parallel.

Either from custom or intention Robur was in no hurry to leave his deck-house. When he came out this morning he contented himself with bowing to his two guests as he passed them in the stern of the aeronef.

And now Frycollin ventured out of his cabin. His eyes red with sleeplessness, and dazed in their look, he tottered along like a man whose foot feels it is not on solid ground. His first glance was at the suspensory screws, which were working with gratifying regularity without any signs of haste.

That done, the negro stumbled along to the rail, and grasped it with both hands, so as to make sure of his balance. Evidently he wished to view the country over which the Albatross was flying at the height of seven hundred feet or more.

At first he kept himself well back behind the rail. Then he shook it to make sure it was firm; then he drew himself up; then he bent forward; then he stretched out his head. It need not be said that while he was executing these different manœuvres he kept his eyes shut. At last he opened them.

What a shout! And how quickly he fled! And how deeply his head sank back into his shoulders!

At the bottom of the abyss he had seen the immense ocean. His hair would have risen on end—if it had not been wool.

"The sea! the sea!" he cried.

And Frycollin would have fallen on the deck had not the cook opened his arms to receive him.

This cook was a Frenchman, and probably a Gascon, his name being François Tapage. If he was not a Gascon he must in his infancy have inhaled the breezes of the Garonne. How did this François Tapage find himself in the service of the engineer? By what chain of accidents had he become one of the crew of the Albatross? We can hardly say; but in any case he spoke English like a Yankee.

"Eh, stand up!" said he, lifting the negro by a vigorous clutch at the waist.

"Master Tapage!" said the poor fellow, giving a despairing look at the screws.

"At your service, Frycollin."

"Did this thing ever smash?"

"No, but it will end by smashing."

"Why? Why?"

"Because everything must end."

"And the sea is beneath us!"

"If we are to fall it is better to fall, in the sea."

"We shall be drowned."

"We shall be drowned, but we shall not be smashed to a jelly."

The next moment Frycollin was on all fours, creeping to the back of his cabin.

During this day the aeronef was only driven at moderate speed. She seemed to skim the placid surface of the sea, which lay glistening in the sunshine about a hundred feet beneath. Uncle Prudent and his companion remained in their cabin, so that they did not meet with Robur, who walked about smoking alone or talking to the mate. Only half the screws were working, yet that was enough to keep the apparatus afloat in the lower zones of the atmosphere.

The crew, as a change from the ordinary routine, would have endeavoured to catch a few fish, had there been any sign of them; but all that could be seen on the surface of the sea were a few of those yellow-bellied whales which measure about eighty feet in length. These are the most formidable cetaceans in the northern seas, and whalers are very careful in attacking them, for their strength is prodigious. However, in harpooning one of these whales, either with the ordinary harpoon, the Fletcher fuse, or the javelin-bomb, of which there was an assortment on board, there would have been no danger to the men of the Albatross.

But what was the good of such useless. massacre? Doubtless to show off the powers of the aeronef to the members of the Weldon Institute. And so Robur gave orders for the capture of one of these monstrous cetaceans.

At the shout of "A whale! a whale!" Uncle Prudent and Phil Evans came out of their cabin. Perhaps there was a whaler in sight! In that case all they had to do to escape from their flying prison was to jump into the sea, and chance being picked up by the vessel.

The crew were all on deck.

"Shall we try, sir?" asked Tom Turner.

"Yes," said Robur.

In the engine-room the engineer and his assistant were at their posts ready to obey the orders signalled to them. The Albatross dropped towards the sea, and remained about fifty feet above it.

There was no ship in sight—of that the two colleagues soon assured themselves—nor was there any land to be seen to which they could swim, providing Robur made no attempt to recapture them.

Several jets of water from the spout holes soon announced the presence of the whales as they came to the surface to breathe.

Tom Turner and one of the men were in the bow. Within his reach was one of those javelin-bombs, of Californian make, which are shot from an arquebus, and which are shaped as a metallic cylinder terminated by a cylindrical shell armed with a shaft having a barbed point. Robur was a little farther aft, and with his right hand signalled to the engineers, while with his left he directed the steersman. He thus controlled the aeronef in every way, horizontally and vertically, and it is almost impossible to conceive with what speed and precision the Albatross answered to his orders. She seemed a living being, of which he was the soul.

"A whale! a whale!" shouted Tom Turner, as the back of a cetacean emerged from the surface about four cable lengths in front of the Albatross.

The Albatross swept towards it, and when she was witnin sixty feet of it she stopped dead.

Tom Turner seized the arquebus, which was resting against a cleat on the rail. He fired, and the projectile, attached to a long line, entered the whale's body. The shell, filled with an explosive compound, burst, and shot out a small harpoon with two branches, which fastened into the animal's flesh.

"Look out!" shouted Turner.

Uncle Prudent and Phil Evans, much against their will, became greatly interested in the spectacle.

The whale, seriously wounded, gave the sea such a slap with his tail, that the water dashed up over the bow of the aeronef. Then he plunged to a great depth, while the line, which had been previously wetted in a tub of water to prevent its taking fire, ran out like lightning. When the whale rose to the surface he started off at full speed in a northerly direction.

It may be imagined with what speed the Albatross was towed in pursuit. Besides, the propellers had been stopped. The whale was let go as he would, and the ship followed him. Turner stood ready to cut the line in case a fresh plunge should render this towing dangerous.

For half an hour, and perhaps for a distance of six miles, the Albatross was thus dragged along, but it was obvious that the whale was tiring. Then, at a gesture from Robur, the assistant engineers started the propellers astern, so as to oppose a certain resistance to the whale, who was gradually getting closer.

Soon the aeronef was gliding about twenty-five feet above him. His tail was beating the waters with incredible violence, and as he turned over on his back an enorous wave was produced.

Suddenly the whale turned up again, so as to take a header, as it were, and then dived with such rapidity that Turner had barely time to cut the line.

The aeronef was dragged to the very surface of the water. A whirlpool was formed where the animal had disappeared. A wave dashed up on to the deck as if the aeronef were a ship driving against wind and tide.

Luckily, with a blow of the hatchet the mate severed the line, and the Albatross, freed from her tug, sprang aloft six hundred feet under the impulse of her ascensional screws. Robur had manœuvred his ship without losing his coolness for a moment.

A few minutes afterwards the whale returned to the surface—dead. From every side the birds flew down on to the carcass, and their cries were enough to deafen a

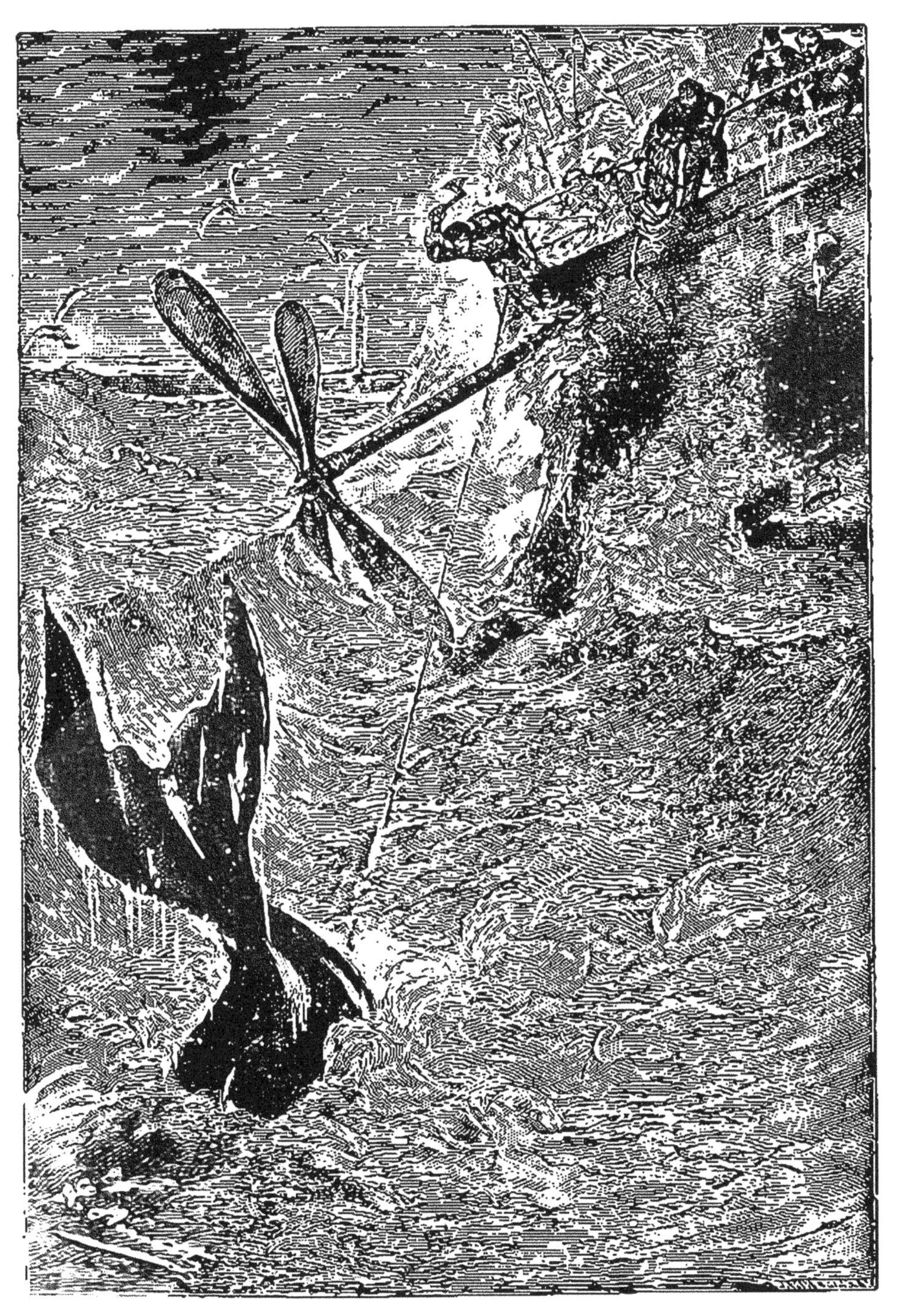

With a blow of the hatchet the mate severed the line.

Page 104.

congress. The Albatross, without stopping to share in the spoil, resumed her course to the west.

In the morning of the 17th of June, at about six o'clock, land was sighted on the horizon. This was the peninsula of Alaska, and the long range of breakers of the Aleutian Islands.

The Albatross glided over the barrier where the fur seals swarm for the benefit of the Russo-American Company. An excellent business is the capture of these amphibians, which are from six to seven feet long, russet in colour, and weigh from three hundred to four hundred pounds. There they were in interminable files, ranged in line of battle, and countable by thousands.

Although they did not move at the passage of the Albatross, it was otherwise with the ducks, divers, and loons, whose husky cries filled the air as they disappeared beneath the waves and fled terrified from the aerial monster.

The twelve hundred miles of the Behring Sea between the first of the Aleutians and the extreme end of Kamtschatka were traversed during the twenty-four hours of this day and the following night. Uncle Prudent and Phil Evans found that there was no present chance of putting their project of escape into execution. Flight was not to be thought of among the deserts of Eastern Asia, nor on the coast of the sea of Okhotsk. Evidently the Albatross was bound for Japan or China, and there, although it was not perhaps quite safe to trust themselves to the mercies of the Chinese or Japanese, the two friends had made up their minds to run if the aeronef stopped.

But would she stop? She was not like a bird which grows fatigued by too long a flight, or like a balloon which has to descend for want of gas. She still had food for many weeks, and her organs were of marvellous strength, defying all weakness and weariness.

During the 18th of June she swept over the peninsula of Kamtschatka, and during the day there was a glimpse of Petropaulovski and the volcano of Kloutschew. Then she rose again to cross the Sea of Okhotsk, running down by the Kurile Isles, which seemed to be a breakwater pierced by hundreds of channels. On the 19th, in the morning, the Albatross was over the strait of La Perouse between Saghalien and Northern Japan, and had reached the mouth of the great Siberian river, the Amoor.

Then there came on a fog so dense that the aeronef had to rise above it. At the altitude she was there was no obstacle to be feared, no elevated monuments to hinder her passage, no mountains against which there was risk of being shattered in her flight. The country was only slightly varied. But the fog was very disagreeable, and made everything on board very damp.

All that was necessary was to get above this bed of mist, which was nearly thirteen hundred feet thick, and the ascensional screws being increased in speed; the Albatross was soon clear of the fog and in the sunny regions of the sky. Under these circumstances, Uncle Prudent and Phil

Evans would have found some difficulty in carrying out their plan of escape, even admitting that they could leave the aeronef.

During the day, as Robur passed them, he stopped for a moment, and without seeming to attach any importance to what he said, addressed them carelessly as follows :—

"Gentlemen, a sailing-ship or a steamship caught in a fog from which it cannot escape is always much delayed. It must not move unless it keeps its whistle or its horn going. It must reduce its speed, and any instant a collision may be expected. The Albatross has none of these things to fear. What does fog matter to her? She can leave it when she chooses. The whole of space is hers."

And Robur continued his stroll without waiting for an answer, and the puffs of his pipe were lost in the sky.

"Uncle Prudent," said Phil Evans, "it seems that this astonishing Albatross never has anything to fear."

"That we shall see!" answered the president of the Weldon Institute.

The fog lasted three days, the 19th, 20th, and 21st of June, with regrettable persistence. An ascent had to be made to clear the Japanese mountain of Fusiyama. When the curtain of mist was drawn aside there lay below them an immense city, with palaces, villas, gardens, and parks. Even without seeing it Robur had recognized it by the barking of the innumerable dogs, the cries of the birds of prey, and above all, by the cadaverous odour which the bodies of its executed criminals gave off into space.

The two colleagues were out on the deck while the engineer was taking his observations in case he thought it best to continue his course through the fog.

"Gentlemen," said he, "I have no reason for concealing from you that this town is Tokio, the capital of Japan."

Uncle Prudent did reply. In the presence of the engineer he was almost choked, as if his lungs were short of air.

"This view of Tokio," continued Robur, "is very curious."

"Curious as it may be—" replied Phil Evans.

"It is not as good as Pekin?" interrupted the engineer. "That is what I think, and very shortly you shall have an opportunity of judging."

Impossible to be more agreeable!

The Albatross then gliding south-east, had her course changed four points so as to head to the eastward.

"This town is Tokio, the capital of Japan."

Page 108.

## CHAPTER XII.

### THROUGH THE HIMALAYAS.

DURING the night the fog cleared off. There were symptoms of an approaching typhoon—a rapid fall of the barometer, a disappearance of vapour, large clouds of ellipsoid form clinging to a copper sky, and, on the opposite horizon, long streaks of carmine on a slate-coloured field, with a large sector quite clear in the north. Then the sea was smooth and calm and at sunset assumed a deep scarlet hue.

Fortunately the typhoon broke more to the south, and had no other result than to sweep away the mist which had been accumulating during the last three days.

In an hour they had traversed the hundred and twenty-five miles of the Corean strait, and while the typhoon was raging on the coast of China, the Albatross was over the Yellow Sea. During the 22nd and 23rd she was over the Gulf of Pechelee, and on the 24th she was ascending the valley of the Peiho on her way to the capital of the Celestial Empire.

Leaning over the rail, the two colleagues, as the

engineer had told them, could see distinctly the immense city, the wall which divides it into two parts—the Manchoo town and the Chinese town—the twelve suburbs which surround it, the large boulevards which radiate from its centre, the temples with their green and yellow roofs bathed in the rising sun, the grounds surrounding the houses of the mandarins; then in the middle of the Manchoo town the eighteen hundred acres of the Yellow town, with its pagodas, its imperial gardens, its artificial lakes, its mountain of coal which towers above the capital; and in the centre of the Yellow town, like a square of a Chinese puzzle enclosed in another, the Red town, that is the imperial palace, with all the peaks of its outrageous architecture.

Below the Albatross the air was filled with a singular harmony. It seemed to be a concert of Æolian harps. In the air were a hundred kites of different forms, made of sheets of palm-leaf, and having at their upper end a sort of bow of light wood with a thin slip of bamboo beneath. In the breath of the wind these slips, with all their notes varied like those of a harmonicon, gave forth a most melancholy murmuring. It seemed as though they were breathing musical oxygen.

It suited Robur's whim to run close up to this aerial orchestra, and the Albatross slowed as she glided through the sonorous waves which the kites gave off through the atmosphere.

But immediately an extraordinary effect was produced

amongst the innumerable population. Beatings of the tomtoms and sounds of other formidable instruments of the Chinese orchestra, gun reports by the thousand, mortars fired in hundreds, all were brought into play to scare away the aeronef. Although the Chinese astronomers may have recognized the aerial machine as the moving body that had given rise to such disputes, it was to the Celestial million, from the humblest tankader to the best-buttoned mandarin, an apocalyptical monster appearing in the sky of Buddha.

The crew of the Albatross troubled themselves very little about these demonstrations. But the strings which held the kites, and were tied to fixed pegs in the imperial gardens, were cut or quickly hauled in; and the kites were either drawn in rapidly, sounding louder as they sank, or else fell like a bird shot through both wings whose song ends with its last sigh.

A noisy fanfare escaped from Tom Turner's trumpet, and drowned the final notes of the aerial concert. It did not interrupt the terrestrial fusillade. At last a shell exploded a few feet below the Albatross, and then she mounted into the inaccessible regions of the sky.

Nothing happened during the few following days of which the prisoners could take advantage. The aeronef kept on her course to the south-west, thereby showing that it was intended to take her to India. Twelve hours after leaving Pekin Uncle Prudent and Phil Evans caught a glimpse of the Great Wall in the neighbourhood of

Chen-Si. Then, avoiding the Lung Mountains, they passed over the valley of the Hoangho and crossed the Chinese border on the Thibet side.

Thibet consists of high table-lands without vegetation, with here and there snowy peaks and barren ravines, torrents fed by glaciers, depressions with glittering beds of salt, lakes surrounded by luxurious forests, with icy winds sweeping over all.

The barometer falling seventeen-tenths of an inch indicated an altitude of thirteen thousand feet above the level of the sea. At that height the temperature, although it was in the warmest months of the northern hemisphere, was only a little above freezing. This cold, combined with the speed of the Albatross, made the voyage somewhat trying, and although the friends had warm travelling wraps, they preferred to keep to their cabin.

It need hardly be said that to keep the aeronef in this rarefied atmosphere the suspensory screws had to be driven at extreme speed. But they worked with perfect regularity, and the sound of their wings almost acted as a lullaby.

During this day, appearing from below about the size of a carrier pigeon, she passed over Garlock, a town of western Thibet, the capital of the province of Gari Khorsum.

On the 27th of June, Uncle Prudent and Phil Evans sighted an enormous barrier, broken here and there by several peaks, lost in the snows that bounded the horizon.

Avoiding the Lung Mountains.

Page 112.

Gliding like a ship between enormous reefs.

Page 113.

Leaning against the fore-cabin, so as to keep their places notwithstanding the speed of the ship, they watched these colossal masses, which seemed to be running away from the aeronef.

"The Himalayas, evidently," said Phil Evans; "and probably Robur is going round their base, so as to pass into India."

"So much the worse," answered Uncle Prudent. "On that immense territory we shall perhaps be able to—"

"Unless he goes round by Burmah to the east, or Nepaul to the west."

"Anyhow, I defy him to go through them."

"Indeed!" said a voice.

The next day, the 28th of June, the Albatross was in front of the huge mass above the province of Zzang. On the other side of the chain was the province of Nepaul.

These ranges block the road into India from the north. The two northern ones, between which the aeronef was gliding like a ship between enormous reefs, are the first steps of the Central Asian barrier. The first was the Kuen Lung, the other the Karakorum, bordering the longitudinal valley parallel to the Himalayas, from which the Indus flows to the west and the Brahmapootra to the east.

What a superb orographical system! More than two hundred summits have been measured, seventeen of which exceed twenty-five thousand feet. In front of the

Albatross, at a height of twenty-nine thousand feet, towered Mount Everest. To the right was Dhawalagiri, reaching twenty-six thousand eight hundred feet, and relegated to second place since the measurement of Mount Everest.

Evidently Robur did not intend to go over the top of these peaks; but probably he knew the passes of the Himalayas, among others that of Ibi Ganim, which the brothers Schlagintweit traversed in 1856 at a height of twenty-two thousand feet. And towards it he went.

Several hours of palpitation, becoming quite painful, followed; and although the rarefaction of the air was not such as to necessitate recourse being had to the special apparatus for renewing the oxygen in the cabins, the cold was excessive.

Robur stood in the bow, his sturdy figure wrapped in a great-coat. He gave the orders, while Tom Turner was at the helm. The engineer kept an attentive watch on his batteries, the acid in which fortunately ran no risk of congelation. The screws, running at the full strength of the current, gave forth a note of intense shrillness in spite of the trifling density of the air. The barometer showed twenty-three thousand feet in altitude.

Magnificent was the grouping of the chaos of mountains! Everywhere were brilliant white summits. There were no lakes, but glaciers descending ten thousand feet towards the base. There was no herbage, only a few phanerogams on the limit of vegetable life. Down on the lower flanks of the range were splendid forests of pines and cedars. Here were none of the gigantic ferns and interminable parasites stretching from tree to tree as in the thickets of the jungle. There were no animals—no wild horses, or yaks, or Thibetan bulls. Occasionally a scared gazelle showed itself far down the slopes. There were no birds, save a couple of those crows which can rise to the utmost limits of the respirable air.

The pass at last was traversed. The Albatross began to descend. Coming from the hills out of the forest region there was now beneath them an immense plain stretching far and wide.

Then Robur stepped up to his guests, and in a pleasant voice remarked,—

" India, gentlemen ! "

## CHAPTER XIII.

### OVER THE CASPIAN.

THE engineer had no intention of taking his ship over the wondrous lands of Hindostan. To cross the Himalayas was to show how admirable was the machine he commanded; to convince those who would not be convinced was all he wished to do.

But if in their hearts Uncle Prudent and his colleague could not help admiring so perfect an engine of aerial locomotion, they allowed none of their admiration to be visible. All they thought of was how to escape. They did not even admire the superb spectacle that lay beneath them as the Albatross flew along the river banks of the Punjab.

At the base of the Himalayas there runs a marshy belt of country, the home of malarious vapours, the Terai, in which fever is endemic. But this offered no obstacle to the Albatross, or in any way affected the health of her crew. She kept on without undue haste towards the angle where India joins on to China and Turkestan, and on the 29th of June, in the early hours of the morning, there opened to view the incomparable valley of Cashmere.

Yes! incomparable is this gorge between the major and minor Himalayas—furrowed by the buttresses in which the mighty range dies out in the basin of the Hydaspes, and watered by the capricious windings of the river which saw the struggle between the armies of Porus and Alexander, when India and Greece contended for Central Asia. The Hydaspes is still there, although the two towns founded by the Macedonian in remembrance of his victory have long since disappeared.

During the morning the aeronef was over Serinuggur, which is better known under the name of Cashmere. Uncle Prudent and his companion beheld the superb city clustered along both banks of the river; its wooden bridges stretching across like threads, its villas and their balconies standing out in bold outline, its hills shaded by tall poplars, its roofs grassed over and looking like molehills; its numerous canals, with boats like nut-shells, and boatmen like ants; its palaces, temples, kiosks, mosques, and bungalows on the outskirts; and its old citadel of Hari-Pawata on the slope of the hill like the most important of the forts of Paris on the slope of Mont Valerien.

"That would be Venice," said Phil Evans, "if we were in Europe."

"And if we were in Europe," answered Uncle Prudent, "we should know how to find the way to America."

The Albatross did not linger over the lake through

which the river flows, but continued her flight down the valley of the Hydaspes.

For half an hour only did she descend to within thirty feet of the river, and remained stationary. Then, by means of an india-rubber pipe, Tom Turner and his men replenished their water supply, which was drawn up by a pump worked by the accumulators. Uncle Prudent and Phil Evans stood watching the operation. The same idea occurred to each of them. They were only a few feet from the surface of the stream. They were both good swimmers. A plunge would give them their liberty; and once they had reached the river, how could Robur get them back again? For his propellers to work, he must keep at least six feet above the ground.

In a moment all the chances pro and con. were run over in their minds. In a moment they were considered, and the prisoners rushed to throw themselves overboard, when several pairs of hands seized them by the shoulders.

They had been watched; and flight was impossible. This time they did not yield without resisting. They tried to throw off those who held them. But these men of the Albatross were no children.

"Gentlemen," said the engineer, "when people have the pleasure of travelling with Robur the Conqueror, as you have so well named him, on board his admirable Albatross, they do not leave him in that way. I may add you never leave him."

Phil Evans drew away his colleague, who was about to

They tried to throw off those who held hem.

Page 118.

commit some act of violence. They retired to their cabin, resolved to escape, even if it cost them their lives.

Immediately the Albatross resumed her course to the west. During the day at moderate speed she passed over the territory of Cabulistan, catching a momentary glimpse of its capital, and crossed the frontier of the kingdom of Herat, nearly seven hundred miles from Cashmere.

In these much-disputed countries, the open road for the Russians to the English possessions in India, there were seen many columns and convoys, and, in a word, everything that constitutes in men and material an army on the march. There were heard also the roar of the cannon and the crackling of musketry. But the engineer never meddled with the affairs of others where his honour or humanity was not concerned. He passed above them. If Herat, as we are told, is the key of Central Asia, it mattered little to him if it was kept in an English or Muscovite pocket. Terrestrial interests were nothing to him who had made the air his domain.

Besides, the country soon disappeared in one of those sandstorms which are so frequent in these regions. The wind called the "tebbad" bears along the seeds of fever in the impalpable dust it raises in its passage. And many are the caravans that perish in its eddies.

To escape this dust, which might have interfered with the working of the screws, the Albatross shot up some six thousand feet into a purer atmosphere.

And thus vanished the Persian frontier and the extensive plains. The speed was not excessive, although there were no rocks ahead, for the mountains marked on the map are of very moderate altitude. But as the ship approached the capital, she had to steer clear of Demavend, whose snowy peak rises some twenty-two thousand feet, and the chain of Elbruz, at whose foot is built Teheran.

As soon as the day broke on the 2nd of July the peak of Demavend appeared above the sandstorm, and the Albatross was steered so as to pass over the town, which the wind had wrapped in a mantle of dust.

However, about six o'clock her crew could see the large ditches that surround it, and the Shah's palace, with its walls covered with porcelain tiles, and its ornamental lakes, which seemed like huge turquoises of beautiful blue.

It was but a hasty glimpse. The Albatross now headed for the north, and a few hours afterwards she was over a little hill at the northern angle of the Persian frontier, on the shores of a vast extent of water which stretched away out of sight to the north and east.

The town was Ashurada, the most southerly of the Russian stations. The vast extent of water was a sea. It was the Caspian.

The eddies of sand had been passed. There was a view of a group of European houses rising along a promontory, with a church tower in the midst of them.

The Albatross swooped down towards the surface of the sea. Towards evening she was running along the coast—which formerly belonged to Turkestan, but now belongs to Russia—and in the morning of the 3rd of July she was about three hundred feet above the Caspian.

There was no land in sight, either on the Asiatic or European side. On the surface of the sea a few white sails were bellying in the breeze. These were native vessels recognizable by their peculiar rig—kesebeys, with two masts; kayuks, the old pirate boats, with one mast; teimils, and smaller craft for trading and fishing. Here and there a few puffs of smoke rose up to the Albatross from the funnels of the Ashurada steamers, which the Russians keep as the police of these Turcoman waters.

That morning Tom Turner was talking to the cook, Tapage, and to a question of his replied,—

"Yes; we shall be about forty-eight hours over the Caspian."

"Good!" said the cook; "then we can have some fishing."

"Just so."

They were to remain for forty-eight hours over the Caspian, which is some six hundred and twenty-five miles long and two hundred wide, because the speed of the Albatross had been much reduced, and while the fishing was going on she would be stopped altogether.

The reply was heard by Phil Evans, who was then in the bow, where Frycollin was overwhelming him with piteous pleadings to be put "on the ground."

Without replying to this preposterous request, Evans

returned aft to Uncle Prudent; and there, taking care not to be overheard, he reported the conversation that had taken place.

"Phil Evans," said Uncle Prudent, "I think there can be no mistake as to this scoundrel's intention with regard to us."

"None," said Phil Evans. "He will only give us our liberty when it suits him, and perhaps not at all."

"In that case we must do all we can to get away from the Albatross."

"A splendid craft she is, I must admit."

"Perhaps so," said Uncle Prudent; "but she belongs to a scoundrel who detains us on board in defiance of all right. For us and ours she is a constant danger. If we do not destroy her—"

"Let us begin by saving ourselves!" answered Phil Evans; "we can see about the destruction afterwards."

"Just so," said Uncle Prudent. "And we must avail ourselves of every chance that comes along. Evidently the Albatross is going to cross the Caspian into Europe, either by the north into Russia or by the west into the southern countries. Well, no matter where we stop, before we get to the Atlantic we shall be safe. And we ought to be ready at any moment."

"But," asked Evans, "how are we to get out?"

"Listen to me," said Uncle Prudent. "It may happen during the night that the Albatross may drop to within a few hundred feet of the ground. Now there are on board several ropes of that length, and, with a little pluck, we might slip down them—"

"Yes," said Evans. "If the case is desperate I don't mind—"

"Nor I. During the night there's no one about except the man at the wheel. And if we can drop one of the ropes forward without being seen or heard—"

"Good! I am glad to see you are so cool; that means business. But just now we are over the Caspian. There are several ships in sight. The Albatross is going down to fish. Cannot we do something now?"

"Sh! They are watching us much more than you think," said Uncle Prudent. "You saw that when we tried to jump into the Hydaspes."

"And who knows that they don't watch us at night?" asked Evans.

"Well, we must end this; we must finish with this Albatross and her master."

It will be seen how in the excitement of their anger the colleagues—Uncle Prudent in particular—were prepared to attempt the most hazardous things. The sense of their powerlessness, the ironical disdain with which Robur treated them, the brutal remarks he indulged in —all contributed towards intensifying the aggravation which daily grew more manifest.

This very day something occurred which gave rise to another most regrettable altercation between Robur and his guests. This was provoked by Frycollin, who, finding himself above the boundless sea, was seized with another fit of terror. Like a child, like the negro he was, he gave himself over to groaning and protesting and crying, and writhing in a thousand contortions and grimaces.

"I want to get out! I want to get out! I am not a bird! Boohoo! I don't want to fly, I want to get out!"

Uncle Prudent, as may be imagined, did not attempt to quiet him. In fact, he encouraged him, and particularly as the incessant howling seemed to have a strangely irritating effect on Robur.

When Tom Turner and his companions were getting ready for fishing, the engineer ordered them to shut up Frycollin in his cabin. But the negro never ceased his jumping about, and began to kick at the wall and yell with redoubled power.

It was noon. The Albatross was only about fifteen or twenty feet above the water. A few ships, terrified at the apparition, sought safety in flight.

As may be guessed, a sharp look-out was kept on the prisoners, whose temptation to escape could not but be intensified. Even supposing they jumped overboard they would have been picked up by the india-rubber boat. As there was nothing to do during the fishing in which Phil Evans intended to take part, Uncle Prudent, raging furiously as usual, retired to his cabin.

The Caspian Sea is a volcanic depression. Into it flow the waters of the Volga, the Ural, the Kour, the Kouma, the Jemba, and others. Without the evaporation which

An hour's work sufficed to fill up the larders.

Page 125.

relieves it of its overflow, this basin, with an area of 17,000 square miles, and a depth of from sixty to four hundred feet, would flood the low marshy ground to its north and east. Although it is not in communication with the Black Sea or the Sea of Aral, being at a much lower level than they are, it contains an immense number of fish—such fish, be it understood, as can live in its bitter waters, the bitterness being due to the naphtha which pours in from the springs on the south.

The crew of the Albatross made no secret of their delight at the change in their food the fishing would bring them.

"Look out!" shouted Turner, as he harpooned a good-sized fish, not unlike a shark.

It was a splendid sturgeon seven feet long, called by the Russians belouga, the eggs of which mixed up with salt, vinegar, and white wine form caviare. Sturgeons from the river are, it may be, rather better than those from the sea; but these were welcomed warmly enough on board the Albatross.

But the best catches were made with the drag-nets, which brought up at each haul carp, bream, salmon, salt-water pike, and a number of medium-sized sterlets, which wealthy gourmets have sent them alive to Astrakhan, Moscow, and Petersburg, and which now passed direct from their natural element into the cook's kettle without any charge for transport.

An hour's work sufficed to fill up the larders of the aeronef, and she resumed her course to the north.

During the fishing Frycollin had continued shouting and kicking at his cabin wall and making a tremendous noise.

"That wretched nigger will not be quiet, then?" said Robur, almost out of patience.

"It seems to me, sir, he has a right to complain," said Phil Evans.

"Yes, and I have a right to look after my ears," replied Robur.

"Engineer Robur!" said Uncle Prudent, who had just appeared on deck.

"President of the Weldon Institute!"

They had stepped up to one another, and were looking into the whites of each other's eyes.

Then Robur shrugged his shoulders.

"Put him at the end of a line," he said.

Turner saw his meaning at once.

Frycollin was dragged out of his cabin.

Loud were his cries when the mate and one of the men seized him and tied him into a tub, which they hitched on to a rope—one of those very ropes, in fact, that Uncle Prudent had intended to use as we know.

The negro at first thought he was going to be hanged. No! he was only going to be towed!

The rope was paid out for a hundred feet and Frycollin found himself hanging in space.

He could then shout at his ease. But fright contracted his larynx and he was mute.

Uncle Prudent and Phil Evans endeavoured to prevent this performance. They were thrust aside.

"It is scandalous! It is cowardly!" said Uncle Prudent, quite beside himself with rage.

"Indeed!" said Robur.

"It is an abuse of power against which I protest."

"Protest away!"

"I will be avenged, Mr. Robur."

"Avenge when you like, Mr. Prudent."

"I will have my revenge on you and yours."

The crew began to close up with anything but peaceful intentions. Robur motioned them away.

"Yes, on you and yours!" said Uncle Prudent, whom his colleague in vain tried to keep quiet.

"Whenever you please!" said the engineer.

"And in every possible way!"

"That is enough now," said Robur, in a threatening tone. "There are other ropes on board. And if you don't be quiet, I'll treat you as I have done your nigger!"

Uncle Prudent was silent, not because he was afraid, but because his wrath had nearly choked him; and Phil Evans led him off to his cabin.

During the last hour the air had been strangely troubled. The symptoms could not be mistaken. A storm was threatening. The electric saturation of the atmosphere had become so great that about half-past two o'clock Robur witnessed a phenomenon that wa new to him.

In the north, whence the storm was travelling, were spirals of half-luminous vapour due to the difference in the electric charges of the various beds of cloud. The reflections of these bands came running along the waves in myriads of lights, growing in intensity as the sky darkened.

The Albatross and the storm were sure to meet, for they were exactly in front of each other.

And Frycollin? Well! Frycollin was being towed—and towed is exactly the word, for the rope made such an angle with the aeronef, now going at over sixty knots an hour, that the tub was a long way behind her.

The crew were busy in preparing for the storm, for the Albatross would either have to rise above it or drive through its lowest layers. She was about three thousand feet above the sea when a clap of thunder was heard. Suddenly the squall struck her. In a few seconds the fiery clouds swept on around her.

Phil Evans went to intercede for Frycollin, and asked for him to be taken on board again.

But Robur had already given orders to that effect, and the rope was being hauled in, when suddenly there took place an inexplicable slackening in the speed of the screws.

The engineer rushed to the central deck-house.

"Power! More power!" he shouted. "We must rise quickly and get over the storm!"

"Impossible, sir!"

"What is the matter?"

"The currents are troubled! They are intermittent!"

And, in fact, the Albatross was falling fast.

As with telegraph wires on land during a storm, so was it with the accumulators of the aeronef. But what is only an inconvenience in the case of messages was here a terrible danger.

"Let her down, then," said Robur, "and get out of the electric zone! Keep cool, my lads!"

He stepped on to his quarter-deck and his crew went to their stations.

Although the Albatross had sunk several hundred feet she was still in the thick of the cloud, and the flashes played across her as if they were fireworks. It seemed as though she was struck. The screws ran more and more slowly, and what began as a gentle descent threatened to become a collapse.

In less than a minute it was evident they would get down to the surface of the sea. Once they were immersed no power could drag them from the abyss.

Suddenly the electric cloud appeared above them. The Albatross was only sixty feet from the crest of the waves. In two or three seconds the deck would be under water.

But Robur, seizing the propitious moment, rushed to the central house and seized the levers. He turned on the currents from the piles no longer neutralized by the electric tension of the surrounding atmosphere. In a moment the screws had regained their normal speed and checked the descent; and the Albatross remained at her slight elevation while her propellers drove her swiftly out of reach of the storm.

Frycollin, of course, had a bath—though only for a few seconds. When he was dragged on deck he was as wet as if he had been to the bottom of the sea. As may be imagined, he cried no more.

In the morning of the 4th of July the Albatross had passed over the northern shore of the Caspian.

Frycollin, of course, had a bath.

Page 130.

## CHAPTER XIV.

### THE AERONEF AT FULL SPEED.

If ever Uncle Prudent and Phil Evans despaired of escaping from the Albatross it was during the two days that followed. It may be that Robur considered it more difficult to keep a watch on his prisoners while he was crossing Europe, and he certainly knew that they had made up their minds to get away.

But any attempt to have done so would have been simply committing suicide. To jump from an express going sixty miles an hour is to risk your life, but to jump from a machine going one hundred and twenty miles an hour would be to seek your death.

And it was at this speed, the greatest that could be given to her, that the Albatross tore along. Her speed exceeded that of the swallow, which is one hundred and twelve miles an hour.

At first the wind was in the north-east, and the Albatross had it fair, her general course being a westerly one. But the wind began to drop, and it soon became impossible for the colleagues to remain on the deck without having their breath taken away by the rapidity of the flight. And on one occasion they would have been blown overboard if they had not been dashed up against the deck-house by the pressure of the wind.

Luckily the steersman saw them through the windows of his cage, and by the electric bell gave the alarm to the men in the fore-cabin. Four of them came aft, creeping along the deck.

Those who have been at sea, beating to windward in half a gale of wind, will understand what the pressure was like. Only here it was the Albatross that by her incomparable speed made her own wind.

To allow Uncle Prudent and Phil Evans to get back to their cabin the speed had to be reduced. Inside the deck-houses the Albatross bore with her a perfectly breathable atmosphere.

To stand such driving the strength of the apparatus must have been prodigious. The propellers spun round so swiftly that they seemed immovable, and it was with irresistible penetrative power that they screwed themselves through the air.

The last town that had been noticed was Astrakhan, situated at the north end of the Caspian Sea. The Star of the Desert—it must have been a poet who so called it—has now sunk from the first rank to the fifth or sixth. A momentary glance was afforded at its old walls, with their useless battlements, the ancient towers in the centre of the city, the mosques and modern churches, the cathedral with its five domes, gilded and dotted with stars as if it were a piece of the sky, as they rose from the bank of the Volga, which here, as it joins the sea, is over a mile in width.

Thenceforward the flight of the Albatross became quite a race through the heights of the sky, as if she had been harnessed to one of those fabulous hippogriffs which cleared a league at every sweep of the wing.

At ten o'clock in the morning of the 4th of July the aeronef, heading north-west, followed for a little the valley of the Volga. The steppes of the Don and the Ural stretched away on each side of the river. Even if it had been possible to get a glimpse of these vast territories there would have been no time to count the towns and villages. In the evening the aeronef passed over Moscow without saluting the flag on the Kremlin. In ten hours she had covered the twelve hundred miles which separate Astrakhan from the ancient capital of all the Russias.

From Moscow to St. Petersburg the railway line measures about seven hundred and fifty miles. This was but a half-day's journey, and the Albatross, as punctual as the mail, reached St. Petersburg and the banks of the Neva at two o'clock in the morning.

Then came the Gulf of Finland, the Archipelago of Abo, the Baltic, Sweden in the latitude of Stockholm, and Norway in the latitude of Christiania. Ten hours only for these twelve hundred miles! Verily it might be thought that no human power would henceforth be able to check the speed of the Albatross, and as if the resultant of her force of projection and the attraction of the earth would maintain her in an unvarying trajectory round the globe.

But she did stop nevertheless, and that was over the famous fall of the Rjukanfos in Norway. Gousta, whose summit dominates this wonderful region of Tellemarken, stood in the west like a gigantic barrier apparently impassable. And when the Albatross resumed her journey at full speed her head had been turned to the south.

And during this extraordinary flight what was Frycollin doing? Frycollin remained silent in a corner of his cabin, sleeping as well as he could, except at meal times.

Tapage then favoured him with his company—and amused himself at his expense.

"Eh! eh! my boy!" said he. "So you are not crying any more? Perhaps it hurt you too much? That two hours' hanging cured you of it! At our present rate, what a splendid air-bath you might have for your rheumatics!"

"It seems to me we shall soon go to pieces!"

"Perhaps so; but we shall go so fast we shan't have time to fall! That is some comfort!"

"Do you think so?"

"I do."

To tell the truth, and not to exaggerate like Tapage, it

was only reasonable that owing to the excessive speed the work of the suspensory screws should be somewhat lessened. The Albatross glided on its bed of air like a Congreve rocket.

"And shall we last long like that?" asked Frycollin.

"Long? Oh, no; only as long as we live!"

"Oh!" said the negro, beginning his lamentations.

"Take care, Fry, take care! for, as they say in my country, the master may send you to the seesaw!"

And Frycollin gulped down his sobs as he gulped down the meat which, in double doses, he was hastily swallowing.

Meanwhile Uncle Prudent and Phil Evans, who were not men to waste time in wrangling when nothing could come of it, agreed upon doing something. It was evident that escape was not to be thought of. But if it was impossible for them to again set foot on the terrestrial globe, could they not make known to its inhabitants what had become of them since their disappearance, and tell them by whom they had been carried off, and provoke—how was not very clear—some audacious attempt on the part of their friends to rescue them from Robur?

Communicate? But how?

Should they follow the example of sailors in distress and enclose in a bottle a document giving the place of shipwreck and throw it into the sea?

But here the sea was the atmosphere. The bottle would not swim. And if it did not fall on somebody and crack his skull it might never be found.

The colleagues were about to sacrifice one of the bottles on board when an idea occurred to Uncle Prudent. He took snuff, as we know, and we may pardon this fault in an American, who might do worse. And as a snuff-taker he possessed a snuff-box, which was now empty. This box was made of aluminium. If it was thrown overboard any honest citizen that found it would pick it up, and, being an honest citizen, he would take it to the police-office, and there they would open it and discover from the document what had become of the two victims of Robur the Conqueror!

And this is what was done. The note was short, but it told all, and it gave the address of the Weldon Institute, with a request that it might be forwarded. Then Uncle Prudent folded up the note, shut it in the box, and bound the box round with a piece of worsted so as to keep it from opening as it fell. And then all that had to be done was to wait for a favourable opportunity.

During this marvellous flight over Europe it was not an easy thing to leave the cabin and creep along the deck at the risk of being suddenly and secretly blown away, and it would not do for the snuff-box to fall into the sea or a gulf or a lake or a watercourse, for it would then perhaps be lost. At the same time it was not impossible that the colleagues might in this way get into communication with the habitable globe.

It was then growing daylight, and it seemed as though it would be better to wait for the night and take advantage of a slackening of speed or a halt to go out on deck and drop the precious snuff-box into some town.

When all these points had been thought over and settled, the prisoners found they could not put their plan into execution—on that day, at all events—for the Albatross, after leaving Gousta, had kept her southerly course, which took her over the North Sea, much to the consternation of the thousands of coasting craft engaged in the English, Dutch, French, and Belgian trade. Unless the snuff-box fell on the deck of one of these vessels there was every chance of its going to the bottom of the sea, and Uncle Prudent and Phil Evans were obliged to wait for a better opportunity. And, as we shall immediately see, an excellent chance was soon to be offered them.

At ten o'clock that evening the Albatross reached the French coast near Dunkerque. The night was rather dark. For a moment they could see the lighthouse at Grisnez cross its electric beam with the lights from Dover on the other side of the strait. Then the Albatross flew over the French territory at a mean height of three thousand feet.

There was no diminution in her speed. She shot like a rocket over the towns and villages so numerous in northern France. She was flying straight on to Paris, and after Dunkerque came Doullens, Amiens, Creil, Saint Denis. She never left the line; and about midnight she was over the "city of light," which merits its name even when its inhabitants are asleep—or ought to be.

By what strange whim was it that she was stopped over the city of Paris? We do not know; but down she came till she was within a few hundred feet of the ground. Robur then came out of his cabin, and the crew came on to the deck to breathe the ambient air.

Uncle Prudent and Phil Evans took care not to miss such an excellent opportunity. They left their deck-house and walked off away from the others so as to be ready at the propitious moment. It was important their action should not be seen.

The Albatross, like a huge coleopter, glided gently over the mighty city. She took the line of the boulevards, then brilliantly lighted by the Edison lamps. Up to her there floated the rumble of the vehicles as they drove along the streets, and the roll of the trains on the numerous railways that converge into Paris. Then she glided over the highest monuments as if she was going to knock the ball off the Pantheon or the cross off the Invalides. She hovered over the two minarets of the Trocadero and the metal tower of the Champ de Mars, where the enormous reflector was inundating the whole capital with its electric rays.

This aerial promenade, this nocturnal loitering, lasted for about an hour. It was a halt for breath before the voyage was resumed.

And probably Robur wished to give the Parisians the sight of a meteor quite unforeseen by their astronomers. The lamps of the Albatross were turned on. Two brilliant sheaves of light shot down and moved along

Away from the others.

Page 138.

The lamps of the Albatross were turned on.

over the squares, the gardens, the palaces, the sixty thousand houses, and swept the space from one horizon to the other.

Assuredly the Albatross was seen this time—and not only well seen but heard, for Tom Turner brought out his trumpet and blew a rousing tarantaratara.

At this moment Uncle Prudent leant over the rail, opened his hand, and let his snuff-box fall.

Immediately the Albatross shot upwards, and past her, higher still, there mounted the noisy cheering of the crowd then thick on the boulevards—a hurrah of stupefaction to greet the imaginary meteor.

Then the lamps of the aeronef were turned off, and the darkness and the silence closed in around as the voyage was resumed at the rate of one hundred and twenty miles an hour.

This was all that was to be seen of the French capital. At four o'clock in the morning the Albatross had crossed the whole country obliquely; and so as to lose no time in traversing the Alps or the Pyrenees, she flew over the face of Provence to the cape of Antibes. At nine o'clock next morning the San Pietrini assembled on the terrace of Saint Peter at Rome were astounded to see her pass over the eternal city. Two hours afterwards she crossed the Bay of Naples and hovered for an instant over the fuliginous wreaths of Vesuvius. Then, after cutting obliquely across the the Mediterranean, in the early hours of the afternoon she was signalled by the look-outs at La Goulette on the Tunisian coast.

After America, Asia! After Asia, Europe! More than eighteen thousand miles had this wonderful machine accomplished in less than twenty-three days!

And now she was off over the known and unknown regions of Africa!

* * * * * *

It may be interesting to know what had happened to the famous snuff-box after its fall?

It had fallen in the Rue de Rivoli, opposite No. 200, when the street was deserted. In the morning it was picked up by an honest sweeper, who took it to the prefecture of police.

There it was at first supposed to be an infernal machine. And it was untied, examined, and opened with extreme care.

Suddenly a sort of explosion took place. It was a terrific sneeze on the part of the inspector.

The document was then extracted from the snuff-box, and, to the general surprise, read as follows:—

"Messrs. Prudent and Phil Evans, president and secretary of the Weldon Institute, Philadelphia, have been carried off in the aeronef Albatross belonging to Robur the engineer..

"Please inform our friends and acquaintances."

"P. and P. E."

Thus was the strange phenomenon at last explained to the people of the two worlds. Thus was peace given to the scientists of the numerous observatories on the surface of the terrestrial globe.

## CHAPTER XV.

### A SKIRMISH IN DAHOMEY.

AT this point in the circumaviatory voyage of the Albatross it is only natural that some such questions as the following should be asked.

Who was this Robur, of whom up to the present we know nothing but the name? Did he pass his life in the air? Did his aeronef never rest? Had he not some retreat in some inaccessible spot in which, if he had need of repose or revictualling, he could betake himself? It would be very strange if it were not so. The most powerful flyers have always an eyrie or nest somewhere.

And what was the engineer going to do with his prisoners? Was he going to keep them in his power and condemn them to perpetual aviation? Or was he going to take them on a trip over Africa, South America, Australasia, the Indian Ocean, the Atlantic, and the Pacific, to convince them against their will, and then dismiss them with, "And now, gentlemen, I hope you will believe a little more in heavier than air"?

To these questions it is now impossible to reply. They

are the secrets of the future. Perhaps the answers will be revealed.

Anyhow the bird-like Robur was not seeking his nest on the northern frontier of Africa. By the end of the day he had traversed Tunis from Cape Bon to Cape Carthage, sometimes hovering, and sometimes darting along at top speed. Soon he reached the interior, and flew down the beautiful valley of Medjeida above its yellow stream hidden under its luxuriant bushes of cactus and oleander ; and scared away the hundreds of parrots that perch on the telegraph wires and seem to wait for the messages to pass to bear them away beneath their wings.

When night came the Albatross was over the frontiers of Kroumiria, and if a Kroumir then existed, he, of course, fell on his face and uttered an invocation to Allah at the apparition of the gigantic eagle.

In the morning she was over Bona and the hills in the neighbourhood ; then she reached Philippeville, now a small Algiers, with its new wharves and arcades and its admirable vineyards, whose verdant shoots clothe the countryside, which seems to be a slice brought hither from Burgundy or the Bordelais.

This promenade of three hundred miles into great and little Kabylia was brought to an end about noon over the Kasbah at Algiers. What a view it was for the passengers on the aeronef—the open roadstead between Cape Matifou and Point Pescade, the shore dotted with palaces, marabouts, villas, irregular valleys clothed in their vineyard mantles, the Mediterranean so blue ploughed by the huge liners now dwarfed to canoes! And so it was at Oran the picturesque, whose inhabitants, loitering in the gardens of the citadel, saw the Albatross appear among the earliest stars of the night.

Two hours after sunset the helm was put up and the Albatross bore off to the south-east; and on the morrow, after clearing the Tell Mountains, she saw the rising of the morning star over the sands of the Sahara.

On the 30th of July there was seen from the aeronef the little village of Geryville, founded like Laghouat on the frontier of the desert to facilitate the future conquest of Kabylia. Next, not without difficulty, the peaks of Stillero were passed against a somewhat boisterous wind. Then the desert was crossed, sometimes leisurely, over the Ksars or green oases, sometimes at terrific speed that far outstripped the flight of the vultures. Often the crew had to fire into the flocks of these birds which a dozen or so at a time fearlessly hurled themselves on to the aeronef to the extreme terror of Frycollin.

But if the vultures could only reply with cries and blows of beaks and talons, the natives, in no way less savage, were not sparing of their musket shots, particularly when crossing the Mountain of Sel, whose green and violet slope bore its cape of white. Then the Albatross was at last over the grand Sahara; and at once she rose into the higher zones so as to escape from a simoom which was sweeping a wave of ruddy sand along the surface of the ground like a bore on the surface of the sea.

Then the desolate table-lands of Chetka scattered their ballast in blackish waves up to the fresh and verdant valley of Ain-Massin. It is difficult to conceive the variety of the territories which could be seen at one view. To the green hills covered with trees and shrubs there succeeded long grey undulations draped like the folds of an Arab burnous and broken in picturesque masses. In the distance could be seen the wadys with their torrential waters, their forests of palm-trees, and blocks of small houses grouped on a hill around a mosque, among them Metlili, where there vegetates a religious chief, the grand marabout Sidi Chick.

Before night several hundred miles had been accomplished above a flattish country ridged occasionally with large sand-hills. If the Albatross had halted, she would have come to the earth in the depths of the Wargla oasis hidden beneath an immense forest of palm-trees. The town was clearly enough displayed with its three distinct quarters, the ancient palace of the Sultan, a kind of fortified Kasbah, houses of brick which had been left to the sun to bake, and artesian wells dug in the valley where the aeronef could have renewed her water supply. But, thanks to her extraordinary speed, the waters of the Hydaspes taken in the vale of Cashmere still filled her tanks in the centre of the African deserts.

Was the Albatross seen by the Arabs, the Mozabites,

and the negroes who share amongst them the town of Wargla? Certainly, for she was saluted with many hundred gunshots, and the bullets fell back before they reached her.

Then came the night, that silent night in the desert of which Felicien David has so poetically told us the secrets.

During the following hours the course lay south-westerly, cutting across the routes of El Golea, one of which was explored in 1859 by the intrepid Duveyrier.

The darkness was profound. Nothing could be seen of the Trans-Saharan Railway constructing on the plans of Duponchel—a long ribbon of iron destined to bind together Algiers and Timbuctoo by way of Laghouat and Gardaia, and destined eventually to run down into the Gulf of Guinea.

Then the Albatross entered the equatorial region below the tropic of Cancer. Six hundred miles from the northern frontier of the Sahara she crossed the route on which Major Laing met his death in 1846, and crossed the road of the caravans from Morocco to the Soudan, and that part of the desert swept by the Tuaregs, where could be heard what is called "the song of the sand," a soft and plaintive murmur that seems to escape from the ground.

Only one thing happened. A cloud of locusts came flying along, and there fell such a cargo of them on board as to threaten to sink the ship. But all hands set to work to clear the deck, and the locusts were thrown over except a few hundreds kept by Tapage for his larder. And he served them up in so succulent a fashion that Frycollin forgot for the moment his perpetual trances and said,—

"These are as good as prawns."

The aeronef was then eleven hundred miles from the Wargla oasis and almost on the northern frontier of the Soudan. About two o'clock in the afternoon a city appeared in the bend of a large river. The river was the Niger. The city was Timbuctoo.

If, up to then, this African Mecca had only been visited by the travellers of the ancient world, Batouta, Khazan, Imbert, Mungo Park, Adams, Laing, Caillé, Barth, Lenz, on that day by a most singular chance the two Americans could boast of having seen, heard, and smelt it, on their return to America—if they ever got back there.

Of having seen it, because their view included the whole triangle of three or four miles in circumference; of having heard it, because the day was one of some rejoicing and the noise was terrible; of having smelt it, because the olfactory nerve could not but be very disagreeably affected by the odours of the Youbou-Kamo square, where the meat-market stands close to the palace of the ancient Somai kings.

The engineer had no notion of allowing the president and secretary of the Weldon Institute to be ignorant that they had the extreme honour of contemplating the Queen of the Soudan, now in the power of the Tuaregs of Taganet.

"Gentlemen, Timbuctoo!" he said, in the same tone as twelve days before he had said,—

"Gentlemen, India!"

Then he continued,—

"Timbuctoo is an important city of from twelve to thirteen thousand inhabitants, formerly illustrious in science and art. Perhaps you would like to stay there for a day or two?"

Such a proposal could only have been made ironically. "But," continued he, "it would be dangerous among the Negroes, Berbers, and Foullanes who occupy it—particularly as our arrival in an aeronef might prejudice them against you."

"Sir," said Phil Evans, in the same tone, "for the pleasure of leaving you we would willingly risk an unpleasant reception from the natives. Prison for prison, we would rather be in Timbuctoo than on the Albatross."

"That is a matter of taste," answered the engineer. "Anyhow, I shall not try the adventure, for I am responsible for the safety of the guests who do me the honour to travel with me."

"And so," said Uncle Prudent, explosively, "you are not content with being our gaoler, but you insult us."

"Oh! a little irony, that is all!"

"Are there any weapons on board?"

"Oh! quite an arsenal."

"Two revolvers will do if I hold one and you the other."

"A duel!" exclaimed Robur, "a duel, which would perhaps cause the death of one of us."

"Which certainly would cause it."

"Well! No, Mr. President of the Weldon Institute, I very much prefer keeping you alive."

"To be sure of living yourself. That is wise."

"Wise or not, it suits me. You are at liberty to think as you like, and to complain to those who have the power to help you—if you can."

"And that we have done, Mr. Robur."

"Indeed!"

"Was it so difficult when we were crossing the inhabited part of Europe to drop a letter overboard?"

"Did you do that?" said Robur, in a paroxysm of rage.

"And if we have done it?"

"If you have done it—you deserve—"

"What, sir?"

"To follow your letter overboard."

"Throw us over, then. We did do it."

Robur stepped towards them. At a gesture from him Tom Turner and some of the crew ran up. The engineer was seriously tempted to put his threat into execution, and, fearful perhaps of yielding to it, he precipitately rushed into his cabin.

"Good!" exclaimed Phil Evans.

"And what he dare not do," said Uncle Prudent, "I will do! Yes, I will do!"

Flocks of elephants and buffaloes.

Page 149.

At the moment the population of Timbuctoo were crowding into the squares and roads and the terraces built like amphitheatres. In the rich quarters of Sankore and Sarahama, as in the miserable huts at Ragüidi, the priests from the minarets were thundering their loudest maledictions against the aerial monster. These were more harmless than the rifle bullets; though assuredly if the aeronef had come to earth she would have been torn to pieces.

For some miles noisy flocks of storks, francolins, and ibises escorted the Albatross and tried to race her, but in her rapid flight she soon distanced them.

The evening came. The air was troubled by the roarings of the numerous flocks of elephants and buffaloes which wander over this land, whose fertility is simply marvellous. For forty-eight hours the whole of the region between the prime meridian and the second degree, in the bend of the Niger, was viewed from the Albatross.

If a geographer had only such an apparatus at his command, with what facility could he map the country, note the elevations, fix the courses of the rivers and their affluents, and determine the positions of the towns and villages! There would then be no huge blanks on the map of Africa, no dotted lines, no vague designations which are the despair of cartographers.

In the morning of the 11th the Albatross crossed the mountains of northern Guinea, between the Soudan and the gulf which bears their name. On the horizon was the confused outline of the Kong mountains in the kingdom of Dahomey.

Since the departure from Timbuctoo Uncle Prudent and Phil Evans noticed that the course had been due south. If that direction was persisted in they would cross the equator in six more degrees. The Albatross would then abandon the continents and fly not over the Behring Sea, or the Caspian Sea, or the North Sea, or the Mediterranean, but over the Atlantic Ocean.

This look-out was not particularly pleasing to the two friends, whose chances of escape had sunk to zero.

But the Albatross had slackened speed as though hesitating to leave Africa behind. Was Robur thinking of going back? No; but his attention had been particularly attracted to the country which he was then crossing.

We know—and he knew—that the kingdom of Dahomey is one of the most powerful on the West Coast of Africa. Strong enough to hold its own with its neighbour Ashantee, its area is somewhat small, being contained within three hundred and sixty leagues from north to south, and one hundred and eighty from east to west. But its population numbers some seven or eight hundred thousand, including the neighbouring independent territories of Whydah and Ardrah.

If Dahomey is not a large country, it is often talked about. It is celebrated for the frightful cruelties which signalize its annual festivals, and by its human sacrifices—fearful hecatombs intended to honour the sovereign it has lost and the sovereign who has succeeded him. It is even a matter of politeness when the King of Dahomey receives a visit from some high personage or some foreign ambassador to give him a surprise present of a dozen heads, cut off in his honour by the minister of justice, the "minghan," who is wonderfully skilful in that branch of his duties.

When the Albatross came flying over Dahomey the old King Bahadou had just died, and the whole population was proceeding to the enthronization of his successor. Hence there was great agitation all over the country, and it did not escape Robur that everybody was on the move.

Long lines of Dahomians were hurrying along the roads from the country into the capital, Abomey. Well-kept roads radiating among vast plains clothed with giant trees, immense fields of manioc, magnificent forests of palms, cocoa-trees, mimosas, orange-trees, mango-trees—such was the country whose perfumes mounted to the Albatross, while thousands of parrots and cardinals swarmed among the trees.

The engineer, leaning over the rail, seemed deep in thought, and exchanged but a few words with Tom Turner.

It did not look as though the Albatross had attracted the attention of those moving masses, which were often invisible under the impenetrable roof of trees. This was doubtless due to her keeping at a good altitude amid a bank of light cloud.

About eleven o'clock in the morning the capital was sighted, surrounded by its walls, defended by a fosse measuring twelve miles round, with wide, regular streets on the flat plain, and a large square on the northern side occupied by the king's palace. This huge collection of buildings is commanded by a terrace not far from the place of sacrifice. During the festival days it is from this high terrace that they throw the prisoners tied up in wicker baskets, and it can be imagined with what fury these unhappy wretches are cut in pieces.

In one of the courtyards which divide the king's palace there were drawn up four thousand warriors, one of the contingents of the royal army—and not the least courageous one.

If it is doubtful if there are any Amazons on the river of that name, there is no doubt of there being Amazons at Dahomey. Some have a blue shirt with a blue or red scarf, with white-and-blue striped trousers and a white cap; others, the elephant-huntresses, have a heavy carbine, a short-bladed dagger, and two antelope horns fixed to their heads by a band of iron. The artillery-women have a blue-and-red tunic, and, as weapons, blunderbusses and old cast cannons; and another brigade, consisting of vestal virgins pure as Diana, have blue tunics and white trousers. If we add to these Amazons five or six thousand men in cotton drawers and shirts, with a knotted tuft to increase their stature, we shall have passed in review the Dahomian army.

Abomey on this day was deserted. The sovereign the royal family, the masculine and feminine army, and the population had all gone out of the capital to a vast plain a few miles away surrounded by magnificent forests.

On this plain the recognition of the new king was to take place. Here it was that thousands of prisoners taken during recent razzias were to be immolated in his honour.

It was about two o'clock when the Albatross arrived over the plain and began to descend among the clouds which still hid her from the Dahomians.

There were sixteen thousand people at least come from all parts of the kingdom, from Whydah, and Kerapay, and Ardrah, and Tombory, and the most distant villages.

The new king—a sturdy fellow named Bou-Nadi—some five-and-twenty years old, was seated on a hillock shaded by a group of wide-branched trees. Before him stood his male army, his Amazons, and his people.

At the foot of the mound fifty musicians were playing on their barbarous instruments, elephants' tusks giving forth a husky note, deerskin drums, calabashes, guitars, bells struck with an iron clapper, and bamboo flutes, whose shrill whistle was heard over all. Every other second came discharges of guns and blunderbusses, discharges of cannons with the carriages jumping so as to imperil the lives of the artillery-women, and a general uproar so intense that even the thunder would be unheard amidst it.

In one corner of the plain, under a guard of soldiers, were grouped the prisoners destined to accompany the defunct king into the other world. At the obsequies of Ghozo, the father of Bahadou, his son had despatched three thousand, and Bou-Nadi could not do less than his predecessor. For an hour there was a series of discourses, harangues, palavers and dances, executed not only by professionals, but by the Amazons, who displayed much martial grace.

But the time for the hecatomb was approaching. Robur, who knew the customs of Dahomey, did not lose sight of the men, women, and children reserved for butchery.

The minghan was standing at the foot of the hillock. He was brandishing his executioner's sword, with its curved blade surmounted by a metal bird, whose weight rendered the cut more certain.

This time he was not alone. He could not have performed the task. Near him were grouped a hundred executioners, all accustomed to cut off heads at one blow.

The Albatross came slowly down in an oblique direction. Soon she emerged from the bed of clouds which hid her till she was within three hundred feet of the ground, and for the first time she was visible from below.

Contrary to what had hitherto happened, the savages saw in her a celestial being come to render homage to King Bahadou. The enthusiasm was indescribable, the shouts were interminable, the prayers were terrific—prayers addressed to this supernatural hippogriff, which had doubtless come to take the king's body to the higher regions of the Dahomian heaven.

The little gun shot forth its shrapnel.

Page 155.

And now the first head fell under the minghan's sword, and the prisoners were led up in hundreds before the horrible executioners.

Suddenly a gun was fired from the Albatross. The minister of justice fell dead on his face.

"Well aimed, Tom!" said Robur.

His comrades, armed as he was, stood ready to fire when the order was given.

But a change came over the crowd below. They had understood. The winged monster was not a friendly spirit it was a hostile spirit. And after the fall of the minghan loud shouts for revenge arose on all sides. Almost immediately a fusillade resounded over the plain.

These menaces did not prevent the Albatross from descending boldly to within a hundred and fifty feet of the ground. Uncle Prudent and Phil Evans, whatever were their feelings towards Robur, could not help joining him in such a work of humanity.

"Let us free the prisoners!" they shouted.

"That is what I am going to do!" said the engineer.

And the magazine rifles of the Albatross in the hands of the colleagues, as in the hands of the crew, began to rain down the bullets, of which not one was lost in the masses below. And the little gun shot forth its shrapnel, which really did marvels.

The prisoners, although they did not understand how the help had come to them, broke their bonds, while the soldiers were firing at the aeronef. The stern screw was shot through by a bullet, and a few holes were made in the hull. Frycollin crouching in his cabin received a graze from a bullet that came through the deck-house.

"Ah! They will have them!" said Tom Turner. And, rushing to the magazine, he returned with a dozen dynamite cartridges, which he distributed to the men. At a sign from Robur these cartridges were fired at the hillock, and as they reached the ground exploded like so many small shells.

The king and his court and army and people were stricken with fear at the turn things had taken. They fled under the trees, while the prisoners ran off without anybody thinking of pursuing them.

In this way was the festival interfered with. And in this way did Uncle Prudent and Phil Evans recognize the power of the aeronef and the services it could render to humanity.

Soon the Albatross rose again to a moderate height, and passing over Whydah lost to view this savage coast which the south-west wind hems round with an inaccessible surf. And she flew out over the Atlantic.

Exploded like so many small shells.

Page 136

## CHAPTER XVI.

### OVER THE ATLANTIC.

YES, the Atlantic! The fears of the two colleagues were realized; but it did not seem as though Robur had the least anxiety about venturing over this vast ocean. Both he and his men seemed quite unconcerned about it, and had gone back to their stations.

Whither was the Albatross bound? Was she going more than round the world as Robur had said? Even if she were, the voyage must end somewhere. That Robur spent his life in the air on board the aeronef and never came to the ground was impossible. How could he make up his stock of provisions and the materials required for working his machines? He must have some retreat, some harbour of refuge in some unknown and inaccessible spot where the Albatross could revictual. That he had broken off all connection with the inhabitants of the land might be true, but with every point on the surface of the earth, certainly not.

That being the case, where was this point? How had the engineer come to choose it? Was he expected by a little colony of which he was the chief? Could he there find a new crew?

What means had he that he should be able to build so costly a vessel as the Albatross and keep her building secret? It is true his living was not expensive. But, finally, who was this Robur? Where did he come from? What had been his history? Here were riddles impossible to solve; and Robur was not the man to willingly assist in their solution.

It is not to be wondered at that these insoluble problems drove the colleagues almost to frenzy. To find themselves whipped off into the unknown without knowing what the end might be, doubting even if the adventure would end, sentenced to perpetual aviation, was this not enough to drive the president and secretary of the Weldon Institute to extremities.

Meanwhile the Albatross drove along above the Atlantic, and in the morning when the sun rose there was nothing to be seen but the circular line where earth met sky. Not a spot of land was in sight in this huge field of vision. Africa had vanished beneath the northern horizon.

When Frycollin ventured out of his cabin and saw all this water beneath him, fear took possession of him.

Beneath him is hardly the correct phrase; we should have said around him, for to an observer above the earth the abyss seems to curve up like a bowl to the horizon on a level with his eye, and the edge of the horizon seems to travel away as he moves towards it.

It is probable that Frycollin could not explain this effect physically, but he felt it all the same, and it produced on him that horror of the abyss from which certain people, brave though they may be, cannot free themselves. The negro was wise enough to say nothing. With eyes shut he felt his way back to his cabin, resolving to stay there for some considerable time.

Of the hundred and forty-five million square miles of which the area of the world's waters consists, the Atlantic claims about a quarter; and it seemed as though the engineer was in no hurry to cross it. There was now no going at full speed, none of the hundred and twenty miles an hour at which the Albatross had flown over Europe. Here, where the south-west winds prevail, the wind was ahead of them, and though it was not very strong, it would not do to defy it. And the Albatross was sent along at a moderate speed, which, however, easily outstripped that of the fastest mail-boat.

On the 13th of July she crossed the line, and the fact was duly announced to the crew. It was then that Uncle Prudent and Phil Evans ascertained that they were bound for the southern hemisphere. The crossing of the line took place without any of the Neptunian ceremonies that still linger on certain ships. Tapage was the only one to mark the event, and he did so by pouring a pint of water down Frycollin's neck.

On the morning of the 15th the Albatross passed between the islands of Ascension and St. Helena, approaching the last, whose higher ground showed above the horizon for some hours. In the evenings of the 16th and 17th of July there was a curious phenomenon at sunset. In a higher latitude it might have been taken for the aurora borealis. The sun as it disappeared shot forth a number of multi-coloured rays, some of which were of a vivid green.

Was this due to cosmic dust which the earth was then passing through, and which reflected the last beams of the day? Some observers have assigned such an origin to these crepuscular lights, but their explanation would not have been maintained for long had they been on board the aeronef, where it was found that there were floating in the air tiny crystals of pyroxene, and glassy globes and slender needles of magnetic iron, analogous to the matter ejected by certain volcanoes. There could be no doubt that a volcanic eruption had projected this cloud into the air, where it was held in suspension while it drifted over the Atlantic.

And other phenomena were observed. On several occasions the sky took a strange greyish tint, and when the curtain of vapour was passed its surface seemed ridged with white feathery clouds and dotted with solid spangles, giving an appearance which could only be explained as due to a form of hail.

In the night between the 17th and 18th there appeared a greenish lunar bow, owing to the aeronef being between the full moon and a curtain of fine rain which went off into vapour before it reached the sea.

A volcanic eruption had projected this cloud into the air.

Page 160.

Did these phenomena portend a change in the weather? Perhaps. Anyhow, the wind, which had blown from the south-west since their leaving the coast of Africa, had now dropped to a calm. And in this tropical zone it was extremely cold, for Robur had risen to get the benefit of the higher air-currents, and taken steps to screen himself from the direct rays of the sun, which would have been almost insupportable.

In the southern hemisphere the month of July answers to the month of January in the northern, that is to say, it is the depth of winter, and if the Albatross was kept on her southerly course she would soon feel the effect of this.

On the 18th of July, when beyond the tropic of Capricorn, another phenomenon was noticed, which would have been somewhat alarming to a ship on the sea.

A strange succession of luminous waves widened out over the surface of the ocean with a speed estimated at quite sixty miles an hour. The waves ran along at about eighty feet from one another, tracing two furrows of light. As night fell a bright reflection rose even to the Albatross, so that she might have been taken for a flaming aerolite. Never before had Robur sailed on a sea of fire—a fire without heat—which there was no need to flee from as it mounted upwards into the sky.

The cause of this light must have been electricity; it could not be attributed to a bank of fish spawn, nor to a crowd of those animalculæ that give phosphorescence to the sea, and this showed that the electrical tension of the atmosphere was considerable.

In the morning an ordinary ship would probably have been lost. But the Albatross played with the winds and waves like the powerful bird whose name she bore. If she did not walk on their surface like the petrels, she could like the eagles find calm and sunshine in the higher zones.

They had now passed the forty-seventh parallel. The day was but little over seven hours long, and would become even less as they approached the Pole.

About one o'clock in the afternoon the Albatross was floating along in a lower current than usual, about a hundred feet from the level of the sea. The air was calm, but in certain parts of the sky were thick black clouds, massed in mountains on their upper surface, and ruled off below by a sharp horizontal line. From these clouds a few lengthy protuberances escaped, and their points as they fell seemed to draw up hills of foaming water to meet them.

Suddenly the water shot up in the form of a gigantic hour-glass, and the Albatross was enveloped in the eddy of an enormous waterspout, while twenty others, black as ink, raged around her. Fortunately the gyratory movement of the water was opposite to that of the suspensory screws, otherwise the aeronef would have been hurled into the sea. But she began to spin round on herself with frightful rapidity.

Enveloped in the eddy of an enormous waterspout.

Page 162.

The danger was immense, and perhaps impossible to escape, for the engineer could not get through the spout which sucked him back in defiance of his propellers. The men, thrown to the ends of the deck by centrifugal force, were grasping the rail to save themselves from being shot off.

"Keep cool!" shouted Robur.

They wanted all their coolness, and their patience too.

Uncle Prudent and Phil Evans, who had just come out of their cabin, were hurled back at the risk of flying overboard.

As she spun the Albatross was carried along by the spout, which pirouetted along the waves with a speed enough to make the helices jealous. And if she escaped from the spout she might be caught by another, and jerked to pieces with the shock.

"Get the gun ready!" said Robur.

The order was given to Tom Turner, who was crouching behind the swivel amidships where the effect of the centrifugal force was least felt. He understood. In a moment he had opened the breech and slipped in a cartridge from the ammunition-box at hand. The gun went off, and the waterspouts collapsed, and with them vanished the platform of cloud they seemed to bear above them.

"Nothing broken on board?" asked Robur.

"No," answered Tom Turner "But we don't want to have another game of humming-top like that!"

For ten minutes or so the Albatross had been in extreme peril. Had it not been for her extraordinary strength of build she would have been lost.

During this passage of the Atlantic many were the hours whose monotony was unbroken by any phenomenon whatever. The days grew shorter and shorter, and the cold became keen. Uncle Prudent and Phil Evans saw little of Robur. Seated in his cabin, the engineer was busy laying out his course and marking it on his maps, taking his observations whenever he could, recording the readings of his barometers, thermometers, and chronometers, and making full entries in his log-book.

The colleagues wrapped themselves well up and eagerly watched for the sight of land to the southward. At Uncle Prudent's request Frycollin tried to pump the cook as to whither the engineer was bound. But what reliance could be placed on the information given by this Gascon? Sometimes Robur was an ex-minister of the Argentine Republic, sometimes a lord of the Admiralty, sometimes an ex-President of the United States, sometimes a Spanish general temporarily retired, sometimes a Viceroy of the Indies who had sought a more elevated position in the air. Sometimes he possessed millions, thanks to successful razzias in the aeronef, and he had been proclaimed for piracy. Sometimes he had been ruined by making the aeronef, and had been forced to fly aloft to escape from his creditors. As to knowing if he were going to stop anywhere, no! But if he thought of going to the moon, and found there a convenient anchorage, he would anchor there!

"Eh! Fry! my boy! That would just suit you to see what was going on up there."

"I shall not go! I refuse!" said the negro, who took all these things seriously.

"And why, Fry, why? You might get married to some pretty bouncing Lunarian!"

Frycollin reported this conversation to his master, who saw it was evident that nothing was to be learnt about Robur. And so he thought still more of how he could have his revenge on him.

"Phil," said he one day, "is it quite certain that escape is impossible?"

"Impossible."

"Be it so! But a man is always his own property; and if necessary, by sacrificing his life—"

"If we are to make that sacrifice," said Phil Evans, "the sooner the better. It is almost time to end this. Where is the Albatross going? Here we are flying obliquely over the Atlantic, and if we keep on we shall get to the coast of Patagonia or Teirra del Fuego. And what are we to do then? Get into the Pacific, or go to the continent at the South Pole? Everything is possible with this Robur. We shall be lost in the end. It is thus a case of legitimate self-defence, and if we must perish—"

"Which we shall not do," answered Uncle Prudent,

"without being avenged, without annihilating this machine and all she carries."

The colleagues had reached a stage of impotent fury and were prepared to sacrifice themselves if they could only destroy the inventor and his secret. A few months only would then be the life of this prodigious aeronef, of whose superiority in aerial locomotion they had such convincing proofs! The idea took such hold of them that they thought of nothing else but how to put it into execution. And how? By seizing on some of the explosives on board and simply blowing her up. But could they get at the magazine!

Fortunately for them, Frycollin had no suspicion of their scheme. At the thought of the Albatross exploding in mid air, he would not have shrunk from betraying his master.

It was on the 23rd of July that the land reappeared in the south-west near Cape Virgins at the entrance of the Straits of Magellan. Under the fifty-second parallel at this time of year the night was eighteen hours long and the temperature was six below freezing.

At first the Albatross, instead of keeping on to the south, followed the windings of the coast as if to enter the Pacific. After passing Lomas Bay, leaving Mount Gregory to the north and the Brecknocks to the west, they sighted Puerto Arena, a small Chilian village, at the moment the church-bells were in full swing; and a few hours later they were over the old settlement at Port Famine.

If the Patagonians, whose fires could be seen occasionally, were really above the average in stature, the passengers in the aeronef were unable to say, for to them they seemed to be dwarfs. But what a magnificent landscape opened around during these short hours of the southern day! Rugged mountains, peaks eternally capped with snow, with thick forest rising on their flanks, inland seas, bays deep set amid the peninsulas and islands of the Archipelago. Clarence Island, Dawson Island, and the Land of Desolation, straits and channels, capes and promontories, all in inextricable confusion, and bound by the ice in one solid mass from Cape Forward, the most southerly point of the American continent, to Cape Horn the most southerly point of the New World.

When she reached Port Famine the Albatross resumed her course to the south. Passing between Mount Tarn on the Brunswick Peninsula and Mount Graves, she steered for Mount Sarmiento, an enormous peak wrapped in snow, which commands the Straits of Magellan, rising six thousand four hundred feet from the sea. And now they were over the land of the Fuegians, Tierra del Fuego, the land of fire. Six months later, in the height of summer, with days from fifteen to sixteen hours long, how beautiful and fertile would most of this country be, particularly in its northern portion! Then, all around would be seen valleys and pasturages that could form the feeding-grounds of thousands of animals; then would appear virgin forests, gigantic trees—birches, beeches, ashtrees, cypresses, tree-ferns—and broad plains overrun by herds of guanacos, vicunas, and ostriches. Now there were armies of penguins and myriads of birds; and when the Albatross turned on her electric lamps the guillemots, ducks, and geese came crowding on board enough to fill Tapage's larder a hundred times and more.

Here was work for the cook, who knew how to bring out the flavour of the game and keep down its peculiar oiliness. And here was work for Frycollin in plucking dozen after dozen of such interesting feathered friends.

That day, as the sun was setting about three o'clock in the afternoon, there appeared in sight a large lake framed in a border of superb forest. The lake was completely frozen over, and a few natives with long snowshoes on their feet were swiftly gliding over it.

At the sight of the Albatross, the Fuegians, overwhelmed with terror, scattered in all directions, and when they could not get away they hid themselves, taking, like the animals, to the holes in the ground.

The Albatross still held her southerly course, crossing the Beagle Channel, and Navarin Island and Wollaston Island, on the shores of the Pacific. Then, having accomplished 4700 miles since she left Dahomey, she passed the last islands of the Magellanic archipelago, whose most southerly outpost, lashed by the everlasting surf, is the terrible Cape Horn.

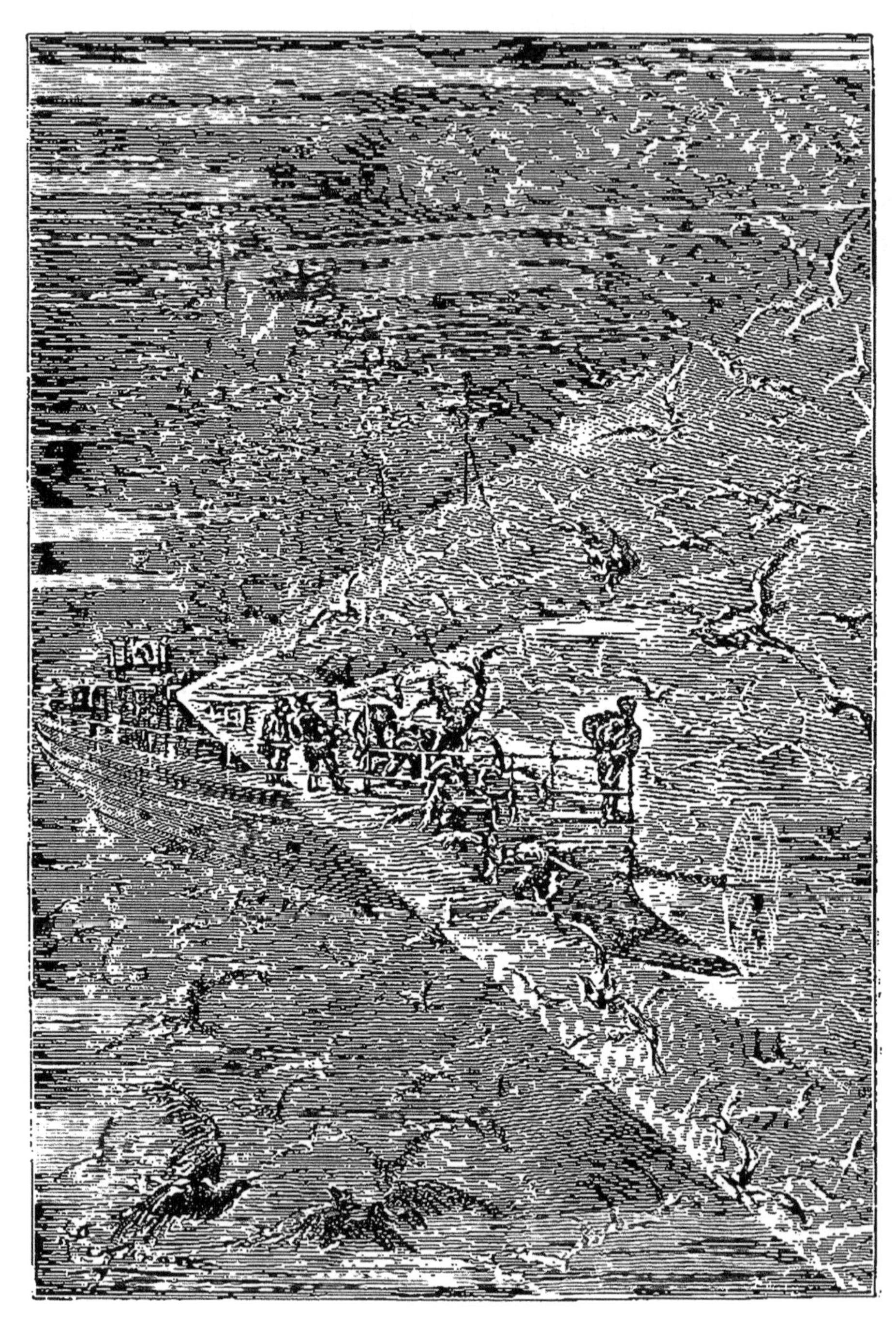

Here was work for the cook.

Page 163.

## CHAPTER XVII.

### THE SHIPWRECKED CREW.

NEXT day was the 24th of July; and the 24th of July in the southern hemisphere corresponds to the 24th of January in the northern. The fifty-sixth degree of latitude had been left behind. The similar parallel in northern Europe runs through Edinburgh.

The thermometer kept steadily below freezing, so that the machinery was called upon to furnish a little artificial heat in the cabins. Although the days begin to lengthen after the 21st of June in the southern hemisphere, yet the advance of the Albatross towards the Pole more than neutralized this increase, and consequently the daylight became very short. There was thus very little to be seen. At night time the cold became very keen; but as there was no scarcity of clothing on board, the colleagues, well wrapped up, remained a good deal on deck thinking over their plans of escape, and watching for an opportunity. Little was seen of Robur; since the high words that had been exchanged in the Timbuctoo country, the engineer had left off speaking to his prisoners.

Frycollin seldom came out of the cook-house, where Tapage treated him most hospitably, on condition that he acted as his assistant. This position was not without its advantages, and the negro, with his master's permission, very willingly accepted it. Shut up in the galley, he saw nothing of what was passing outside, and might even consider himself beyond the reach of danger. He was, in fact, very like the ostrich, not only in his stomach, but in his folly.

But whither went the Albatross? Was she in mid-winter bound for the southern seas or continents round the Pole? In this icy atmosphere, even granting that the elements of the batteries were unaffected by such frost, would not all the crew succumb to a horrible death from the cold? That Robur should attempt to cross the Pole in the warm season was bad enough, but to attempt such a thing in the depth of the winter night would be the act of a madman.

Thus reasoned the President and Secretary of the Weldon Institute, now they had been brought to the end of the continent of the New World, which is still America, although it does not belong to the United States.

What was this intractable Robur going to do? Had not the time arrived for them to end the voyage by blowing up the ship?

It was noticed that during the 24th of July the engineer had frequent consultations with his mate. He and Tom Turner kept constant watch on the barometer—not so much to keep themselves informed of the height at which they were travelling as to be on the look-out for a change in the weather. Evidently some indications had been observed of which it was necessary to make careful note.

Uncle Prudent also remarked that Robur had been taking stock of the provisions and stores, and everything seemed to show that he was contemplating turning back.

"Turning back!" said Phil Evans. "But where to?"

"Where he can re-provision the ship," said Uncle Prudent.

"That ought to be in some lonely island in the Pacific with a colony of scoundrels worthy of their chief."

"That is what I think. I fancy he is going west, and with the speed he can get up it would not take him long to get home."

"But we should not be able to put our plan into execution. If we get there—"

"We shall not get there!"

The colleagues had partly guessed the engineer's intentions. During the day it became no longer doubtful that when the Albatross reached the confines of the Antarctic Sea her course was to be changed. When the ice has formed about Cape Horn the lower regions of the Pacific are covered with ice-fields and icebergs. The floes then form an impenetrable barrier to the strongest ships and the boldest navigators.

Of course, by increasing the speed of her wings the Albatross could clear the mountain of ice accumulated on the ocean as she could the mountains of earth on the polar continent—if it is a continent that forms the cap of the southern pole. But would she attempt it in the middle of the polar night, in an atmosphere of sixty below freezing?

After she had advanced about a hundred miles to the south the Albatross headed westerly, as if for some unknown island of the Pacific. Beneath her stretched the liquid plain between Asia and America. The waters now had assumed that singular colour which has earned for them the name of the Milky Sea. In the half shadow, which the enfeebled rays of the sun were unable to dissipate, the surface of the Pacific was a milky white. It seemed like a vast snowfield, whose undulations were imperceptible at such a height. If the sea had been solidified by the cold, and converted into an immense icefield, its aspect could not have been much different. They knew that the phenomenon was produced by myriads of luminous particles or phosphorescent corpuscles; but it was surprising to come across such an opalescent mass beyond the limits of the Indian Ocean.

Suddenly the barometer fell after keeping somewhat high during the earlier hours of the day. Evidently the indications were such as a shipmaster might feel anxious at, though the master of an aeronef might despise them. There was every sign that a terrible storm had recently raged in the Pacific.

It was one o'clock in the afternoon when Tom Turner came up to the engineer and said, "Do you see that black spot on the horizon, sir—there away to due north of us? That is not a rock?"

"No, Tom; there is no land out there."

"Then it must be a ship or a boat."

Uncle Prudent and Phil Evans, who were in the bow, looked in the direction pointed out by the mate.

Robur asked for the glass and attentively observed the object.

"It is a boat," said he, "and there are some men in it."

"Shipwrecked?" asked Tom.

"Yes! They have had to abandon their ship, and knowing nothing of the nearest land, are perhaps dying of hunger and thirst! Well, it shall not be said that the Albatross did not come to their help!"

The orders were given, and the aeronef began to sink towards the sea. At three hundred yards from it the descent was stopped, and the propellers drove ahead full speed towards the north.

It was a boat. Her sail flapped against the mast as she rose and fell on the waves. There was no wind, and she was making no progress. Doubtless there was no one on board with strength enough left to work the oars. In the boat were five men asleep or helpless, if they were not dead.

The Albatross had arrived above them, and slowly descended.

On the boat's stern was the name of the ship to which she belonged—the Jeannette of Nantes.

"Hallo, there!" shouted Turner, loud enough for the men to hear, for the boat was only eighty feet below him.

There was no answer.

"Fire a gun!" said Robur.

The gun was fired and the report rang out over the sea.

One of the men looked up feebly. His eyes were haggard and his face was that of a skeleton. As he caught sight of the Albatross he made a gesture as of fear.

"Don't be afraid," said Robur in French, "we have come to help you. Who are you?"

"We belong to the barque Jeannette, and I am the mate. We left her a fortnight ago as she was sinking. We have no water and no food."

The four other men had now sat up. Wan and exhausted, in a terrible state of emaciation, they lifted their hands towards the Albatross.

"Look out!" shouted Robur.

A line was let down, and a pail of fresh water was lowered into the boat. The men snatched at it and drank it with an eagerness awful to see.

"Bread, Bread!" they exclaimed.

Immediately a basket with some food and five pints of coffee descended towards them. The mate with difficulty restrained them in their ravenousness.

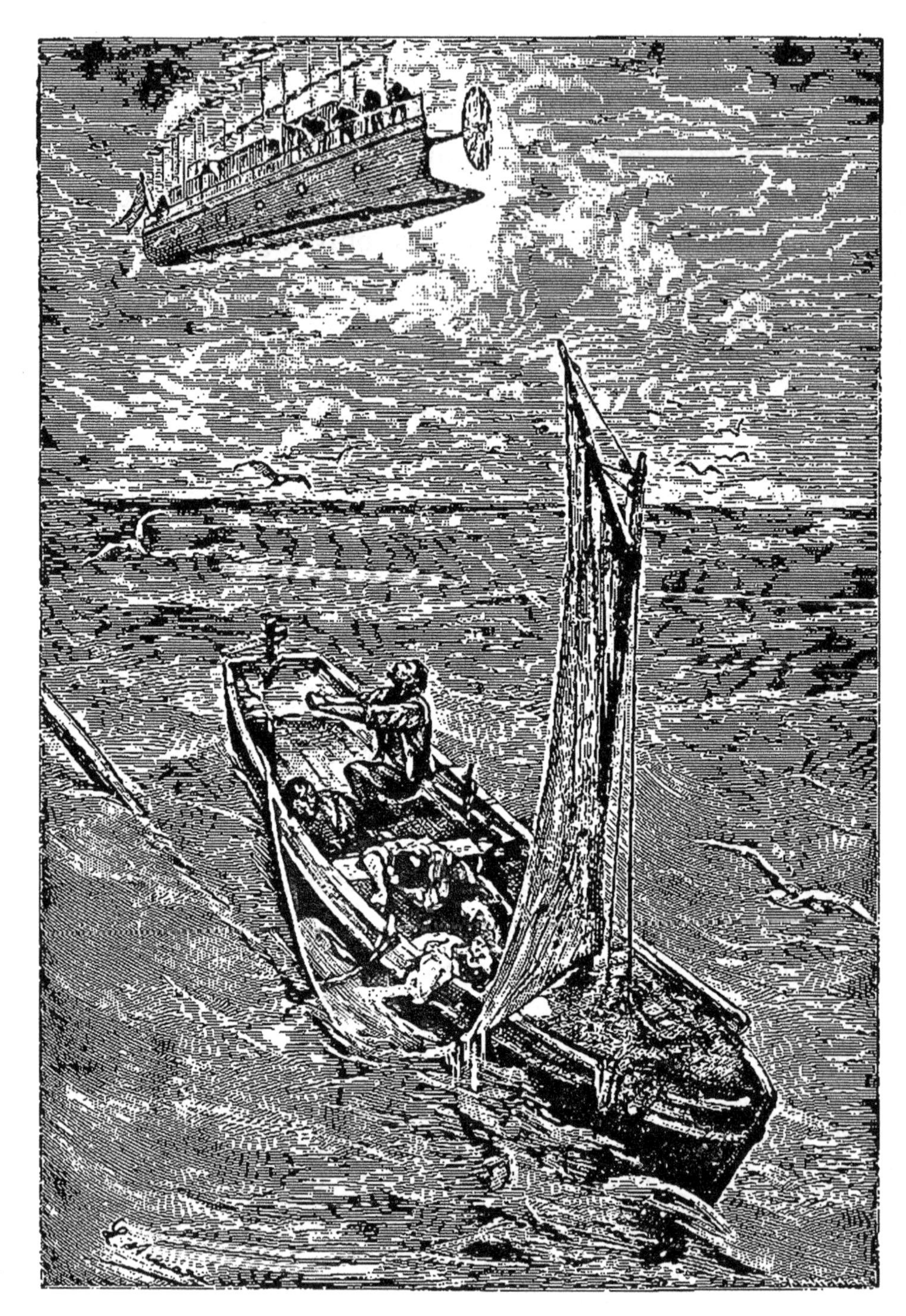

"Who are you?"

Page 174.

"Where are we?" asked the mate at last.

"Fifty miles from the Chili coast and the Chonos Archipelago," answered Robur.

"Thanks. But we are becalmed, and—"

"We are going to tow you."

"Who are you?"

"People who are glad to be of assistance to you," said Robur.

The mate understood that the incognito was to be respected. But had the flying machine sufficient power to tow them through the water?

Yes; and the boat, attached to a hundred feet of rope, began to move off towards the east. At ten o'clock at night the land was sighted—or rather they could see the lights which indicated its position. This rescue from the sky had come just in time for the survivors of the Jeannette, and they had good reason to believe it miraculous.

When they had been taken to the mouth of the channel leading among the Chonos Islands, Robur shouted to them to cast off the tow-line. This, with many a blessing to those who had saved them, they did, and the Albatross headed out to the offing.

Certainly there was some good in this aeronef, which could thus help those who were lost at sea! What balloon, perfect as it might be, would be able to perform such a service? And between themselves Uncle Prudent and Phil Evans could not but admit it, although they were quite disposed to deny the evidence of their senses.

## CHAPTER XVIII.

### OVER THE VOLCANO.

THE sea was as rough as ever, and the symptoms became alarming. The barometer fell several millimetres. The wind came in violent gusts, and then for a moment or so failed altogether. Under such circumstances a sailing vessel would have had two reefs in her topsails and a reef in her foresail. Everything showed that the wind was rising in the north-west. The storm-glass became much troubled and its movements were most disquieting.

At one o'clock in the morning the wind came on again with extreme violence. Although the aeronef was going right in its teeth she was still making progress at a rate of from twelve to fifteen miles an hour. But that was the utmost she could do.

Evidently preparations must be made for a cyclone, a very rare occurrence in these latitudes. Whether it be called a hurricane, as in the Atlantic, a typhoon, as in Chinese waters, a simoom, as in the Sahara, or a tornado, as on the western coast, such a storm is always a gyratory one, and most dangerous for any ship caught in the current, which increases from the circumference to the centre, and has only one spot of calm, the middle of the vortex.

Robur knew this. He also knew it was best to escape from the cyclone and get beyond its zone of attraction by ascending to the higher strata. Up to then he had always succeeded in doing this, but now he had not an hour, perhaps not a minute, to lose.

In fact the violence of the wind sensibly increased. The crests of the waves were swept off as they rose and blown into white dust on the surface of the sea. It was manifest that the cyclone was advancing with fearful velocity straight towards the regions of the pole.

"Higher!" said Robur.

"Higher it is," said Tom Turner.

An extreme ascensional power was communicated to the aeronef, and she shot up slantingly as if she was travelling on a plane sloping downwards from the south-west. Suddenly the barometer fell more than a dozen millimetres and the Albatross paused in her ascent.

What was the cause of the stoppage? Evidently she was pulled back by the air; some formidable current had diminished the resistance to the screws. When a steamer travels up stream more work is got out of her screw than when the water is running between the blades. The recoil is then considerable, and may perhaps be as great as the current. It was thus with the Albatross at this moment.

But Robur was not the man to give in. His seventy-four screws, working perfectly together, were driven at their maximum speed. But the aeronef could not escape ; the attraction of the cyclone was irresistible. During the few moments of calm she began to ascend, but the heavy pull soon drew her back, and she sunk like a ship as she founders.

Evidently if the violence of the cyclone went on increasing the Albatross would be but as a straw caught in one of those whirlwinds that root up the trees, carry off roofs, and blow down walls.

Robur and Tom could only speak by signs. Uncle Prudent and Phil Evans clung to the rail and wondered if the cyclone was not playing their game in destroying the aeronef and with her the inventor, and with the inventor the secret of his invention.

But if the Albatross could not get out of the cyclone vertically could she not do something else ? Could she not gain the centre, where it was comparatively calm, and where they would have more control over her ? Quite so ; but to do this she would have to break through the circular currents which were sweeping her round with them. Had she sufficient mechanical power to escape through them ?

Suddenly the upper part of the cloud fell in. The vapour condensed in torrents of rain. It was two o'clock in the morning. The barometer, oscillating over a range of twelve millimetres, had now fallen to 27.91, and from this something should be taken on account of the height of the aeronef above the level of the sea.

Strange to say, the cyclone was out of the zone to which

such storms are generally restricted, such zone being bounded by the thirtieth parallel of north latitude and the twenty-sixth parallel of south latitude. This may perhaps explain why the eddying storm suddenly turned into a straight one. But what a hurricane! The tempest in Connecticut on the 22nd of March, 1882, could only have been compared to it, and the speed of that was more than three hundred miles an hour.

The Albatross had thus to fly before the wind, or rather she had to be left to be driven by the current, from which she could neither mount nor escape. But in following this unchanging trajectory she was bearing due south, towards those polar regions which Robur had endeavoured to avoid. And now he was no longer master of her course; she would go where the hurricane took her.

Tom Turner was at the helm, and it required all his skill to keep her straight. In the first hours of the morning—if we can so call the vague tint which began to rise over the horizon—the Albatross was fifteen degrees below Cape Horn; twelve hundred miles more and she would cross the antarctic circle. Where she was, in this month of July, the night lasted nineteen hours and a half. The sun's disk—without warmth, without light—only appeared above the horizon to disappear almost immediately. At the pole the night lengthened into one of a hundred and seventy-nine hours. Everything showed that the Albatross was about to plunge into an abyss.

During the day an observation, had it been possible

would have given 66° 40′ south latitude. The aeronef was within fourteen hundred miles of the pole.

Irresistibly was she drawn towards this inaccessible corner of the globe, her speed eating up, so to speak, her weight, although she weighed less than before, owing to the flattening of the earth at the pole. It seemed as though she could have dispensed altogether with her suspensory screws. And soon the fury of the storm reached such a height that Robur thought it best to reduce the speed of her helices as much as possible, so as to avoid disaster. And only enough speed was given to keep the aeronef under control of the rudder.

Amid these dangers the engineer retained his imperturbable coolness, and the crew obeyed him as if their leader's mind had entered into them. Uncle Prudent and Phil Evans had not for a moment left the deck; they could remain without being disturbed. The air made but slight resistance. The aeronef was like an aerostat, which drifts with the fluid mass in which it is plunged.

Is the domain of the southern pole a continent or an archipelago? Or is it a palæocrystic sea, whose ice melts not even during the long summer? We know not. But what we do know is that the southern pole is colder than the northern one—a phenomenon due to the position of the earth in its orbit during winter in the antarctic regions.

During this day there was nothing to show that the storm was abating. It was by the seventy-fifth meridian to the west that the Albatross crossed into the circumpolar region. By what meridian would she come out—if she ever came out?

As she descended more to the south the length of the day diminished. Before long she would be plunged in that continuous night which is illuminated only by the rays of the moon or the pale streamers of the aurora. But the moon was then new, and the companions of Robur might see nothing of the regions whose secret has hitherto defied human curiosity.

There was not much inconvenience on board from the cold, for the temperature was not nearly so low as was expected. It seemed as though the hurricane was a sort of Gulf Stream, carrying a certain amount of heat along with it.

Great was the regret that the whole region was in such profound obscurity. Even if the moon had been in full glory but few observations could have been made. At this season of the year an immense curtain of snow, an icy carapace, covers up the polar surface. There was none of that ice "blink" to be seen, that whitish tint of which the reflection is absent from dark horizons. Under such circumstances how could they distinguish the shape of the ground, the extent of the seas, the position of the islands? How could they recognize the hydrographic network of the country or the orographic configuration, and distinguish the hills and mountains from the icebergs and floes?

A little after midnight an aurora illuminated the darkness. With its silver fringes and spangles radiating over space, it seemed like a huge fan open over half the sky. Its farthest electric effluences were lost in the Southern Cross, whose four bright stars were gleaming overhead. The phenomenon was one of incomparable magnificence, and the light showed the face of the country as a confused mass of white.

It need not be said that they had approached so near to the pole that the compass was constantly affected, and gave no precise indication of the course pursued. Its inclination was such that at one time Robur felt certain they were passing over the magnetic pole discovered by Sir James Ross. And an hour later, in calculating the angle the needle made with the vertical, he exclaimed,—

"The South Pole is beneath us!"

A white cap appeared, but nothing could be seen of what it hid under its ice.

A few minutes afterwards the aurora died away, and the point where all the world's meridians cross is still to be discovered.

If Uncle Prudent and Phil Evans wished to bury in the most mysterious solitudes the aeronef and all she bore, the moment was propitious. If they did not do so it was doubtless because the explosive they required was still denied to them.

The hurricane still raged, and swept along with such rapidity that had a mountain been met with the aeronef would have been dashed to pieces like a ship on a lee shore. Not only had the power gone to steer her horizontally, but the control of her elevation had also vanished.

And it was not unlikely, that mountains did exist in these antarctic lands. Any instant a shock might happen which would destroy the Albatross. Such a catastrophe became more probable as the wind shifted more to the east after they passed the prime meridian. Two luminous points then showed themselves ahead of the Albatross. These were the two volcanos of the Ross Mountains—Erebus and Terror. Was the Albatross to be shrivelled up in their flames like a gigantic butterfly?

An hour of intense excitement followed. One of the volcanoes, Erebus, seemed to be rushing at the aeronef, which could not move from the bed of the hurricane. The cloud of flame grew as they neared it. A network of fire barred their road. A brilliant light shone round over all. The figures on board stood out in the bright light as if come from another world. Motionless, without a sound or a gesture, they waited for the terrible moment when the furnace would wrap them in its fires.

But the storm that bore the Albatross saved them from such a fearful fate. The flames of Erebus were blown down by the hurricane as it passed, and the Albatross flew over unhurt. She swept through a hail of ejected material, which was fortunately kept at bay by the centrifugal action of the suspensory screws. And she harmlessly passed over the crater while it was in full eruption.

An hour afterwards the horizon hid from their view the

two colossal torches which light the confines of the world during the long polar night.

At two o'clock in the morning Balleny Island was sighted on the coast of Discovery Land, though it could not be recognized owing to its being bound to the mainland by a cement of ice.

And the Albatross emerged from the polar circle on the hundred and seventy-fifth meridian. The hurricane had carried her over the icebergs and icefloes, against which she was in danger of being dashed a hundred times or more. She was not in the hands of the helmsman, but in the hand of God—and God is a good pilot.

The aeronef sped along to the north, and at the sixtieth parallel the storm showed signs of dying away. Its violence sensibly diminished. The Albatross began to come under control again. And, what was a great comfort, had again entered the lighted regions of the globe; and the day reappeared about eight o'clock in the morning.

Robur had been carried by the storm into the Pacific over the polar region, accomplishing four thousand three hundred and fifty miles in nineteen hours, or about three miles a minute, a speed almost double that which the Albatross was equal to with her propellers under ordinary circumstances. But he did not know where he then was owing to the disturbance of the needle in the neighbourhood of the magnetic pole, and he would have to wait till the sun shone out under convenient conditions for observation. Unfortunately, heavy clouds covered the sky all that day and the sun did not appear.

This was a disappointment more keenly felt as both propelling screws had sustained damage during the tempest. Robur, much disconcerted at this accident, could only advance at a moderate speed during this day, and when he passed over the antipodes of Paris was only going about eighteen miles an hour. It was necessary not to aggravate the damage to the screws, for if the propellers were rendered useless the situation of the aeronef above the vast seas of the Pacific would be a very awkward one. And the engineer began to consider if he could not effect his repairs on the spot, so as to make sure of continuing his voyage.

In the morning of the 27th of July, about seven o'clock, land was sighted to the north. It was soon seen to be an island. But which island was it of the thousands that dot the Pacific? However, Robur decided to stop at it without landing. He thought that he could repair damages during the day and start in the evening.

The wind had died away completely, and this was a favourable circumstance for the manœuvre he desired to execute. At least, if she did not remain stationary the Albatross would not be carried he knew not where.

A cable one hundred and fifty feet long with an anchor at the end was dropped overboard. When the aeronef reached the shore of the island the anchor dragged up the first few rocks and then got firmly fixed between two large blocks. The cable then stretched to full length under the influence of the suspensory screws, and the Albatross remained motionless, riding like a ship in a roadstead.

It was the first time she had been fastened to the earth since she left Philadelphia.

## CHAPTER XIX.

### ANCHORED AT LAST.

WHEN the Albatross was high in the air the island could be seen to be of moderate size. But on what parallel was it situated? What meridian ran through it? Was it an island in the Pacific, in Australasia, or in the Indian Ocean? When the sun appeared, and Robur had taken his observations, they would know; but although they could not trust to the indications of the compass there was reason to think they were in the Pacific.

At this height—one hundred and fifty feet—the island which measured about fifteen miles round, was like a three-pointed star in the sea.

Off the south-west point was an islet and a range of rocks. On the shore there were no tide-marks, and this tended to confirm Robur in his opinion as to his position, for the ebb and flow are almost imperceptible in the Pacific.

At the north-west point there was a conical mountain about two hundred feet high.

No natives were to be seen, but they might be on the

opposite coast. In any case, if they had perceived the aeronef, terror had made them hide themselves or run away.

The Albatross had anchored on the south-west point of the island. Not far off, down a little creek, a small river flowed in among the rocks. Beyond were several winding valleys; trees of different kinds; and birds—partridges and bustards—in great numbers. If the island was not inhabited it was habitable. Robur might surely have landed on it; if he had not done so it was probably because the ground was uneven and did not offer a convenient spot to beach the aeronef.

While he was waiting for the sun the engineer began the repairs he reckoned on completing before the day was over. The suspensory screws were undamaged and had worked admirably amid all the violence of the storm, which, as we have said, had considerably lightened their work. At this moment half of them were in action, enough to keep the Albatross fixed to the shore by the taut cable. But the two propellers had suffered, and more than Robur had thought. Their blades would have to be adjusted and the gearing seen to by which they received their rotatory movement.

It was the screw at the bow which was first attacked under Robur's superintendence. It was the best to commence with, in case the Albatross had to leave before the work was finished. With only this propeller he could easily keep a proper course.

Meanwhile Uncle Prudent and his colleague, after walking about the deck, had sat down aft. Frycollin was strangely reassured. What a difference! To be suspended only one hundred and fifty feet from the ground!

The work was only interrupted for a moment while the elevation of the sun above the horizon allowed Robur to take an horary angle, so that at the time of its culmination he could calculate his position.

The result of the observation, taken with the greatest exactitude, was as follows:—

Longitude, 176 deg. 10 min. west.
Latitude, 44 deg. 25 min. south.

This point on the map answered to the position of the Chatham Islands, and particularly of Pitt Island, one of the group.

"That is nearer than I supposed," said Robur to Tom Turner.

"How far off are we?"

"Forty-six degrees south of X Island, or two thousand eight hundred miles."

"All the more reason to get our propellers into order," said the mate. "We may have the wind against us this passage, and with the little stores we have left we ought to get to X as soon as possible."

"Yes, Tom, and I hope to get under way to-night, even if I go with one screw, and put the other to-rights on the voyage."

"Mr. Robur," said Tom, "what is to be done with those two gentlemen and their servant?"

"Do you think they would complain if they became colonists of X Island?"

But where was this X? It was an island lost in the immensity of the Pacific Ocean between the Equator and the Tropic of Cancer—an island most appropriately named by Robur in this algebraic fashion. It was in the north of the South Pacific, a long way out of the route of inter-oceanic communication. There it was that Robur had founded his little colony, and there the Albatross rested when tired with her flight. There she was provisioned for all her voyages. In X Island, Robur, a man of immense wealth, had established a ship-yard, in which he built his aeronef. There he could repair it, and even rebuild it. In his warehouses were materials and provisions of all sorts stored for the fifty inhabitants who lived on the island.

When Robur had doubled Cape Horn a few days before, his intention had been to regain X Island by crossing the Pacific obliquely. But the cyclone had seized the Albatross, and the hurricane had carried her away to the south. In fact, he had been brought back to much the same latitude as before, and if his propellers had not been damaged the delay would have been of no importance.

His object was therefore to get back to X Island; but as the mate had said, the voyage would be a long one, and the winds would probably be against them. The

While they were busy in the bow.

Page 191.

mechanical power of the Albatross was, however, quite equal to taking her to her destination, and under ordinary circumstances she would be there in three or four days.

Hence Robur's resolve to anchor on the Chatham Islands. There was there every opportunity for repairing at least the fore-screw. He had no fear that if the wind were to rise he would be driven to the south instead of to the north. When night came the repairs would be finished, and he would have to manœuvre so as to weigh his anchor. If it were too firmly fixed in the rocks he could cut the cable and resume his flight towards the equator.

The crew of the Albatross, knowing there was no time to lose, set to work vigorously.

While they were busy in the bow of the aeronef, Uncle Prudent and Phil Evans held a little conversation together which had exceptionally important consequences.

"Phil Evans," said Uncle Prudent, "you have resolved, as I have, to sacrifice your life?"

"Yes, like you."

"It is evident that we can expect nothing from Robur."

"Nothing."

"Well, Phil Evans, I have made up my mind. If the Albatross leaves this place to-night, the night will not pass without our having accomplished our task. We will smash the wings of this bird of Robur's! This night I will blow it into the air!"

"The sooner the better," said Phil Evans.

It will be seen that the two colleagues were agreed on

all points, even in accepting with indifference the frightful death in store for them.

"Have you all you want?" asked Phil Evans.

"Yes. Last night, while Robur and his people had enough to do to look after the safety of the ship, I slipped into the magazine and got hold of a dynamite cartridge."

"Let us set to work, Uncle Prudent."

"No. Wait till to-night. When the night comes we will go into our cabin, and you shall see something that will surprise you."

At six o'clock the colleagues dined together as usual. Two hours afterwards they retired to their cabin like men who wished to make up for a sleepless night.

Neither Robur nor any of his companions had a suspicion of the catastrophe that threatened the Albatross.

This was Uncle Prudent's plan.

As he had said, he had stolen into the magazine, and there had possessed himself of some powder and a cartridge like those used by Robur in Dahomey. Returning to his cabin, he had carefully concealed the cartridge with which he had resolved to blow up the Albatross in mid-air.

Phil Evans, screened by his companion, was now examining the infernal machine, which was a metallic canister containing about two pounds of dynamite, enough to shatter the aeronef to atoms. If the explosion did not destroy her at once, it would do so in her fall. Nothing was easier than to place this cartridge in a corner of the cabin, so that it would blow in the deck and tear away the framework of the hull.

But to obtain the explosion it was necessary to adjust the fulminating cap with which the cartridge was fitted. This was the most delicate part of the operation, for the explosion would have to be carefully timed, so as not to occur too soon or too late.

Uncle Prudent had carefully thought over the matter. His conclusions were as follows. As soon as the fore propeller was repaired the aeronef would resume her course to the north, and that done Robur and his crew would probably come aft to put the other screw into order. The presence of these people about the cabin might interfere with his plans, and so he had resolved to make a slow match do duty as a time-fuse.

"When I got the cartridge," said he to Phil Evans, "I took some gunpowder as well. With the powder I will make a fuse that will take some time to burn, and which will lead into the fulminate. My idea is to light it about midnight, so that the explosion will take place about three or four o'clock in the morning."

"Well planned!" said Phil Evans.

The colleagues, as we see, had arrived at such a stage as to look with the greatest nonchalance on the awful destruction in which they were about to perish. Their hatred against Robur and his people had so increased that they would sacrifice their own lives to destroy the Albatross and all she bore. The act was that of madmen, it was horrible; but at such a pitch had they arrived after five weeks of anger that could not vent itself, of rage that could not be gratified.

"And Frycollin?" asked Phil Evans, "have we the right to dispose of his life?"

"We shall sacrifice ours as well!" said Uncle Prudent.

It is doubtful if Frycollin would have thought the reason sufficient.

Immediately Uncle Prudent set to work, while Evans kept watch in the neighbourhood of the cabin.

The crew were all at work forward. There was no fear of being surprised.

Uncle Prudent began by rubbing a small quantity of the powder very fine; and then, having slightly moistened it, he wrapped it up in a piece of rag in the shape of a match. When it was lighted he calculated it would burn about an inch in five minutes, or a yard in three hours. The match was tried and found to answer, and was then wound round with string and attached to the cap of the cartridge. Uncle Prudent had all finished about ten o'clock in the evening without having excited the least suspicion.

During the day the work on the fore screw had been actively carried on, but it had had to be taken on board to adjust the twisted blades. Of the piles and accumulators and the machinery that drove the ship nothing was damaged.

When night fell Robur and his men knocked off work. The fore propeller had not been got into place, and to finish it would take another three hours. After some conversation with Tom Turner it was decided to give the crew a rest, and postpone what required to be done to the next morning.

The final adjustment was a matter of extreme nicety, and the electric lamps did not give so suitable a light for such work as the daylight.

Uncle Prudent and Phil Evans were not aware of this. They had understood that the screw would be in place during the night, and that the Albatross would be on her way to the north.

The night was dark and moonless. Heavy clouds made the darkness deeper. A light breeze began to rise. A few puffs came from the south-west, but they had no effect on the Albatross. She remained motionless at her anchor, and the cable stretched vertically downwards to the ground.

Uncle Prudent and his colleague, imagining they were under way again, sat shut up in their cabin, exchanging but a few words, and listening to the f-r-r-r of the suspensory screws, which drowned every other sound on board. They were waiting till the time of action arrived.

A little before midnight Uncle Prudent said, "It is time!"

Under the berths in the cabin was a sliding box, forming a small locker, and in this locker Uncle Prudent put the dynamite and the slow-match. In this way the match would burn without betraying itself by its smoke or spluttering. Uncle Prudent lighted the end and pushed back the box under the berth with,—

"Now let us go aft, and wait."

They then went out, and were astonished not to find the steersman at his post.

Phil Evans leant out over the rail.

"The Albatross is where she was," said he in a low voice. "The work is not finished. They have not started!"

Uncle Prudent made a gesture of disappointment. "We shall have to put out the match," said he.

"No," said Phil Evans, "we must escape."

"Escape?"

"Yes! down the cable! fifty yards is nothing!"

"Nothing, of course, Phil Evans, and we should be fools not to take the chance now it has come."

But first they went back to the cabin and took away all they could carry, with a view to a more or less prolonged stay on the Chatham Islands. Then they shut the door and noiselessly crept forward, intending to wake Frycollin and take him with them.

The darkness was intense. The clouds were racing up from the south-west, and the aeronef was tugging at her anchor, and thus throwing the cable more and more out of the vertical. There would be no difficulty in slipping down it.

The colleagues made their way along the deck, stopping

Uncle Prudent lighted the end.

Page 196.

in the shadow of the deckhouses to listen if there was any sound. The silence was unbroken. No light shone from the portholes. The aeronef was not only silent; she was asleep.

Uncle Prudent was close to Frycollin's cabin when Phil Evans stopped him.

"The look-out!" he said.

A man was crouching near the deck-house. He was only half asleep. All flight would be impossible if he were to give the alarm.

Close by were a few ropes, and pieces of rag and waste used in the work at the screw.

An instant afterwards the man was gagged and blindfolded and lashed to the rail unable to utter a sound or move an inch.

This was done almost without a whisper.

Uncle Prudent and Phil Evans listened. All was silent within the cabins. Every one on board was asleep.

They reached Frycollin's cabin. Tapage was snoring away in a style worthy of his name, and that promised well.

To his great surprise, Uncle Prudent had not even to push Frycollin's door. It was open. He stepped into the doorway and looked round.

"Nobody here!" he said.

"Nobody! Where can he be?" asked Phil Evans.

They went into the bow, thinking Frycollin might perhaps be asleep in the corner.

Still they found nobody.

"Has the fellow got the start of us?" asked Uncle Prudent.

"Whether he has or not," said Phil Evans, "we can't wait any longer. Down you go."

Without hesitation the fugitives one after the other clambered over the side and, seizing the cable with hands and feet, slipped down it safe and sound to the ground.

Think of their joy at again treading the earth they had lost for so long—at walking on solid ground and being no longer the playthings of the atmosphere!

They were starting up the creek for the interior of the island when suddenly a form rose in front of them.

It was Frycollin.

The negro had had the same idea as his master and the audacity to start without telling him.

But there was no time for recriminations, and Uncle Prudent was in search of a refuge in some distant part of the island when Phil Evans stopped him.

"Uncle Prudent," said he. "Here we are safe from Robur. He is doomed like his companions to a terrible death. He deserves it, we know. But if he would swear on his honour not to take us prisoners again—"

"The honour of such a man—"

Uncle Prudent did not finish his sentence.

There was a noise on the Albatross. Evidently the alarm had been given. The escape was discovered.

"Help! Help!" shouted somebody.

"Down you go."

Page 198.

In a few seconds the cable was cut.

Page 199.

It was the look-out man, who had got rid of his gag. Hurried footsteps were heard on deck. Almost immediately the electric lamps shot beams over a large circle.

"There they are! There they are!" shouted Tom Turner.

The fugitives were seen.

At the same instant an order was given by Robur, and, the suspensory screws being slowed, the cable was hauled in on board, and the Albatross sank towards the ground.

At this moment the voice of Phil Evans was heard shouting,—

"Engineer Robur, will you give us your word of honour to leave us free on this island?"

"Never!" said Robur.

And the reply was followed by the report of a gun, and the bullet grazed Phil's shoulder.

"Ah! The brutes!" said Uncle Prudent.

Knife in hand, he rushed towards the rocks where the anchor had fixed itself. The aeronef was not more than fifty feet from the ground.

In a few seconds the cable was cut, and the breeze, which had increased considerably, striking the Albatross on the quarter, carried her out over the sea.

# CHAPTER XX.

## THE WRECK OF THE ALBATROSS.

IT was then twenty minutes after midnight. Five or six shots had been fired from the aeronef. Uncle Prudent and Frycollin, supporting Phil Evans, had taken shelter among the rocks. They had not been hit. For the moment there was nothing to fear.

As the Albatross drifted off from Pitt Island she rose obliquely to nearly three thousand feet. It was necessary to increase the ascensional power to prevent her falling into the sea.

When the look-out man had got clear of his gag and shouted, Robur and Tom Turner had rushed up to him and torn off his bandage. The mate had then run back to the stern cabin. It was empty!

Tapage had searched Frycollin's cabin, and that also was empty.

When he saw that the prisoners had escaped, Robur was seized with a paroxysm of anger. The escape meant the revelation of his secret to the world. He had not been much concerned at the document thrown overboard while they were crossing Europe, for there were so many chances that it would be lost in its fall; but now—!"

As he grew calm,—

"They have escaped," said he. "Be it so! but they cannot get away from Pitt Island, and in a day or so I will go back! I will recapture them! And then—"

In fact, the safety of the three fugitives was by no means assured. The Albatross would be repaired, and return well in hand. Before the day was out they might again be in the power of the engineer.

Before the day was out! But in two hours the Albatross would be annihilated! The dynamite cartridge was like a torpedo fastened to her hull, and would accomplish her destruction in mid-air.

The breeze freshened, and the aeronef was carried to the north-east. Although her speed was but moderate, she would be out of sight of the Chatham Islands before sunrise.

To return against the wind she must have her propellers going, particularly the one in the bow.

"Tom," said the engineer, "turn the lights full on."

"Yes, sir."

"And all hands to work."

"Yes, sir."

There was no longer any idea of putting off the work till to-morrow. There was now no thought of fatigue. Not one of the men of the Albatross failed to share in the feelings of his chief. Not one but was ready to do anything to recapture the fugitives!

As soon as the screw was in place they would return to the island, and drop another anchor, and give chase to the fugitives. Then only would they begin repairing the stern-screw ; and then the aeronef could resume her voyage across the Pacific to X Island.

It was important, above all things, that the Albatross should not be carried too far to the north-east, but unfortunately the breeze grew stronger, and she could not head against it, or even remain stationary. Deprived of her propellers she was an unguidable balloon. The fugitives on the shore knew that she would have disappeared before the explosion blew her to pieces.

Robur felt much disappointment at seeing his plans so interfered with. Would it not take him much longer than he thought to get back to his old anchorage?

While the work at the screw was actively pushed on, he resolved to descend to the surface of the sea, in the hope that the wind would there be lighter. Perhaps the Albatross would be able to remain in the neighbourhood until she was again fit to work to windward.

The manœuvre was instantly executed. If a passing ship had sighted the aerial machine as she sunk through the air, with her electric lights in full blaze, with what terror would she have been seized !

When the Albatross was a few hundred feet from the waves she stopped.

Unfortunately Robur found that the breeze was stronger here than above, and the aeronef drifted off more rapidly.

He risked being blown a long way off to the north-east, and that would delay his return to Pitt Island.

In short, after several experiments, he found it better to keep his ship well up in the air, and the Albatross went aloft to about ten thousand feet. There, if she did not remain stationary, the drifting was very slight. The engineer could thus hope that by sunrise at such an altitude he would still be in sight of the island.

Robur did not trouble himself about the reception the fugitives might have received from the natives—if there were any natives. That they might help them mattered little to him. With the powers of offence possessed by the Albatross they would be promptly terrified and dispersed. The capture of the prisoners was certain, and once he had them again,—

"They will not escape from X Island!"

About one o'clock in the morning the fore-screw was finished, and all that had to be done was to get it back to its place. This would take about an hour. That done, the Albatross would be headed south-west and the stern-screw could be taken in hand.

And how about the match that was burning in the deserted cabin?—the match of which more than a third was now consumed? And the spark that was creeping along to the dynamite?

Assuredly if the men of the aeronef had not been so busy one of them would have heard the feeble sputtering that was going on in the deck-house. Perhaps he would have smelt the burning powder! He would doubtless have become uneasy! And told Tom Turner! And then they would have looked about, and found the box and the infernal machine; and then there would have been time to save this wonderful Albatross and all she bore!

But the men were at work in the bow, twenty yards away from the cabin. Nothing brought them to that part of the deck; nothing called off their attention from their work.

Robur was there working with his hands, excellent mechanic as he was. He hurried on the work, but nothing was neglected, everything was carefully done. Was it not necessary that he should again become absolute master of his invention? If he did not recapture the fugitives they would get away home. They would begin inquiring into matters. They might even discover X Island, and there would be an end to this life, which the men of the Albatross had created for themselves, a life that seemed superhuman and sublime.

And here Tom Turner came up to the engineer. It was a quarter past one.

"It seems to me, sir, that the breeze is falling, and going round to the west."

"What does the barometer say?" asked Robur, after looking up at the sky.

"It is almost stationary, and the clouds seem gathering below us."

"So they are, and it may be raining down at the sea;

but if we keep above the rain it makes no difference to us. It will not interfere with the work."

"If it is raining it is not a heavy rain," said Tom. "The clouds do not look like it, and probably the wind has dropped altogether."

"Perhaps so, but I think we had better not go down yet. Let us get into going order as soon as we can, and then we can do as we like."

At a few minutes after two the first part of the work was finished. The fore-screw was in its place, and the power was turned on. The speed was gradually increased, and the Albatross, heading to the south-west, returned at moderate speed towards the Chatham Islands.

"Tom," said Robur, "it is about two hours and a half since we got adrift. The wind has not changed all the time. I think we ought to be over the island in an hour."

"Yes, sir. We are going about forty feet a second. We ought to be there about half-past three."

"All the better. It would suit us best to get back while it is dark, and even beach the Albatross if we can. Those fellows will fancy we are a long way off to the northward, and never think of keeping a look-out. If we have to stop a day or two on the island—"

"We'll stop, and if we have to fight an army of natives—"

"We'll fight," said Robur. "We'll fight then for our Albatross."

The engineer went forward to the men, who were waiting for orders.

"My lads," he said to them, "we cannot knock off yet. We must work till day comes."

They were all ready to do so.

The stern-screw had now to be treated as the other had been. The damage was the same, a twisting from the violence of the hurricane during the passage across the southern pole.

But to get the screw on board it seemed best to stop the progress of the aeronef for a few minutes, and even to drive her backwards. The engines were reversed. The aeronef began to fall astern, when Tom Turner was surprised by a peculiar odour.

This was from the gas given off by the match, which had accumulated in the box, and was now escaping from the cabin.

"Hallo!" said the mate, with a sniff.

"What is the matter?" asked Robur.

"Don't you smell something? Isn't it burning powder?"

"So it is, Tom."

"And it comes from that cabin."

"Yes, the very cabin—"

"Have those scoundrels set it on fire?"

"Suppose it is something else!" exclaimed Robur. "Force the door, Tom; drive in the door!"

But the mate had not made one step towards it when a

The Albatross dropped into the abyss.

Page 207.

fearful explosion shook the Albatross. The cabins flew into splinters. The lamps went out. The electric current suddenly failed. The darkness was complete. Most of the suspensory screws were twisted or broken, but a few in the bow still revolved.

At the same instant the hull of the aeronef opened just behind the first deck-house, where the engines for the fore-screw were placed; and the after-part of the deck collapsed in space.

Immediately the last suspensory screw stopped spinning, and the Albatross dropped into the abyss.

It was a fall of ten thousand feet for the eight men who were clinging to the wreck; and the fall was even faster than it might have been, for the fore propeller was vertical in the air and still working!

It was then that Robur, with extraordinary coolness, climbed up to the broken deck-house, and seizing the lever reversed the rotation, so that the propeller became a suspender.

The fall continued, but it was checked, and the wreck did not fall with the accelerating swiftness of bodies influenced solely by gravitation; and if it was death to the survivors of the Albatross from their being hurled into the sea, it was not death by asphyxia amid air which the rapidity of descent rendered unbreathable.

Eighty seconds after the explosion, all that remained of the Albatross plunged into the waves!

## CHAPTER XXI.

### THE INSTITUTE AGAIN.

SOME weeks before, on the 13th of June, on the morning after the sitting during which the Weldon Institute had been given over to such stormy discussions, the excitement of all classes of the Philadelphian population, black or white, had been much easier to imagine than to describe.

From a very early hour conversation was entirely occupied with the unexpected and scandalous incident of the night before. A stranger, calling himself an engineer, and answering to the name of Robur, a person of unknown origin, of anonymous nationality, had unexpectedly presented himself in the club-room, insulted the balloonists, made fun of the aeronauts, boasted of the marvels of machines heavier than air, and raised a frightful tumult by the remarks with which he greeted the menaces of his adversaries. After leaving the desk, amid a volley of revolver shots, he had disappeared, and, in spite of every endeavour, no trace could be found of him.

Assuredly here was enough to exercise every tongue and excite every imagination. But by how much was this excitement increased when in the evening of the 13th of June it was found that neither the president nor secretary of the Weldon Institute had returned to their homes! Was it by chance only that they were absent? No, or at least there was nothing to lead people to think so. It had even been agreed that in the morning they would be back at the club, one as president, the other as secretary, to take their places during a discussion on the events of the preceding evening.

And not only was there the complete disappearance of these two considerable personages in the state of Pennsylvania, but there was no news of the valet Frycollin. He was as undiscoverable as his master. Never had a negro since Toussaint L'Ouverture, Soulouque, or Dessaline had so much talked about him.

The next day there was no news. Neither the colleagues nor Frycollin had been found. The anxiety become serious. Agitation commenced. A numerous crowd besieged the post and telegraph offices in case any news should be received.

There was no news.

And they had been seen coming out of the Weldon Institute loudly talking together, and with Frycollin in attendance, go down Walnut Street towards Fairmont Park!

Jem Chip, the vegetarian, had even shaken hands with the president and left him with "To-morrow!"

And William T. Forbes, the manufacturer of sugar from

rags, had received a cordial shake from Phil Evans who had said to him twice,—

"Au revoir! au revoir!"

Miss Doll and Miss Mat Forbes, so attached to Uncle Prudent by the bonds of purest friendship, could not get over the disappearance, and in order to obtain news of the absent, talked even more than they were accustomed to.

Three, four, five, six days passed. Then a week, then two weeks, and there was nothing to give a clue to the missing three.

The most minute search had been made in every quarter. Nothing! In the streets going down to the harbour. Nothing! In the park, even under the trees and brushwood. Nothing! Always nothing! although here it was noticed that the grass looked to be pressed down in a way that seemed suspicious and certainly was inexplicable; and at the edge of the clearing there were traces of a recent struggle. Perhaps a band of scoundrels had attacked the colleagues here in the deserted park in the middle of the night!

It was possible. The police proceeded with their inquiries in all due form and with all lawful slowness. They dragged the Sckuylkill river, and cut into the thick bushes that fringe its banks; and if this was useless it was not quite a waste, for the Schuylkill is in great want of a good weeding, and it got it on this occasion! Practical people are the authorities of Philadelphia!

Then the newspapers were tried. Advertisements and

The grass looked to be pressed down.

Page 210.

notices and articles were sent to all the journals in the Union without distinction of colour. The "Daily Negro," the special organ of the black race, published a portrait of Frycollin after his latest photograph. Rewards were offered to whoever would give news of the three absentees, and even to those who would find some clue to put the police on the track.

"Five thousand dollars! five thousand dollars to any citizen who would—"

Nothing was done. The five thousand dollars remained with the treasurer of the Weldon Institute.

Undiscoverable! undiscoverable! undiscoverable! Uncle Prudent and Phil Evans, of Philadelphia!

It need hardly be said that the club was put to serious inconvenience by this disappearance of its president and secretary. And at first the assembly voted urgency to a measure which suspended the work on the Goahead. How, in the absence of the principal promoters of the affair, of those who had devoted to the enterprise a certain part of their fortune in time and money—how could they finish the work when these were not present? It were better, then, to wait.

And just then came the first news of the strange phenomenon which had exercised people's minds some weeks before.

The mysterious object had been again seen at different times in the higher regions of the atmosphere. But nobody dreamt of establishing a connection between this singular reappearance and the no less singular disappearance of the members of the Weldon Institute. In fact, it would have required a very strong dose of imagination to connect one of these facts with the other.

Whatever it might be, asteroid or aerolite or aerial monster, it had reappeared in such a way that its dimensions and shape could be much better appreciated, first in Canada, over the country between Ottawa and Quebec, on the very morning after the disappearance of the colleagues, and later over the plains of the Far West, where it had tried its speed against an express train on the Union Pacific.

At the end of this day the doubts of the learned world were at an end. The body was not a product of nature, it was a flying machine, the practical application of the theory of "heavier than air." And if the inventor of the aeronef had wished to keep himself unknown he could evidently have done better than to try it over the Far West. As to the mechanical force he required, or the engines by which it was communicated, nothing was known, but there could be no doubt the aeronef was gifted with an extraordinary faculty of locomotion. In fact, a few days afterwards it was reported from the Celestial Empire, then from the southern part of India, then from the Russian steppes.

Who was then this bold mechanician that possessed such powers of locomotion, for whom States had no frontiers and oceans no limits, who disposed of the terrestrial atmosphere as if it were his domain? Could it be this Robur whose theories had been so brutally thrown in the face of the Weldon Institute the day he led the attack against the utopia of guidable balloons?

Perhaps such a notion occurred to some of the wide-awake people, but none dreamt that the said Robur had anything to do with the disappearance of the president and secretary of the Institute.

Things remained in this state of mystery when a telegram arrived from France through the New York cable at 11.37 a.m. on July 13.

And what was this telegram? It was the text of the document found at Paris in a snuff-box revealing what had happened to the two personages for whom the Union was in mourning.

So, then, the perpetrator of this kidnapping was Robur the engineer, come expressly to Philadelphia to destroy in its egg the theory of the balloonists. He it was who commanded the Albatross! He it was who carried off by way of reprisal Uncle Prudent, Phil Evans, and Frycollin; and they might be considered lost for ever. At least until some means were found of constructing an engine capable of contending with this powerful machine their terrestrial friends would never bring them back to earth.

What excitement! What stupor! The telegram from Paris had been addressed to the members of the Weldon Institute. The members of the club were immediately informed of it. Ten minutes later all Philadelphia received the news through its telephones, and in less than an hour all America heard of it through the innumerable electric wires of the new continent.

No one would believe it! "It is an unseasonable joke," said some. "It is all smoke," said others. How could such a thing be done in Philadelphia, and so secretly, too? How could the Albatross have been beached in Fairmont Park without its appearance having been signalled all over Pennsylvania?

Very good. These were the arguments. The incredulous had the right of doubting. But the right did not last long. Seven days after the receipt of the telegram the French mail-boat *Normandie* came into the Hudson, bringing the famous snuff-box. The railway took it in all haste from New York to Philadelphia.

It was indeed the snuff-box of the President of the Weldon Institute. Jem Chip would have done better on that day to take some more substantial nourishment, for he fell into a swoon when he recognized it. How many a time had he taken from it the pinch of friendship! And Miss Doll and Miss Mat also recognized it, and so did William T. Forbes, Truck Milnor, Batt T. Fyn, and many other members.

And not only was it the president's snuff-box, it was the president's writing.

Then did the people lament and stretch out their hands in despair to the skies. Uncle Prudent and his colleague carried away in a flying machine, and no one able to deliver them!

The Niagara Falls Company, in which Uncle Prudent was the largest shareholder, thought of suspending its business and turning off its cataracts. The Wheelton Watch Company thought of winding up its machinery now it had lost its manager.

Nothing more was heard of the aeronef. July passed, and there was no news. August ran its course, and the uncertainty on the subject of Robur's prisoners was as great as ever. Had he, like Icarus, fallen a victim to his own temerity?

The first twenty-seven days of September went by without result, but on the 28th a rumour spread through Philadelphia that Uncle Prudent and Phil Evans had during the afternoon quietly walked into the president's house. And, what was more extraordinary, the rumour was true, although very few believed it.

They had, however, to give in to the evidence. There could be no doubt these were the two men, and not their shadows. And Frycollin also had come back!

The members of the club, then their friends, then the crowd, swarmed into the president's house, and shook hands with the president and secretary, and cheered them again and again.

Jem Chip was there, having left his luncheon—a joint of boiled lettuces—and William T. Forbes and his daughters, and all the members of the club. It is a mystery how

Uncle Prudent and Phil Evans emerged alive from the thousands who welcomed them.

On that evening was the weekly meeting of the Institute. It was expected that the colleagues would take their places at the desk. As they had said nothing of their adventures, it was thought they would then speak, and relate the impressions of their voyage.

But for some reason or other both were silent. And so also was Frycollin, whom his congeners in their delirium had failed to dismember.

But though the colleagues did not tell what had happened to them, that is no reason why we should not.

We know what occurred on the night of the 27th and 28th of July: the daring escape to the earth, the scramble among the rocks, the bullet fired at Phil Evans, the cut cable, and the Albatross deprived of her propellers, drifting off to the north-east at a great altitude.

Her electric lamps rendered her visible for some time. And then she disappeared.

The fugitives had little to fear. How could Robur get back to the island for three or four hours if his screws were out of gear? By that time the Albatross would have been destroyed by the explosion, and be no more than a wreck floating on the sea; those whom she bore would be mangled corpses, which the ocean would not even give up again.

The act of vengeance would be accomplished in all its horror.

They worshipped them, we ought rather to say.

Page 217.

Uncle Prudent and Phil Evans looked upon it as an act of legitimate self-defence, and felt no remorse whatever.

Evans was but slightly wounded by the rifle bullet, and the three made their way up from the shore in the hope of meeting some of the natives.

The hope was realized. About fifty natives were living by fishing off the western coast. They had seen the aeronef descend on the island, and they welcomed the fugitives as if they were supernatural beings. They worshipped them, we ought rather to say. They accommodated them in the most comfortable of their huts.

As they had expected, Uncle Prudent and Phil Evans saw nothing more of the aeronef. They concluded that the catastrophe had taken place in some high region of the atmosphere, and that they would hear no more of Robur and his prodigious machine.

Meanwhile they had to wait for an opportunity of returning to America. The Chatham Islands are not much visited by navigators, and all August passed without sign of a ship. The fugitives began to ask themselves if they had not exchanged one prison for another.

At last, on September 3rd, a ship came to water at the Chatham Islands. It will not have been forgotten that when Uncle Prudent was seized he had on him several thousand paper dollars, much more than would take him back to America. After thanking their adorers, who were not sparing of their most respectful demonstrations, Uncle Prudent, Phil Evans, and Frycollin embarked for

Auckland. They said nothing of their adventures, and in two days landed in New Zealand.

At Auckland, a mail-boat on the 20th of September took them on board as passengers, and after a splendid passage the survivors of the Albatross, stepped ashore at San Francisco. They said nothing as to who they were or whence they had come, but as they had paid full price for their berths no American captain would trouble them further.

At San Francisco they took the first train out on the Pacific Railway, and on the 27th they arrived at Philadelphia.

That is the compendious history of what had occurred since the escape of the fugitives. And that is why this very evening the president and secretary of the Weldon Institute took their seats amid a most extraordinary attendance.

But never before had either of them been so calm. To look at them it did not seem as though anything abnormal had happened since the memorable sitting of the 12th of June. Three months and a half had gone, and seemed to be counted as nothing.

After the first round of cheers, which both received without showing the slightest emotion, Uncle Prudent took off his hat and spoke.

"Worthy citizens," said he, "the meeting is now open."

Tremendous applause. And properly so, for if it was not extraordinary that the meeting was open, it was extraordinary that it should be opened by Uncle Prudent and Phil Evans.

The president allowed the enthusiasm to subside in shouts and clappings; then he continued:—

"At our last meeting, gentlemen, the discussion was somewhat animated—(hear, hear)—between the partisans of the screw before and those of the screw behind for our balloon the Goahead. (Marks of surprise.) We have found a way to bring the beforists and the behindists in agreement. That way is as follows: we are going to use two screws, one at each end of the car!" (Silence and complete stupefaction.)

That was all.

Yes, all! Of the kidnapping of the president and secretary of the Weldon Institute not a word! Not a word of the Albatross nor of Robur! Not a word of the voyage! Not a word of the way in which the prisoners had escaped! Not a word of what had become of the aeronef, if it still flew through space, or if they were to be prepared for new reprisals on the members of the club!

Of course the balloonists were longing to ask Uncle Prudent and the secretary about all these things, but they looked so close and so serious that they thought it best to respect their attitude. When they thought fit to speak they would do so, and it would be an honour to hear.

After all, there might be in all this some secret which could not yet be divulged.

And then Uncle Prudent, resuming his speech amid a silence up to then unknown in the meetings of the Weldon Institute, said, "Gentlemen, it now only remains for us to finish the aerostat Goahead. It is left to her to effect the conquest of the air! The meeting is at an end!"

## CHAPTER XXII.

### THE GOAHEAD IS LAUNCHED.

ON the following 19th of April, seven months after the unexpected return of Uncle Prudent and Phil Evans, Philadelphia was in a state of unwonted excitement. There were neither elections nor meetings this time. The aerostat Goahead, built by the Weldon Institute, was to take possession of her natural element.

The celebrated Harry W. Tinder, whose name we mentioned at the beginning of this story, had been engaged as aeronaut. He had no assistant, and the only passengers were to be the president and secretary of the Weldon Institute. Did they not merit such an honour? Did it not come to them appropriately to rise in person to protest against any apparatus that was heavier than air?

During the seven months, however, they had said nothing of their adventures; and even Frycollin had not uttered a whisper of Robur and his wonderful clipper. Probably Uncle Prudent and his friend desired that no question should arise as to the merits of the aeronef, or any other flying machine. Although the Goahead might not claim the first place among aerial locomotives, they would have nothing to say about the inventions of other aviators. They believed, and would always believe, that the true atmospheric vehicle was the aerostat, and that to it alone belonged the future.

Besides, he on whom they had been so terribly—and in their idea so justly—avenged, existed no longer. None of those who accompanied him had survived. The secret of the Albatross was buried in the depths of the Pacific!

That Robur had a retreat, an island in the middle of that vast ocean, where he could put into port, was only a hypothesis; and the colleagues reserved to themselves the right of making inquiries on the subject—later on.

The grand experiment which the Weldon Institute had been preparing for so long was at last to take place. The Goahead was the most perfect type of what had up to then been invented in aerostatic art—she was what an Inflexible or a Formidable is in ships of war.

She possessed all the qualities of a good aerostat. Her dimensions allowed of her rising to the greatest height a balloon could attain; her impermeability enabled her to remain for an indefinite time in the atmosphere; her solidity would defy any dilatation of gas or violence of wind or rain; her capacity gave her sufficient ascensional force to lift with all their accessories an electric engine that would communicate to her propellers a power superior to anything yet obtained. The Goahead was of elongated form, so as to facilitate her horizontal displacement. Her car was a platform somewhat like that of the balloon used by Krebs and Renard; and it carried all the necessary outfit, instruments, cables, grapnels, guide-ropes, &c., and the piles and accumulators for the mechanical power. The car had a screw in front, and a screw and rudder behind. But probably the work done by the machines would be very much less than that done by the machines of the Albatross.

The Goahead had been taken to the clearing in Fairmont Park, to the very spot where the aeronef had landed for a few hours.

Her ascensional power was due to the very lightest of gaseous bodies. Ordinary lighting gas possesses an elevating force of about 700 grammes for every cubic metre. But hydrogen possesses an ascensional force estimated at 1100 grammes per cubic metre. Pure hydrogen prepared according to the method of the celebrated Henry Gifford filled the enormous balloon. And as the capacity of the Goahead was 40,000 cubic metres, the ascensional power of the gas she contained was 40,000 multiplied by 1100, or 44,000 kilogrammes.

On this 29th of April everything was ready. Since eleven o'clock the enormous aerostat had been floating a few feet from the ground ready to rise in mid-air. It was splendid weather and seemed to have been made specially for the experiment, although if the breeze had been stronger the results might have been more conclusive. There had never been any doubt that a balloon could be guided in a calm atmosphere; but to guide it when the atmosphere is in motion is quite another thing; and it is under such circumstances that the experiment should be tried.

But there was no wind to-day, nor any sign of any. Strange to say, North America on that day omitted to send on to Europe one of those first-class storms which it seems to have in such inexhaustible numbers. A better day could not have been chosen for an aeronautic experiment.

The crowd was immense in Fairmont Park; trains had poured into the Pennsylvanian capital sightseers from the neighbouring states; industrial and commercial life came to a standstill that the people might troop to the show—masters, workmen, women, old men, children, members of Congress, soldiers, magistrates, reporters, white natives and black natives, all were there. We need not stop to describe the excitement, the unaccountable movements, the sudden pushings, which made the mass heave and swell. Nor need we recount the number of cheers which rose from all sides like fireworks when Uncle Prudent and Phil Evans appeared on the platform and hoisted the American colours. Need we say that the majority of the crowd had come from afar not so much to see the Goahead as to gaze on these extraordinary men?

Why two and not three? Why not Frycollin? Because Frycollin thought his campaign in the Albatross sufficient for his fame. He had declined the honour of accompanying his master, and he took no part in the frenzied acclamations that greeted the president and secretary of the Weldon Institute.

Of the members of the illustrious assembly not one was absent from the reserved places within the ropes. There were Truck Milnor, Batt T. Fyn, and William T. Forbes with his two daughters on his arm. All had come to affirm by their presence that nothing could separate them from the partisans of "lighter than air."

About twenty minutes past eleven a gun announced the end of the final preparations.

The Goahead only waited the signal to start. At twenty-five minutes past eleven the second gun was fired.

The Goahead was about one hundred and fifty feet above the clearing, and was held by a rope. In this way the platform commanded the excited crowd. Uncle Prudent and Phil Evans stood upright and placed their left hands on their hearts, to signify how deeply they were touched by their reception. Then they extended their right hands towards the zenith, to signify that the greatest of known balloons was about to take possession of the supra-terrestrial domain.

A hundred thousand hands were placed in answer on a hundred thousand hearts, and a hundred thousand other hands were lifted to the sky.

The third gun was fired at half-past eleven.

"Let go!" shouted Uncle Prudent; and the Goahead

"Let go!" shouted Uncle Prudent.

Page 224.

rose "majestically"—an adverb consecrated by custom to all aerostatic ascents.

And it really was a superb spectacle. It seemed as if a vessel were just launched from the stocks. And was she not a vessel launched into the aerial sea?

The Goahead went up in a perfectly vertical line—a proof of the calmness of the atmosphere—and stopped at an altitude of eight hundred feet.

Then she began her horizontal manœuvring. With her screws going she moved to the east at a speed of twelve yards a second. That is the speed of the whale—not an inappropriate comparison, for the balloon was somewhat of the shape of the giant of the northern seas.

A salvo of cheers mounted towards the skilful aeronauts.

Then, under the influence of her rudder, the Goahead went through all the evolutions that her steersman could give her. She turned in a small circle; she moved forwards and backwards in a way to convince the most refractory disbeliever in the guiding of balloons. And if there had been any disbeliever there he would have been simply annihilated.

But why was there no wind to assist at this magnificent experiment? It was regrettable. Doubtless the spectators would have seen the Goahead unhesitatingly execute all the movements of a sailing-vessel in beating to windward, or of a steamer driving in the wind's eye.

At this moment the aerostat rose a few hundred yards.

The manœuvre was understood below. Uncle Prudent

and his companions were going in search of a breeze in the higher zones, so as to complete the experiment. The system of cellular balloons—analogous to the swimming bladder in fishes—into which could be introduced a certain amount of air by pumping, had provided for this vertical motion. Without throwing out ballast or losing gas the aeronaut was able to rise or sink at his will. Of course there was a valve in the upper hemisphere which would permit of a rapid descent if found necessary. All these contrivances are well known, but they were here fitted in perfection.

The Goahead then rose vertically. Her enormous dimensions gradually grew smaller to the eye, and the necks of the crowd were almost ricked as they gazed into the air. Gradually the whale became a porpoise, and the porpoise became a gudgeon.

The ascensional movement did not cease until the Goahead had reached a height of fourteen thousand feet. But the air was so free from mist that she remained clearly visible.

However, she remained over the clearing as if she were a fixture. An immense bell had imprisoned the atmosphere and deprived it of movement; not a breath of wind was there, high or low.

The aerostat manœuvred without encountering any resistance, seeming very small owing to the distance, much as if she were being looked at through the wrong end of a telescope.

Suddenly there was a shout among the crowd, a shout followed by a hundred thousand more.

All hands were stretched towards a point on the horizon.

That point was the north-west.

There in the deep azure appeared a moving body, which was approaching and growing larger.

Was it a bird beating with its wings the higher zones of space? Was it an aerolite shooting obliquely through the atmosphere? In any case, its speed was terrific, and it would soon be above the crowd.

A suspicion communicated itself electrically to the brains of all on the clearing.

But it seemed as though the Goahead had sighted this strange object. Assuredly it seemed as though she feared some danger, for her speed was increased, and she was going east as fast as she could.

Yes, the crowd saw what it meant! A name uttered by one of the members of the Weldon Institute was repeated by a hundred thousand mouths—

"The Albatross! the Albatross!"

## CHAPTER XXIII.

### THE GRAND COLLAPSE.

It was indeed the Albatross! It was indeed Robur who had reappeared in the heights of the sky! It was he who like a huge bird of prey was going to strike the Goahead.

And yet, nine months before, the aeronef, shattered by the explosion, her screws broken, her deck smashed in two, had been apparently annihilated.

Without the prodigious coolness of the engineer, who reversed the gyratory motion of the fore propeller and converted it into a suspensory screw, the men of the Albatross would all have been asphyxiated by the fall. But if they had escaped asphyxia, how had they escaped being drowned in the Pacific?

The remains of the deck, the blades of the propellers, the compartments of the cabins, all formed a sort of raft. When a wounded bird falls on the waves its wings keep it afloat. For several hours Robur and his men remained unhelped, at first on the wreck, and afterwards in the india-rubber boat that had fallen uninjured. A few hours after sunrise they were sighted by a passing ship, and a boat was lowered to their rescue.

Robur and his companions were saved, and so was much of what remained of the aeronef. The engineer said that his ship had perished in a collision, and no further questions were asked him.

The ship was an English three-master, the *Two Friends*, bound to Melbourne, where she arrived a few days afterwards.

Robur was in Australia, but a long way from X Island, to which he desired to return as soon as possible.

In the ruins of the aftermost cabin he had found a considerable sum of money, quite enough to provide for himself and companions without applying to any one for help. A short time after he arrived in Melbourne he became the owner of a small brigantine of about a hundred tons, and in her he sailed for X Island.

There he had but one idea—to be avenged. But to secure his vengeance he would have to make another Albatross. This after all was an easy task for him who made the first. He used up what he could of the old material ; the propellers and engines he had brought back in the brigantine. The mechanism was fitted with new piles and new accumulators, and, in short, in less than eight months the work was finished and a new Albatross, identical with the one destroyed by the explosion, was ready to take flight. And he had the same crew.

The Albatross left X Island in the first week of April·

During this aerial passage Robur did not want to be seen from the earth, and he came along almost always above the clouds. When he arrived over North America he descended in a desolate spot in the Far West. There the engineer, keeping a profound incognito, learnt with considerable pleasure that the Weldon Institute was about to begin its experiments, and that the Goahead, with Uncle Prudent and Phil Evans, was going to start from Philadelphia on the 29th of April.

Here was a chance for Robur and his crew to gratify their longing for revenge! Here was a chance of inflicting on their foes a terrible vengeance, which in the Goahead they could not escape! A public vengeance, which would at the same time prove the superiority of the aeronef to all aerostats and contrivances of that nature!

And that is why, on this very day, like a vulture from the clouds, the aeronef appeared over Fairmont Park.

Yes! It was the Albatross, easily recognized by all those who had never before seen her.

The Goahead was in full flight; but it soon appeared that she could not escape horizontally, and so she sought her safety in a vertical direction, not dropping to the ground, for the aeronef would have cut her off, but rising to a zone where she could not perhaps be reached. This was very daring, and at the same time very logical.

But the Albatross began to rise after her. Although she was smaller than the Goahead, it was a case of the swordfish and the whale.

This could easily be seen from below, and with what anxiety! In a few moments the aerostat had attained a height of sixteen thousand feet.

The Albatross followed her as she rose. She flew round her flanks, and manœuvred round her in a circle with a constantly diminishing radius. She could have annihilated her at a stroke, and Uncle Prudent and his companions would have been dashed to atoms in a frightful fall.

The people, mute with horror, gazed breathlessly; they were seized with that sort of fear which presses on the chest and grips the legs when we see any one fall from a height. An aerial combat was beginning in which there were none of the chances of safety as in a sea-fight. It was the first of its kind, but it would not be the last, for progress is one of the laws of this world. And if the Goahead was flying the American colours, did not the Albatross display the stars and golden sun of Robur the Conqueror.

The Goahead tried to distance her enemy by rising still higher. She threw away the ballast she had in reserve; she made a new leap of three thousand feet; she was now but a dot in space. The Albatross, which followed her round and round at top speed, was now invisible.

Suddenly a shout of terror rose from the crowd. The Goahead increased rapidly in size, and the aeronef appeared dropping with her. This time it was a fall. The gas had dilated in the higher zones of the atmosphere and had burst the balloon, which, half inflated still, was falling rapidly.

But the aeronef, slowing her suspensory screws, came down just as fast. She ran alongside the Goahead when she was not more than four thousand feet from the ground.

Would Robur destroy her?

No; he was going to save her crew!

And so cleverly did he handle his vessel that the aeronaut jumped on board.

Would Uncle Prudent and Phil Evans refuse to be saved by him? They were quite capable of doing so. But the crew threw themselves on them and dragged them by force from the Goahead to the Albatross.

Then the aeronef glided off and remained stationary, while the balloon, quite empty of gas, fell on the trees of the clearing and hung there like a gigantic rag.

An appalling silence reigned on the ground. It seemed as though life were suspended in each of the crowd; and many eyes had been closed so as not to behold the final catastrophe.

Uncle Prudent and Phil Evans had again become the prisoners of the redoubtable Robur. Now he had recaptured them, would he carry them off into space, where it was impossible to follow him?

It seemed so.

However, instead of mounting into the sky the Albatross continued falling. Was she coming down to the ground? It looked like it, and the crowd divided

He was going to save her crew.

Page 232.

so as to leave a space for her in the centre of the clearing.

The excitement was at its maximum. The Albatross stopped six feet from the ground. Then, amid profound silence, the engineer's voice was heard.

"Citizens of the United States," he said, "the president and secretary of the Weldon Institute are again in my power. In keeping them I am only within my right. But from the passion kindled in them by the success of the Albatross I see that their minds are not prepared for that important revolution which the conquest of the air will one day bring. Uncle Prudent and Phil Evans, you are free!"

The president, the secretary, and the aeronaut had only to jump down.

The Albatross then mounted to about forty feet from the ground.

Then Robur continued:—

"Citizens of the United States, my experiment is finished; but my advice to those present is to be premature in nothing, not even in progress. It is evolution and not revolution that we should seek. In a word, we must not be before our time. I have come too soon to-day to withstand such contradictory and divided interests as yours. Nations are not yet fit for union.

"I go, then; and I take my secret with me. But it will not be lost to humanity. It will belong to you the day you are educated enough to profit by it and wise enough not to abuse it. Citizens of the United States! Good-bye!"

And the Albatross, beating the air with her seventy-four screws, and driven by her propellers, shot off towards the east amid a tempest of cheers.

The two colleagues, profoundly humiliated, as through them was the whole Weldon Institute, did the only thing they could. They went home.

And the crowd by a sudden change of front greeted them with particularly keen sarcasms, and, at their expense, are sarcastic still.

* * * * * *

And now, who is this Robur? Shall we ever know?

We know to-day. Robur is the science of the future. Perhaps the science of to-morrow! Certainly the science that will come!

Does the Albatross still cruise in the atmosphere in the realm that none can take from her? There is no reason to doubt it. Will Robur, the Conqueror, appear one day as he said? Yes! He will come to declare the secret of his invention, which will greatly change the social and political conditions of the world.

As for the future of aerial locomotion, it belongs to the aeronef and not the aerostat.

It is to the Albatross that the conquest of the air will assuredly fall.

THE END.

GILBERT AND RIVINGTON, LIMITED, ST. JOHN'S HOUSE, CLERKENWELL ROAD, E.C.

# BOOKS BY JULES VERNE.

| Large Crown 8vo. | Containing 350 to 600 pp. and from 50 to 100 full-page illustrations. | | Containing the whole of the text with some illustrations. | |
|---|---|---|---|---|
| WORKS. | In very handsome cloth binding, gilt edges. | In plainer binding, plain edges. | In cloth binding, gilt edges, smaller type. | Coloured boards. |
| | *s.* *d.* | *s.* *d.* | *s.* *d.* | |
| 20,000 Leagues under the Sea. Parts I. and II. | 10 6 | 5 0 | 3 6 | 2 vols., 1*s.* each. |
| Hector Servadac | 10 6 | 5 0 | 3 6 | 2 vols., 1*s.* each. |
| The Fur Country | 10 6 | 5 0 | 3 6 | 2 vols., 1*s.* each. |
| The Earth to the Moon and a Trip round it | 10 6 | 5 0 | 2 vols., 2*s.* ea. | 2 vols., 1*s.* each. |
| Michael Strogoff | 10 6 | 5 0 | 3 6 | 2 vols., 1*s.* each. |
| Dick Sands, the Boy Captain | 10 6 | 5 0 | 3 6 | 2 vols., 1*s.* each. |
| Five Weeks in a Balloon | 7 6 | 3 6 | 2 0 | 1*s.* 0*d.* |
| Adventures of Three Englishmen and Three Russians | 7 6 | 3 6 | 2 0 | 1 0 |
| Round the World in Eighty Days | 7 6 | 3 6 | 2 0 | 1 0 |
| A Floating City } | 7 6 | 3 6 | 2 0 | 1 0 |
| The Blockade Runners } | | | 2 0 | 1 0 |
| Dr. Ox's Experiment | — | — | 2 0 | 1 0 |
| A Winter amid the Ice | — | — | 2 0 | 1 0 |
| Survivors of the "Chancellor" } | 7 6 | 3 6 | 3 6 | 2 vols., 1*s.* each. |
| Martin Paz } | | | 2 0 | 1*s.* 0*d.* |
| The Mysterious Island, 3 vols.:— | 22 6 | 10 6 | 6 0 | 3 0 |
| I. Dropped from the Clouds | 7 6 | 3 6 | 2 0 | 1 0 |
| II. Abandoned | 7 6 | 3 6 | 2 0 | 1 0 |
| III. Secret of the Island | 7 6 | 3 6 | 2 0 | 1 0 |
| The Child of the Cavern | 7 6 | 3 6 | 2 0 | 1 0 |
| The Begum's Fortune | 7 6 | 3 6 | 2 0 | 1 0 |
| The Tribulations of a Chinaman | 7 6 | 3 6 | 2 0 | 1 0 |
| The Steam House, 2 vols.:— | | | | |
| I. Demon of Cawnpore | 7 6 | 3 6 | 2 0 | 1 0 |
| II. Tigers and Traitors | 7 6 | 3 6 | 2 0 | 1 0 |
| The Giant Raft, 2 vols.:— | | | | |
| I. 800 Leagues on the Amazon | 7 6 | 3 6 | 2 0 | 1 0 |
| II. The Cryptogram | 7 6 | 3 6 | 2 0 | 1 0 |
| The Green Ray | 6 0 | 5 0 | — | 1 0 |
| Godfrey Morgan | 7 6 | 3 6 | 2 0 | 1 0 |
| Kéraban the Inflexible:— | | | | |
| I. Captain of the "Guidara" | 7 6 | 3 6 | 2 0 | 1 0 |
| II. Scarpante the Spy | 7 6 | 3 6 | 2 0 | 1 0 |
| The Archipelago on Fire | 7 6 | | | |
| The Vanished Diamond | 7 6 | | | |
| Mathias Sandorf | 10 6 | | | |
| The Lottery Ticket | 7 6 | | | |

CELEBRATED TRAVELS AND TRAVELLERS. 3 vols. 8vo, 600 pp., 100 full-page illustrations, 12*s.* 6*d.*, gilt edges, 14*s.* each:—(1) THE EXPLORATION OF THE WORLD. (2) THE GREAT NAVIGATORS OF THE EIGHTEENTH CENTURY. (3) THE GREAT EXPLORERS OF THE NINETEENTH CENTURY.

*A Catalogue of American and Foreign Books Published or Imported by* MESSRS. SAMPSON LOW & CO. *can be had on application.*

*Crown Buildings*, 188, *Fleet Street, London*, *October*, 1886.

# A Selection from the List of Books

PUBLISHED BY

# SAMPSON LOW, MARSTON, SEARLE, & RIVINGTON.

---

## ALPHABETICAL LIST.

ABBOTT (*C. C.*) *Poaetquissings Chronicle: Upland and Meadow.* 10*s.* 6*d.*

*About Some Fellows.* By an ETON BOY, Author of "A Day of my Life." Cloth limp, square 16mo, 2*s.* 6*d.*

*Adams* (*C. K.*) *Manual of Historical Literature.* Cr. 8vo, 12*s.* 6*d.*

*Alcott* (*Louisa M.*) *Joe's Boys.* 5*s.*

——— *Lulu's Library.* 3*s.* 6*d.*

——— *Old-Fashioned Thanksgiving Day.* 3*s.* 6*d.*

——— *Proverb Stories.* 16mo, 3*s.* 6*d.*

——— *Spinning-Wheel Stories.* 16mo, 5*s.*

——— See also "Rose Library."

*Alden* (*W. L.*) *Adventures of Jimmy Brown, written by himself.* Illustrated. Small crown 8vo, cloth, 2*s.* 6*d.*

*Aldrich* (*T. B.*) *Friar Jerome's Beautiful Book, &c.* Very choicely printed on hand-made paper, parchment cover, 3*s.* 6*d.*

——— *Poetical Works.* *Édition de luxe.* 8vo, 21*s.*

*Alford* (*Lady Marian*) *Needlework as Art.* With over 100 Woodcuts, Photogravures, &c. Royal 8vo, 42*s.*; large paper, 84*s.*

*Amateur Angler's Days in Dove Dale: Three Weeks' Holiday* in July and August, 1884. By E. M. Printed by Whittingham, at the Chiswick Press. Cloth gilt, 1*s.* 6*d.*; fancy boards, 1*s.*

*American Men of Letters.* Thoreau, Irving, Webster. 2*s.* 6*d.* each.

*Andersen. Fairy Tales.* With over 500 Illustrations by Scandinavian Artists. 6*s.* per vol.

*Anderson* (*W.*) *Pictorial Arts of Japan.* With 80 full-page and other Plates, 16 of them in Colours. Large imp. 4to, 8*l.* 8*s.* (in four folio parts, 2*l.* 2*s.* each); Artist's Proofs, 12*l.* 12*s.*

*Angler's Strange Experiences (An).* By COTSWOLD ISYS. With numerous Illustrations, 4to, 5*s.* New Edition, 3*s.* 6*d.*

*Angling.* See Amateur, "British Fisheries," "Cutcliffe," "Halford," "Hamilton," "Martin," "Orvis," "Pennell," "Pritt," "Stevens," "Theakston," "Walton," "Wells," and "Willis-Bund."

*Arnold (Edwin) Birthday Book.* 4*s.* 6*d.*

*Art Education.* See "Biographies of Great Artists," "Illustrated Text Books," "Mollett's Dictionary."

*Artists at Home.* Photographed by J. P. MAYALL, and reproduced in Facsimile. Letterpress by F. G. STEPHENS. Imp. folio, 42*s.*

*Audsley (G. A.) Ornamental Arts of Japan.* 90 Plates, 74 in Colours and Gold, with General and Descriptive Text. 2 vols., folio, £15 15*s.*; in specally designed leather, 23*l.* 2*s.*

—— *The Art of Chromo-Lithography.* Coloured Plates and Text. Folio, 63*s.*

*Auerbach (B.) Brigitta.* (B. Tauchnitz Collection.) 2*s.*

—— *On the Heights.* 3 vols., 6*s.*

—— *Spinoza.* 2 vols., 18mo, 4*s.*

*BALDWIN (J.) Story of Siegfried.* 6*s.*

—— *Story of Roland.* Crown 8vo, 6*s.*

*Barlow (Alfred) Weaving by Hand and by Power.* With several hundred Illustrations. Third Edition, royal 8vo, 1*l.* 5*s.*

*Barrow (J.) Mountain Ascents in Cumberland and Westmoreland.* 7*s.* 6*d.*

*Bassett (F. S.) Legends and Superstitions of the Sea and of* Sailors. 7*s.* 6*d.*

---

## THE BAYARD SERIES.

Edited by the late J. HAIN FRISWELL.

Comprising Pleasure Books of Literature produced in the Choicest Style as Companionable Volumes at Home and Abroad.

"We can hardly imagine better books for boys to read or for men to ponder over."—*Times.*

*Price 2s. 6d. each Volume, complete in itself, flexible cloth extra, gilt edges, with silk Headbands and Registers.*

The Story of the Chevalier Bayard. By M. De Berville.

De Joinville's St. Louis, King of France.

The Essays of Abraham Cowley, including all his Prose Works.

Abdallah; or, The Four Leaves. By Edouard Laboullaye.

Table-Talk and Opinions of Napoleon Buonaparte.

Vathek: An Oriental Romance. By William Beckford.

*Bayard Series (continued)* :—

Words of Wellington: Maxims and Opinions of the Great Duke.

Dr. Johnson's Rasselas, Prince of Abyssinia. With Notes.

Hazlitt's Round Table. With Biographical Introduction.

The Religio Medici, Hydriotaphia, and the Letter to a Friend. By Sir Thomas Browne, Knt.

Coleridge's Christabel, and other Imaginative Poems. With Preface by Algernon C. Swinburne.

Lord Chesterfield's Letters, Sentences, and Maxims. With Introduction by the Editor, and Essay on Chesterfield by M. de Ste.-Beuve, of the French Academy.

Ballad Poetry of the Affections. By Robert Buchanan.

The King and the Commons. A Selection of Cavalier and Puritan Songs. Edited by Professor Morley.

Essays in Mosaic. By Thos. Ballantyne.

My Uncle Toby; his Story and his Friends. Edited by P. Fitzgerald.

Reflections; or, Moral Sentences and Maxims of the Duke de la Rochefoucauld.

Socrates: Memoirs for English Readers from Xenophon's Memorabilia. By Edw. Levien.

Prince Albert's Golden Precepts

*A Case containing 12 Volumes, price 31s. 6d.; or the Case separately, price 3s. 6d.*

*Behnke and Browne. Child's Voice.* Small 8vo, 3*s*. 6*d*.

*Beyschlag. Female Costume Figures of various Centuries.* 12 designs in portfolio, imperial. 21*s*.

*Bickersteth (Bishop E. H.) The Clergyman in his Home.* Small post 8vo, 1*s*.

——— *Evangelical Churchmanship and Evangelical Eclecticism.* 8vo, 1*s*.

——— *From Year to Year: Original Poetical Pieces.* Small post 8vo, 3*s*. 6*d*.; roan, 6*s*. and 5*s*.; calf or morocco, 10*s*. 6*d*.

——— *Hymnal Companion to the Book of Common Prayer.* May be had in various styles and bindings from 1*d*. to 31*s*. 6*d*. *Price List and Prospectus will be forwarded on application.*

——— *The Master's Home-Call; or, Brief Memorials of Alice* Frances Bickersteth. 20th Thousand. 32mo, cloth gilt, 1*s*.

——— *The Master's Will.* A Funeral Sermon preached on the Death of Mrs. S. Gurney Buxton. Sewn, 6*d*.; cloth gilt, 1*s*.

——— *The Reef, and other Parables.* Crown 8vo, 2*s*. 6*d*.

——— *The Shadow of the Rock.* A Selection of Religious Poetry. 18mo, cloth extra, 2*s*. 6*d*.

——— *The Shadowed Home and the Light Beyond.* New Edition, crown 8vo, cloth extra, 5*s*.

*Biographies of the Great Artists (Illustrated).* Crown 8vo, emblematical binding, 3*s.* 6*d.* per volume, except where the price is given.

Claude Lorrain.
Correggio, by M. E. Heaton, 2*s.* 6*d.*
Della Robbia and Cellini, 2*s.* 6*d.*
Albrecht Dürer, by R. F. Heath.
Figure Painters of Holland.
Fra Angelico, Masaccio, and Botticelli.
Fra Bartolommeo, Albertinelli, and Andrea del Sarto.
Gainsborough and Constable.
Ghiberti and Donatello, 2*s.* 6*d.*
Giotto, by Harry Quilter.
Hans Holbein, by Joseph Cundall.
Hogarth, by Austin Dobson.
Landseer, by F. G. Stevens.
Lawrence and Romney, by Lord Ronald Gower, 2*s.* 6*d.*
Leonardo da Vinci.
Little Masters of Germany, by W. B. Scott.
Mantegna and Francia.
Meissonier, by J. W. Mollett, 2*s.* 6*d.*
Michelangelo Buonarotti, by Clément.
Murillo, by Ellen E. Minor, 2*s.* 6*d.*
Overbeck, by J. B. Atkinson.
Raphael, by N. D'Anvers.
Rembrandt, by J. W. Mollett.
Reynolds, by F. S. Pulling.
Rubens, by C. W. Kett.
Tintoretto, by W. R. Osler.
Titian, by R. F. Heath.
Turner, by Cosmo Monkhouse.
Vandyck and Hals, by P. R Head.
Velasquez, by E. Stowe.
Vernet and Delaroche, by J. Rees.
Watteau, by J. W. Mollett, 2*s.* 6*d.*
Wilkie, by J. W. Mollett.

*Bird (F. J.) American Practical Dyer's Companion.* 8vo, 42*s.*

*Bird (H. E.) Chess Practice.* 8vo, 2*s.* 6*d.*

*Black (Robert) Horse Racing in France.* 14*s.*

*Black (Wm.) Novels.* See "Low's Standard Library."

*Blackburn (Charles F.) Hints on Catalogue Titles and Index* Entries, with a Vocabulary of Terms and Abbreviations, chiefly from Foreign Catalogues. Royal 8vo, 14*s.*

*Blackburn (Henry) Breton Folk.* With 171 Illust. by RANDOLPH CALDECOTT. Imperial 8vo, gilt edges, 21*s.*; plainer binding, 10*s.* 6*d.*

——— *Pyrenees.* With 100 Illustrations by GUSTAVE DORÉ, corrected to 1881. Crown 8vo, 7*s.* 6*d.* See also CALDECOTT.

*Blackmore (R. D.) Lorna Doone. Edition de luxe.* Crown 4to, very numerous Illustrations, cloth, gilt edges, 31*s.* 6*d.*; parchment, uncut, top gilt, 35*s.*; new issue, plainer, 21*s.*; small post 8vo, 6*s.*

——— *Novels.* See "Low's Standard Library."

*Blaikie (William) How to get Strong and how to Stay so.* Rational, Physical, Gymnastic, &c., Exercises. Illust., sm. post 8vo, 5*s.*

——— *Sound Bodies for our Boys and Girls.* 16mo, 2*s.* 6*d.*

*Bonwick. British Colonies.* Asia, 1*s.*; Africa, 1*s.*; America, 1*s.*; Australasia, 1*s.* One vol., 5*s.*

*Bosanquet (Rev. C.) Blossoms from the King's Garden: Sermons* for Children. 2nd Edition, small post 8vo, cloth extra, 6*s.*

——— *Jehoshaphat; or, Sunlight and Clouds.* 1*s.*

*Boulton (Major) North-West Rebellion in Canada.* 9*s.*
*Boussenard (L.) Crusoes of Guiana.* Illustrated. 5*s.*
——— *Gold-seekers, a Sequel.* Illustrated. 16mo, 5*s.*
*Bowker (R. R.) Copyright: its Law and its Literature.* 15*s.*
*Boyesen (F.) Story of Norway.* 7*s.* 6*d.*
*Boy's Froissart. King Arthur. Mabinogion. Percy.* See LANIER.
*Bradshaw (J.) New Zealand as it is.* 8vo, 12*s.* 6*d.*
*Brassey (Lady) Tahiti.* With 31 Autotype Illustrations after Photos. by Colonel STUART-WORTLEY. Fcap. 4to, 21*s.*
*Bright (John) Public Letters.* Crown 8vo, 7*s.* 6*d.*
*Brisse (Baron) Ménus* (366). A *ménu*, in French and English, for every Day in the Year. Translated by Mrs. MATTHEW CLARKE. 2nd Edition. Crown 8vo, 5*s.*
*British Fisheries Directory*, 1883-84. Small 8vo, 2*s.* 6*d.*
*Brittany.* See BLACKBURN.
*Britons in Brittany.* By G. H. F. 2*s.* 6*d.*
*Brown. Life and Letters of John Brown, Liberator of Kansas,* and Martyr of Virginia. By F. B. SANBORN. Illustrated. 8vo, 12*s.* 6*d.*
*Browne (G. Lennox) Voice Use and Stimulants.* Sm. 8vo, 3*s.* 6*d.*
——— *and Behnke (Emil) Voice, Song, and Speech.* Illustrated, 3rd Edition, medium 8vo, 15*s.*
*Bryant (W. C.) and Gay (S. H.) History of the United States.* 4 vols., royal 8vo, profusely Illustrated, 60*s.*
*Bryce (Rev. Professor) Manitoba.* With Illustrations and Maps. Crown 8vo, 7*s.* 6*d.*
*Bunyan's Pilgrim's Progress.* With 138 original Woodcuts. Small post 8vo, cloth gilt, 2*s.* 6*d.*; gilt edges, 3*s.*
*Burnaby (Capt.) On Horseback through Asia Minor.* 2 vols., 8vo, 38*s.* Cheaper Edition, 1 vol., crown 8vo, 10*s.* 6*d.*
*Burnaby (Mrs. F.) High Alps in Winter; or, Mountaineering* in Search of Health. By Mrs. FRED BURNABY. With Portrait of the Authoress, Map, and other Illustrations. Handsome cloth, 14*s.*
*Butler (W. F.) The Great Lone Land; an Account of the Red* River Expedition, 1869-70. New Edition, cr. 8vo, cloth extra, 7*s.* 6*d.*
——— *Invasion of England, told twenty years after, by an* Old Soldier. Crown 8vo, 2*s.* 6*d.*
——— *Red Cloud; or, the Solitary Sioux.* Imperial 16mo, numerous illustrations, gilt edges, 5*s.*
——— *The Wild North Land; the Story of a Winter Journey* with Dogs across Northern North America. 8vo, 18*s.* Cr. 8vo, 7*s.* 6*d.*

*CADOGAN (Lady A.) Illustrated Games of Patience.* Twenty-four Diagrams in Colours, with Text. Fcap. 4to, 12*s.* 6*d.*

*Caldecott (Randolph) Memoir.* By HENRY BLACKBURN. With 170 (chiefly unpublished) Examples of the Artist's Work. 14*s.*; large paper, 21*s.*

*California.* See NORDHOFF.

*Cambridge Staircase (A).* By the Author of "A Day of my Life at Eton." Small crown 8vo, cloth, 2*s.* 6*d.*

*Cambridge Trifles; from an Undergraduate Pen.* By the Author of "A Day of my Life at Eton," &c. 16mo, cloth extra, 2*s.* 6*d.*

*Campbell (Lady Colin) Book of the Running Brook: and of Still Waters.* 5*s.*

*Canadian People: Short History.* Crown 8vo, 7*s.* 6*d.*

*Carleton (Will) Farm Ballads, Farm Festivals, and Farm Legends.* 1 vol., small post 8vo, 3*s.* 6*d.*

—— *City Ballads.* With Illustrations. 12*s.* 6*d.*

—— See also "Rose Library."

*Carnegie (A.) American Four-in-Hand in Britain.* Small 4to, Illustrated, 10*s.* 6*d.* Popular Edition, 1*s.*

—— *Round the World.* 8vo, 10*s.* 6*d.*

—— *Triumphant Democracy.* 6*s.*; also 1*s.* 6*d.* and 1*s.*

*Chairman's Handbook (The).* By R. F. D. PALGRAVE, Clerk of the Table of the House of Commons. 5th Edition, 2*s.*

*Changed Cross (The),* and other Religious Poems. 16mo, 2*s.* 6*d.*; calf or morocco, 6*s.*

*Charities of London.* See Low's.

*Chattock (R. S.) Practical Notes on Etching.* 8vo, 10*s.* 6*d.*

*Chess.* See BIRD (H. E.).

*Children's Praises. Hymns for Sunday-Schools and Services.* Compiled by LOUISA H. H. TRISTRAM. 4*d.*

*Choice Editions of Choice Books.* 2*s.* 6*d.* each. Illustrated by C. W. COPE, R.A., T. CRESWICK, R.A., E. DUNCAN, BIRKET FOSTER, J. C. HORSLEY, A.R.A., G. HICKS, R. REDGRAVE, R.A., C. STONEHOUSE, F. TAYLER, G. THOMAS, H. J. TOWNSHEND, E. H. WEHNERT, HARRISON WEIR, &c.

Bloomfield's Farmer's Boy.
Campbell's Pleasures of Hope.
Coleridge's Ancient Mariner.
Goldsmith's Deserted Village.
Goldsmith's Vicar of Wakefield.
Gray's Elegy in a Churchyard.
Keat's Eve of St. Agnes.
Milton's L'Allegro.
Poetry of Nature. Harrison Weir.
Rogers' (Sam.) Pleasures of Memory.
Shakespeare's Songs and Sonnets.
Tennyson's May Queen.
Elizabethan Poets.
Wordsworth's Pastoral Poems.

"Such works are a glorious beatification for a poet."—*Athenæum.*

*Christ in Song.* By PHILIP SCHAFF. New Ed., gilt edges, 6s.

*Chromo-Lithography.* See AUDSLEY.

*Collingwood (Harry) Under the Meteor Flag.* The Log of a Midshipman. Illustrated, small post 8vo, gilt, 6s.; plainer, 5s.

—— *The Voyage of the "Aurora."* Illustrated, small post 8vo, gilt, 6s.; plainer, 5s.

*Composers.* See "Great Musicians."

*Cook (Dutton) Book of the Play.* New Edition. 1 vol., 3s. 6d.

—— *On the Stage: Studies of Theatrical History and the* Actor's Art. 2 vols., 8vo, cloth, 24s.

*Cowen (Jos., M.P.) Life and Speeches.* By MAJOR JONES. 8vo, 14s.

*Cozzens (F.) American Yachts.* 27 Plates, 22 × 28 inches. Proofs, 21l.; Artist's Proofs, 31l. 10s.

*Crown Prince of Germany: a Diary.* 7s. 6d.

*Cundall (Joseph) Annals of the Life and Work of Shakespeare.* With a List of Early Editions. 3s. 6d.; large paper, 5s.

*Cushing (W.) Initials and Pseudonyms: a Dictionary of Literary* Disguises. Large 8vo, top edge gilt, 21s.

*Custer (E. B.) Boots and Saddles. Life in Dakota with General* Custer. Crown 8vo, 8s. 6d.

*Cutcliffe (H. C.) Trout Fishing in Rapid Streams.* Cr. 8vo, 3s. 6d.

*D'ANVERS (N.) An Elementary History of Art.* Crown 8vo, 10s. 6d.

—— *Elementary History of Music.* Crown 8vo, 2s. 6d.

—— *Handbooks of Elementary Art—Architecture; Sculpture;* Old Masters; Modern Painting. Crown 8vo, 3s. 6d. each.

*Davis (Clement) Modern Whist.* 4s.

*Davis (C. T.) Manufacture of Bricks, Tiles, Terra-Cotta, &c.* Illustrated. 8vo, 25s.

—— *Manufacture of Leather.* With many Illustrations. 52s. 6d.

—— *Manufacture of Paper.* 28s.

*Dawidowsky (F.) Glue, Gelatine, Isinglass, Cements, &c.* 8vo, 12s. 6d.

*Day of My Life (A); or, Every-Day Experiences at Eton.* By an ETON BOY. 16mo, cloth extra, 2s. 6d.

*Day's Collacon: an Encyclopædia of Prose Quotations.* Imperial 8vo, cloth, 31s. 6d.

*Decoration.* Vols. II. to XI. New Series, folio, 7s. 6d. each.

*Dogs in Disease: their Management and Treatment.* By ASHMONT. Crown 8vo, 7*s.* 6*d.*

*Donnelly (Ignatius) Atlantis; or, the Antediluvian World.* 7th Edition, crown 8vo, 12*s.* 6*d.*

——— *Ragnarok: The Age of Fire and Gravel.* Illustrated, crown 8vo, 12*s.* 6*d.*

*Doré (Gustave) Life and Reminiscences.* By BLANCHE ROOSEVELT. With numerous Illustrations from the Artist's previously unpublished Drawings. Medium 8vo, 24*s.*

*Dougall (James Dalziel) Shooting: its Appliances, Practice,* and Purpose. New Edition, revised with additions. Crown 8vo, 7*s.* 6*d.*

"The book is admirable in every way. . . . . We wish it every success."—*Globe.*
"A very complete treatise. . . . . Likely to take high rank as an authority on shooting."—*Daily News.*

*Drama.* See COOK (DUTTON).

*Dyeing.* See BIRD (F. J.).

*Dunn (J. R.) Massacres of the Mountains: Indian Wars of* the Far West. 21*s.*

*Duprè (Giovanni).* By H. S. FRIEZE. With Dialogues on Art by AUGUSTO CONTI. 7*s.* 6*d.*

*EDUCATIONAL List and Directory for* 1886-87. 5*s.*

*Educational Works* published in Great Britain. A Classified Catalogue. Second Edition, 8vo, cloth extra, 5*s.*

*Egypt.* See "Foreign Countries."

*Eight Months on the Gran Chaco of the Argentine Republic.* 8vo, 8*s.* 6*d.*

*Electricity.* See GORDON.

*Elliott (H. W.) An Arctic Province: Alaska and the Seal* Islands. Illustrated from Drawings; also with maps. 16*s.*

*Ellis (W.) Royal Jubilees of England.* 3*s.* 6*d.*

*Emerson (Dr. P. H.) and Goodall. Life and Landscape on* the Norfolk Broads. Plates 12 × 8 inches (before publication, 105*s.*), 126*s.*

*Emerson (R. W.) Life.* By G. W. COOKE. Crown 8vo, 8*s.* 6*d.*

*English Catalogue of Books.* Vol. III., 1872—1880. Royal 8vo, half-morocco, 42*s.* See also "Index."

*English Etchings.* A Periodical published Quarterly. 3*s.* 6*d.*

*English Philosophers.* Edited by E. B. IVAN MÜLLER, M.A.

A series intended to give a concise view of the works and lives of English thinkers. Crown 8vo volumes of 180 or 200 pp., price 3*s.* 6*d.* each.

Francis Bacon, by Thomas Fowler.
Hamilton, by W. H. S. Monck.
Hartley and James Mill, by G. S. Bower.
*John Stuart Mill, by Miss Helen Taylor.
Shaftesbury and Hutcheson, by Professor Fowler.
Adam Smith, by J. A. Farrer.

* *Not yet published.*

*Etching.* See CHATTOCK, and ENGLISH ETCHINGS.

*Etchings (Modern) of Celebrated Paintings.* 4to, 31*s.* 6*d.*

*FARINI (G. A.) Through the Kalahari Desert: Fauna,* Flora, and Strange Tribes. 21*s.*

*Farm Ballads, Festivals, and Legends.* See "Rose Library."

*Fauriel (Claude) Last Days of the Consulate.* Cr. 8vo, 10*s.* 6*d.*

*Fawcett (Edgar) A Gentleman of Leisure.* 1*s.*

*Federighi. Seven Ages of Man.* Lithographs from Drawings, 7 plates. 25*s.*

*Feilden (H. St. C.) Some Public Schools, their Cost and* Scholarships. Crown 8vo, 2*s.* 6*d.*

*Fenn (G. Manville) Off to the Wilds: A Story for Boys.* Profusely Illustrated. Crown 8vo, 7*s.* 6*d.*; also 5*s.*

——— *The Silver Cañon: a Tale of the Western Plains.* Illustrated, small post 8vo, gilt, 6*s.*; plainer, 5*s.*

*Fennell (Greville) Book of the Roach.* New Edition, 12mo, 2*s.*

*Ferns.* See HEATH.

*Field (H. M.) Greek Islands and Turkey after the War.* 8*s.* 6*d.*

*Fields (J. T.) Yesterdays with Authors.* New Ed., 8vo, 10*s.* 6*d.*

*Fitzgerald (Percy) Book Fancier: Romance of Book Collecting.*

*Fleming (Sandford) England and Canada: a Summer Tour.* Crown 8vo, 6*s.*

*Florence.* See YRIARTE.

*Folkard (R., Jun.) Plant Lore, Legends, and Lyrics.* Illustrated, 8vo, 16*s.*

*Forbes (H. O.) Naturalist's Wanderings in the Eastern Archipelago.* Illustrated, 8vo, 21*s*.

*Foreign Countries and British Colonies.* A series of Descriptive Handbooks. Crown 8vo, 3*s*. 6*d*. each.

Australia, by J. F. Vesey Fitzgerald.
Austria, by D. Kay, F.R.G.S.
*Canada, by W. Fraser Rae.
Denmark and Iceland, by E. C. Otté.
Egypt, by S. Lane Poole, B.A.
France, by Miss M. Roberts.
Germany, by S. Baring-Gould.
Greece, by L. Sergeant, B.A.
*Holland, by R. L. Poole.
Japan, by S. Mossman.
*New Zealand.
*Persia, by Major-Gen. Sir F. Goldsmid.
Peru, by Clements R. Markham, C.B.
Russia, by W. R. Morfill, M.A.
Spain, by Rev. Wentworth Webster.
Sweden and Norway, by F. H. Woods.
*Switzerland, by W. A. P. Coolidge, M.A.
*Turkey-in-Asia, by J. C. McCoan, M.P.
West Indies, by C. H. Eden, F.R.G.S.

* *Not ready yet.*

*Fortnight in Heaven: an Unconventional Romance.* 3*s*. 6*d*.

*Fortunes made in Business.* Vols. I., II., III. 16*s*. each.

*Frampton (Mary) Journal, Letters, and Anecdotes*, 1799—1846. 8vo, 14*s*.

*Franc (Maud Jeanne).* The following form one Series, small post 8vo, in uniform cloth bindings, with gilt edges:—

Emily's Choice. 5*s*.
Hall's Vineyard. 4*s*.
John's Wife: A Story of Life in South Australia. 4*s*.
Marian; or, The Light of Some One's Home. 5*s*.
Silken Cords and Iron Fetters. 4*s*.
Into the Light. 4*s*.
Vermont Vale. 5*s*.
Minnie's Mission. 4*s*.
Little Mercy. 4*s*.
Beatrice Melton's Discipline. 4*s*.
No Longer a Child. 4*s*.
Golden Gifts. 4*s*.
Two Sides to Every Question. 4*s*.
Master of Ralston. 4*s*.

*Frank's Ranche; or, My Holiday in the Rockies.* A Contribution to the Inquiry into What we are to Do with our Boys. 5*s*.

*French.* See JULIEN.

*Froissart.* See LANIER.

*Fuller (Edward) Fellow Travellers.* 3*s*. 6*d*.

*GALE (F.; the Old Buffer) Modern English Sports: their* Use and Abuse. Crown 8vo, 6*s*.; a few large paper copies, 10*s*. 6*d*.

*Galloway (W. B.) Chalk and Flint Formation.* 2*s*. 6*d*.

*Gane (D. N.) New South Wales and Victoria in* 1885. 5*s.*

*Geary (Grattan) Burma after the Conquest.* 7*s.* 6*d.*

*Gentle Life* (Queen Edition). 2 vols. in 1, small 4to, 6*s.*

## THE GENTLE LIFE SERIES.

Price 6*s.* each; or in calf extra, price 10*s.* 6*d.*; Smaller Edition, cloth extra, 2*s.* 6*d.*, except where price is named.

*The Gentle Life.* Essays in aid of the Formation of Character of Gentlemen and Gentlewomen.

*About in the World.* Essays by Author of "The Gentle Life."

*Like unto Christ.* A New Translation of Thomas à Kempis' "De Imitatione Christi."

*Familiar Words.* An Index Verborum, or Quotation Handbook. 6*s.*

*Essays by Montaigne.* Edited and Annotated by the Author of "The Gentle Life."

*The Gentle Life.* 2nd Series.

*The Silent Hour: Essays, Original and Selected.* By the Author of "The Gentle Life."

*Half-Length Portraits.* Short Studies of Notable Persons. By J. HAIN FRISWELL.

*Essays on English Writers,* for the Self-improvement of Students in English Literature.

*Other People's Windows.* By J. HAIN FRISWELL. 6*s.*

*A Man's Thoughts.* By J. HAIN FRISWELL.

*The Countess of Pembroke's Arcadia.* By Sir PHILIP SIDNEY. New Edition, 6*s.*

---

*George Eliot: a Critical Study of her Life.* By G. W. COOKE. Crown 8vo, 10*s.* 6*d.*

*Germany.* By S. BARING-GOULD. Crown 8vo, 3*s.* 6*d.*

*Gilder (W. H.) Ice-Pack and Tundra.* An Account of the Search for the "Jeannette." 8vo, 18*s.*

—— *Schwatka's Search.* Sledging in quest of the Franklin Records. Illustrated, 8vo, 12*s.* 6*d.*

*Gisborne (W.) New Zealand Rulers and Statesmen.* With Portraits. Crown 8vo, 7*s.* 6*d.*

*Gordon (General) Private Diary in China.* Edited by S. MOSSMAN. Crown 8vo, 7*s.* 6*d.*

*Gordon (J. E. H., B.A. Cantab.) Four Lectures on Electric* Induction at the Royal Institution, 1878-9. Illust., square 16mo, 3*s.*

—— *Electric Lighting.* Illustrated, 8vo, 18*s.*

—— *Physical Treatise on Electricity and Magnetism.* 2nd Edition, enlarged, with coloured, full-page, &c., Illust. 2 vols., 8vo, 42*s.*

—— *Electricity for Schools.* Illustrated. Crown 8vo, 5*s.*

*Gouffé (Jules) Royal Cookery Book.* Translated and adapted for English use by ALPHONSE GOUFFÉ, Head Pastrycook to the Queen. New Edition, with plates in colours, Woodcuts, &c., 8vo, gilt edges, 42*s.*

—— Domestic Edition, half-bound, 10*s.* 6*d.*

*Grant (General, U.S.) Personal Memoirs.* With numerous Illustrations, Maps, &c. 2 vols., 8vo, 28*s.*

*Great Artists.* See "Biographics."

*Great Musicians.* Edited by F. HUEFFER. A Series of Biographies, crown 8vo, 3*s.* each :—

| | | |
|---|---|---|
| Bach. | Handel. | Purcell. |
| *Beethoven. | Haydn. | Rossini. |
| *Berlioz. | *Marcello. | Schubert. |
| English Church Composers. By BARETT. | Mendelssohn. | Schumann. |
| | Mozart. | Richard Wagner. |
| *Glück. | *Palestrina. | Weber. |

* *In preparation.*

*Greenwood (H.) Our Land Laws as they are.* 2*s.* 6*d.*

*Grimm (Hermann) Literature.* 8*s.* 6*d.*

*Groves (J. Percy) Charmouth Grange : a Tale of the Seventeenth Century.* Illustrated, small post 8vo, gilt, 6*s.*; plainer 5*s.*

*Guizot's History of France.* Translated by ROBERT BLACK. Super-royal 8vo, very numerous Full-page and other Illustrations. In 8 vols., cloth extra, gilt, each 24*s.* This work is re-issued in cheaper binding, 8 vols., at 10*s.* 6*d.* each.

"It supplies a want which has long been felt, and ought to be in the hands of all students of history."—*Times.*

—— —— *Masson's School Edition.* Abridged from the Translation by Robert Black, with Chronological Index, Historical and Genealogical Tables, &c. By Professor GUSTAVE MASSON, B.A. With 24 full-page Portraits, and other Illustrations. 1 vol., 8vo, 600 pp., 10*s.* 6*d.*

*Guyon (Mde.) Life.* By UPHAM. 6th Edition, crown 8vo, 6*s.*

*HALFORD (F. M.) Floating Flies, and how to Dress them.* Coloured plates. 8vo, 15*s.*; large paper, 30*s.*

*Hall (W. W.) How to Live Long; or,* 1408 *Health Maxims,* Physical, Mental, and Moral. 2nd Edition, small post 8vo, 2*s.*

*Hamilton (E.) Recollections of Fly-fishing for Salmon, Trout,* and Grayling. With their Habits, Haunts, and History. Illustrated, small post 8vo, 6*s.*; large paper (100 numbered copies), 10*s.* 6*d.*

*Hands (T.) Numerical Exercises in Chemistry.* Cr. 8vo, 2*s.* 6*d.* and 2*s.*; Answers separately, 6*d.*

*Hardy (Thomas).* See LOW'S STANDARD NOVELS.

*Harland (Marian) Home Kitchen: a Collection of Practical* and Inexpensive Receipts. Crown 8vo, 5*s.*

*Harley (T.) Southward Ho! to the State of Georgia.* 5*s.*

*Harper's Magazine.* Published Monthly. 160 pages, fully Illustrated, 1*s.* Vols., half yearly, I.—XII. (December, 1880, to November, 1886), super-royal 8vo, 8*s.* 6*d.* each.

"'Harper's Magazine' is so thickly sown with excellent illustrations that to count them would be a work of time; not that it is a picture magazine, for the engravings illustrate the text after the manner seen in some of our choicest *éditions de luxe.*"—*St. James's Gazette.*

"It is so pretty, so big, and so cheap. . . . An extraordinary shillingsworth—160 large octavo pages, with over a score of articles, and more than three times as many illustrations."—*Edinburgh Daily Review.*

"An amazing shillingsworth . . . combining choice literature of both nations."—*Nonconformist.*

*Harper's Young People.* Vols. I.-II., profusely Illustrated with woodcuts and 12 coloured plates. Royal 4to, extra binding, each 7*s.* 6*d.*; gilt edges, 8*s.* Published Weekly, in wrapper, 1*d.* 12mo. Annual Subscription, post free, 6*s.* 6*d.*; Monthly, in wrapper, with coloured plate, 6*d.*; Annual Subscription, post free, 7*s.* 6*d.*

*Harrison (Mary) Skilful Cook: a Practical Manual of Modern* Experience. Crown 8vo, 5*s.*

*Hatton (Frank) North Borneo.* With Biography by JOSEPH HATTON. New Map, and Illustrations, 18*s.*

*Hatton (Joseph) Journalistic London: with Engravings and* Portraits of Distinguished Writers of the Day. Fcap. 4to, 12*s.* 6*d.*

—— *Three Recruits, and the Girls they left behind them.* Small post 8vo, 6*s.*

"It hurries us along in unflagging excitement."—*Times.*

*Heath (Francis George) Fern World.* With Nature-printed Coloured Plates. Crown 8vo, gilt edges, 12*s.* 6*d.* Cheap Edition, 6*s.*

*Heldmann (Bernard) Mutiny on Board the Ship "Leander."* Small post 8vo, gilt edges, numerous Illustrations, 5*s.*

*Henty (G. A.) Winning his Spurs.* Illustrations. Cr. 8vo, 5*s.*

——— *Cornet of Horse: A Story for Boys.* Illust., cr. 8vo, 5*s.*

——— *Jack Archer: Tale of the Crimea.* Illust., crown 8vo, 5*s.*

——— *(Richmond) Australiana: My Early Life.* 5*s.*

*Herrick (Robert) Poetry.* Preface by AUSTIN DOBSON. With numerous Illustrations by E. A. ABBEY. 4to, gilt edges, 42*s.*

*Hicks (E. S.) Our Boys: How to Enter the Merchant Service.* 5*s.*

*Higginson (T. W.) Larger History of the United States.* 14*s.*

*Hill (Staveley, Q.C., M.P.) From Home to Home: Two Long* Vacations at the Foot of the Rocky Mountains. With Wood Engravings and Photogravures. 8vo, 21*s.*

*Hitchman. Public Life of the Earl of Beaconsfield.* 3*s.* 6*d.*

*Hofmann. Scenes from the Life of our Saviour.* 12 mounted plates, 12 × 9 inches, 21*s.*

*Holder (C. F.) Marvels of Animal Life.* 8*s.* 6*d.*

——— *Ivory King: the Elephant and its Allies.* Illustrated. 8*s.* 6*d.*

*Holmes (O. Wendell) Poetical Works.* 2 vols., 18mo, exquisitely printed, and chastely bound in limp cloth, gilt tops, 10*s.* 6*d.*

——— *Last Leaf: a Holiday Volume.* 42*s.*

——— *Mortal Antipathy.* 8*s.* 6*d.*

*Homer, Iliad I.-XII., done into English Verse.* By ARTHUR S. WAY. 9*s.*

——— *Odyssey.* Translated by A. S. WAY. 7*s.* 6*d.*

*Hore (Mrs.) To Lake Tanganyika in a Bath Chair.* Portraits and maps.

*Hundred Greatest Men (The).* 8 portfolios, 21*s.* each, or 4 vols., half-morocco, gilt edges, 10 guineas. New Ed., 1 vol., royal 8vo, 21*s.*

*Hutchinson (T.) Diary and Letters.* Vol. I., 16*s.*; Vol. II., 16*s.*

*Hygiene and Public Health.* Edited by A. H. BUCK, M.D. Illustrated. 2 vols., royal 8vo, 42*s.*

*Hymnal Companion of Common Prayer.* See BICKERSTETH.

*ILLUSTRATED Text-Books of Art-Education.* Edited by EDWARD J. POYNTER, R.A. Each Volume contains numerous Illustrations, and is strongly bound for Students, price 5*s*. Now ready:—

PAINTING.

**Classic and Italian.** By PERCY R. HEAD.
**German, Flemish, and Dutch.**
**French and Spanish.**
**English and American.**

ARCHITECTURE.

**Classic and Early Christian.**
**Gothic and Renaissance.** By T. ROGER SMITH.

SCULPTURE.

**Antique: Egyptian and Greek.**
**Renaissance and Modern.** By LEADER SCOTT.

*Index to the English Catalogue, Jan.,* 1874, *to Dec.,* 1880. Royal 8vo, half-morocco, 18*s*.

*Indian Garden Series.* See ROBINSON (PHIL.).

*Irving* (*Henry*) *Impressions of America.* By J. HATTON. 2 vols., 21*s*.; New Edition, 1 vol., 6*s*.

*Irving* (*Washington*). Complete Library Edition of his Works in 27 Vols., Copyright, Unabridged, and with the Author's Latest Revisions, called the "Geoffrey Crayon" Edition, handsomely printed in large square 8vo, on superfine laid paper. Each volume, of about 500 pages, fully Illustrated. 12*s*. 6*d*. per vol. *See also* "Little Britain."

——— ("American Men of Letters.") 2*s*. 6*d*.

*JAMES* (*C.*) *Curiosities of Law and Lawyers.* 8vo, 7*s*. 6*d*

*Japan.* See ANDERSON, AUDSLEY, also MORSE.

*Jerdon* (*Gertrude*) *Key-hole Country.* Illustrated. Crown 8vo, cloth, 5*s*.

*Johnston* (*H. H.*) *River Congo, from its Mouth to Bolobo.* New Edition, 8vo, 21*s*.

*Jones* (*Major*) *Heroes of Industry.* Biographies with Portraits 7*s*. 6*d*.

——— *The Emigrants' Friend.* A Complete Guide to the United States. New Edition. 2*s*. 6*d*.

*Julien* (*F.*) *English Student's French Examiner.* 16mo, 2*s*.

——— *First Lessons in Conversational French Grammar.* Crown 8vo, 1*s*.

———*French at Home and at School.* Book I., Accidence, &c. Square crown 8vo, 2*s*.

*Julien (F.) Conversational French Reader.* 16mo, cloth, 2*s*. 6*d*.
——— *Petites Leçons de Conversation et de Grammaire.* 3*s*.
——— *Phrases of Daily Use.* Limp cloth, 6*d*.
——— *Petites Leçons and Phrases.* 3*s*. 6*d*.

*KEMPIS (Thomas à) Daily Text-Book.* Square 16mo, 2*s*. 6*d*.; interleaved as a Birthday Book, 3*s*. 6*d*.

*Kent's Commentaries: an Abridgment for Students of American* Law. By EDEN F. THOMPSON. 10*s*. 6*d*.

*Kerr (W. M.) Far Interior: Cape of Good Hope, across the* Zambesi, to the Lake Regions. Illustrated from Sketches, 2 vols. 8vo, 32*s*.

*Kershaw (S. W.) Protestants from France in their English* Home. Crown 8vo, 6*s*.

*Kielland. Skipper Worsé.* By the Earl of Ducie. Cr. 8vo, 10*s*. 6*d*.

*Kingston (W. H. G.) Works.* Illustrated, 16mo, gilt edges 7*s*. 6*d*.; plainer binding, plain edges, 5*s*. each.

- Heir of Kilfinnan.
- Dick Cheveley.
- Snow-Shoes and Canoes.
- Two Supercargoes.
- With Axe and Rifle.

*Kingsley (Rose) Children of Westminster Abbey: Studies in* English History. 5*s*.

*Knight (E. F.) Albania and Montenegro.* Illust. 8vo, 12*s*. 6*d*.

*Knight (E. J.) Cruise of the "Falcon."* A Voyage to South America in a 30-Ton Yacht. Illust. New Ed. 2 vols., cr. 8vo, 24*s*.

*Kunhardt. Small Yachts: Design and Construction.* 35*s*.

*LAMB (Charles) Essays of Elia.* With over 100 designs by C. O. MURRAY. 6*s*.

*Lanier's Works.* Illustrated, crown 8vo, gilt edges, 7*s*. 6*d*. each.

- Boy's King Arthur.
- Boy's Froissart.
- Boy's Mabinogion; Original Welsh Legends of King Arthur.
- Boy's Percy: Ballads of Love and Adventure, selected from the "Reliques."

*Lansdell (H.) Through Siberia.* 2 vols., 8vo, 30*s*.; 1 vol., 10*s*. 6*d*.
——— *Russia in Central Asia.* Illustrated. 2 vols, 42*s*.

*Larden (W.) School Course on Heat.* Second Edition, Illust. 5*s*.

*Leonardo da Vinci's Literary Works.* Edited by Dr. JEAN PAUL RICHTER. Containing his Writings on Painting, Sculpture, and Architecture, his Philosophical Maxims, Humorous Writings, and Miscellaneous Notes on Personal Events, on his Contemporaries, on Literature, &c.; published from Manuscripts. 2 vols., imperial 8vo, containing about 200 Drawings in Autotype Reproductions, and numerous other Illustrations. Twelve Guineas.

*Le Plongeon. Sacred Mysteries among the Mayas and the* Quiches. 12*s*. 6*d*.

*Library of Religious Poetry.* Best Poems of all Ages. Edited by SCHAFF and GILMAN. Royal 8vo, 21*s*.; cheaper binding, 10*s*. 6*d*.

*Lindsay (W. S.) History of Merchant Shipping.* Over 150 Illustrations, Maps, and Charts. In 4 vols., demy 8vo, cloth extra. Vols. 1 and 2, 11*s*. each; vols. 3 and 4, 14*s*. each. 4 vols., 50*s*.

*Little Britain, The Spectre Bridegroom,* and *Legend of Sleeepy* Hollow. By WASHINGTON IRVING. An entirely New *Édition de luxe.* Illustrated by 120 very fine Engravings on Wood, by Mr. J. D. COOPER. Designed by Mr. CHARLES O. MURRAY. Re-issue, square crown 8vo, cloth, 6*s*.

*Low's Standard Library of Travel and Adventure.* Crown 8vo, uniform in cloth extra, 7*s*. 6*d*., except where price is given.

1. **The Great Lone Land.** By Major W. F. BUTLER, C.B.
2. **The Wild North Land.** By Major W. F. BUTLER, C.B.
3. **How I found Livingstone.** By H. M. STANLEY.
4. **Through the Dark Continent.** By H. M. STANLEY. 12*s*. 6*d*.
5. **The Threshold of the Unknown Region.** By C. R. MARKHAM. (4th Edition, with Additional Chapters, 10*s*. 6*d*.)
6. **Cruise of the Challenger.** By W. J. J. SPRY, R.N.
7. **Burnaby's On Horseback through Asia Minor.** 10*s*. 6*d*.
8. **Schweinfurth's Heart of Africa.** 2 vols., 15*s*.
9. **Marshall's Through America.**
10. **Lansdell's Through Siberia.** Illustrated and unabridged, 10*s*. 6*d*.

*Low's Standard Novels.* Small post 8vo, cloth extra, 6*s*. each, unless otherwise stated.

**A Daughter of Heth.** By W. BLACK.
**In Silk Attire.** By W. BLACK.
**Kilmeny.** A Novel. By W. BLACK.
**Lady Silverdale's Sweetheart.** By W. BLACK.
**Sunrise.** By W. BLACK.
**Three Feathers.** By WILLIAM BLACK.
**Alice Lorraine.** By R. D. BLACKMORE.
**Christowell, a Dartmoor Tale.** By R. D. BLACKMORE.
**Clara Vaughan.** By R. D. BLACKMORE.

*Low's Standard Novels—continued.*

Cradock Nowell. By R. D. BLACKMORE.
Cripps the Carrier. By R. D. BLACKMORE.
Erema; or, My Father's Sin. By R. D. BLACKMORE.
Lorna Doone. By R. D. BLACKMORE. 25th Edition.
Mary Anerley. By R. D. BLACKMORE.
Tommy Upmore. By R. D. BLACKMORE.
An English Squire. By Miss COLERIDGE.
Some One Else. By Mrs. B. M. CROKER.
A Story of the Dragonnades. By Rev. E. GILLIAT, M.A.
A Laodicean. By THOMAS HARDY.
Far from the Madding Crowd. By THOMAS HARDY.
Pair of Blue Eyes. By THOMAS HARDY.
Return of the Native. By THOMAS HARDY.
The Hand of Ethelberta. By THOMAS HARDY.
The Trumpet Major. By THOMAS HARDY.
Two on a Tower. By THOMAS HARDY.
Three Recruits. By JOSEPH HATTON.
A Golden Sorrow. By Mrs. CASHEL HOEY. New Edition.
Out of Court. By Mrs. CASHEL HOEY.
Don John. By JEAN INGELOW.
John Jerome. By JEAN INGELOW. 5*s.*
Sarah de Berenger. By JEAN INGELOW.
Adela Cathcart. By GEORGE MAC DONALD.
Guild Court. By GEORGE MAC DONALD.
Mary Marston. By GEORGE MAC DONALD.
Stephen Archer. New Ed. of "Gifts." By GEORGE MAC DONALD.
The Vicar's Daughter. By GEORGE MAC DONALD.
Weighed and Wanting. By GEORGE MAC DONALD.
Diane. By Mrs. MACQUOID.
Elinor Dryden. By Mrs. MACQUOID.
My Lady Greensleeves. By HELEN MATHERS.
Alaric Spenceley. By Mrs. J. H. RIDDELL.
Daisies and Buttercups. By Mrs. J. H. RIDDELL.
The Senior Partner. By Mrs. J. H. RIDDELL.
A Struggle for Fame. By Mrs. J. H. RIDDELL.
Jack's Courtship. By W. CLARK RUSSELL.
John Holdsworth. By W. CLARK RUSSELL.
A Sailor's Sweetheart. By W. CLARK RUSSELL.
Sea Queen. By W. CLARK RUSSELL.
Watch Below. By W. CLARK RUSSELL.
Strange Voyage. By W. CLARK RUSSELL.
Wreck of the Grosvenor. By W. CLARK RUSSELL.
The Lady Maud. By W. CLARK RUSSELL.
Little Loo. By W. CLARK RUSSELL.
The Late Mrs. Null. By FRANK R. STOCKTON.
My Wife and I. By Mrs. BEECHER STOWE.
Poganuc People, their Loves and Lives. By Mrs. B. STOWE.

*Low's Standard Novels—continued.*

**Ben Hur: a Tale of the Christ.** By LEW. WALLACE.
**Anne.** By CONSTANCE FENIMORE WOOLSON.
**East Angels.** By CONSTANCE FENIMORE WOOLSON.
**For the Major.** By CONSTANCE FENIMORE WOOLSON. 5*s.*
**French Heiress in her own Chateau.**

*Low's Handbook to the Charities of London.* Edited and revised to date. Yearly, cloth, 1*s.* 6*d.*; paper, 1*s.*

MCCORMICK (*R.*). *Voyages of Discovery in the Arctic and* Antarctic Seas in the "Erebus" and "Terror," in Search of Sir John Franklin, &c. With Maps and Lithos. 2 vols., royal 8vo, 52*s.* 6*d.*

*MacDonald* (*G.*) *Orts.* Small post 8vo, 6*s.*

——— See also "Low's Standard Novels."

*Mackay* (*Charles*) *New Glossary of Obscure Words in Shakespeare.* 21*s.*

*Macgregor* (*John*) "*Rob Roy*" *on the Baltic.* 3rd Edition, small post 8vo, 2*s.* 6*d.*; cloth, gilt edges, 3*s.* 6*d.*

——— *A Thousand Miles in the* "*Rob Roy*" *Canoe.* 11th Edition, small post 8vo, 2*s.* 6*d.*; cloth, gilt edges, 3*s.* 6*d.*

——— *Voyage Alone in the Yawl* "*Rob Roy.*" New Edition with additions, small post 8vo, 5*s.*; 3*s.* 6*d.* and 2*s.* 6*d.*

*McLellan's Own Story: The War for the Union.* Illustrations and maps. 18*s.*

*Macquoid* (*Mrs.*). See LOW'S STANDARD NOVELS.

*Magazine.* See DECORATION, ENGLISH ETCHINGS, HARPER.

*Maginn* (*W.*) *Miscellanies. Prose and Verse. With Memoir.* 2 vols., crown 8vo, 24*s.*

*Main* (*Mrs.; Mrs. Fred Burnaby*) *High Life and Towers of Silence.* Illustrated, square 8vo, 10*s.* 6*d.*

*Manitoba.* See BRYCE.

*Manning* (*E. F.*) *Delightful Thames.* Illustrated. 4to, fancy-boards, 5*s.*

*Markham* (*C. R.*) *The Threshold of the Unknown Region.* Crown 8vo, with Four Maps. 4th Edition. Cloth extra, 10*s.* 6*d.*

——— *War between Peru and Chili,* 1879-1881. Third Ed. Crown 8vo, with Maps, 10*s.* 6*d.*

——— See also "Foreign Countries."

*Marshall* (*W. G.*) *Through America.* New Ed., cr. 8vo, 7*s.* 6*d.*

*Martin (J. W.) Float Fishing and Spinning in the Nottingham* Style. New Edition. Crown 8vo, 2*s*. 6*d*.

*Maury (Commander) Physical Geography of the Sea, and its* Meteorology. New Edition, with Charts and Diagrams, cr. 8vo, 6*s*.

*Men of Mark: a Gallery of Contemporary Portraits of the most* Eminent Men of the Day, specially taken from Life. Complete in Seven Vols., 4to, handsomely bound, cloth, gilt edges, 25*s*. each.

*Mendelssohn Family (The)*, 1729—1847. From Letters and Journals. Translated. New Edition, 2 vols., 8vo, 30*s*.

*Mendelssohn.* See also "Great Musicians."

*Merrifield's Nautical Astronomy.* Crown 8vo, 7*s*. 6*d*.

*Merrylees (J.) Carlsbad and its Environs.* 7*s*. 6*d*.; roan, 9*s*.

*Mitchell (D. G.; Ik. Marvel) Works.* Uniform Edition, small 8vo, 5*s*. each.

Bound together.
Doctor Johns.
Dream Life.
Out-of-Town Places.
Reveries of a Bachelor.
Seven Stories, Basement and Attic.
Wet Days at Edgewood.

*Mitford (Mary Russell) Our Village.* With 12 full-pape and 157 smaller Cuts. Cr. 4to, cloth, gilt edges, 21*s*.; cheaper binding, 10*s*. 6*d*.

*Milford (P.) Ned Stafford's Experiences in the United States.* 5*s*.

*Mollett (J. W.) Illustrated Dictionary of Words used in Art and* Archæology. Terms in Architecture, Arms, Bronzes, Christian Art, Colour, Costume, Decoration, Devices, Emblems, Heraldry, Lace, Personal Ornaments, Pottery, Painting, Sculpture, &c. Small 4to, 15*s*.

*Money (E.) The Truth about America.* 5*s*.

*Morley (H.) English Literature in the Reign of Victoria.* 2000th volume of the Tauchnitz Collection of Authors. 18mo, 2*s*. 6*d*.

*Morse (E. S.) Japanese Homes and their Surroundings.* With more than 300 Illustrations. 21*s*.

*Morwood. Our Gipsies in City, Tent, and Van.* 8vo, 18*s*.

*Moxley. Barbados, West Indian Sanatorium.* 3*s*. 6*d*.

*Muller (E.) Noble Words and Noble Deeds.* 7*s*. 6*d*.; plainer binding, 5*s*.

*Murray (E. C. Grenville) Memoirs.* By his widow, COMTESSE DE RETHEL D'ARAGON.

*Music.* See "Great Musicians."

*Mustard Leaves: Glimpses of London Society.* By D.T.S. 3*s*. 6*d*.

*NAPOLEON and Marie Louise: Memoirs.* By Madame DURAND. 7*s.* 6*d.*

*New Zealand.* See BRADSHAW.

*New Zealand Rulers and Statesmen.* See GISBORNE.

*Nicholls (J. H. Kerry) The King Country: Explorations in* New Zealand. Many Illustrations and Map. New Edition, 8vo, 21*s.*

*Nordhoff (C.) California, for Health, Pleasure, and Residence.* New Edition, 8vo, with Maps and Illustrations, 12*s.* 6*d.*

*Northbrook Gallery.* Edited by LORD RONALD GOWER. 36 Permanent Photographs. Imperial 4to, 63*s.*; large paper, 105*s.*

*Nott (Major) Wild Animals Photographed and Described.* 35*s.*

*Nursery Playmates (Prince of).* 217 Coloured Pictures for Children by eminent Artists. Folio, in coloured boards, 6*s.*

*O'BRIEN (R. B.) Fifty Years of Concessions to Ireland.* With a Portrait of T. Drummond. Vol. I., 16*s.*, II., 16*s.*

*Orient Line Guide Book.* By W. J. LOFTIE. 5*s.*

*Orvis (C. F.) Fishing with the Fly.* Illustrated. 8vo, 12*s.* 6*d.*

*Our Little Ones in Heaven.* Edited by the Rev. H. ROBBINS. With Frontispiece after Sir JOSHUA REYNOLDS. New Edition, 5*s.*

*Outing: Magazine of Outdoor Sports.* 1*s.* Monthly.

*Owen (Douglas) Marine Insurance Notes and Clauses.* New Edition, 14*s.*

*PALLISER (Mrs.) A History of Lace.* New Edition, with additional cuts and text. 8vo, 21*s.*

—— *The China Collector's Pocket Companion.* With upwards of 1000 Illustrations of Marks and Monograms. Small 8vo, 5*s.*

*Pascoe (C. E.) London of To-Day.* Illust., crown 8vo, 3*s.* 6*d.*

*Payne (T. O.) Solomon's Temple and Capitol, Ark of the Flood* and Tabernacle (four sections at 24*s.*), extra binding, 105*s.*

*Pennell (H. Cholmondeley) Sporting Fish of Great Britain.* 15*s.*; large paper, 30*s.*

*Pharmacopœia of the United States of America.* 8vo, 21*s.*

*Philpot (H. J.) Diabetes Mellitus.* Crown 8vo, 5*s.*

—— *Diet System.* Tables. I. Dyspepsia; II. Gout; III. Diabetes; IV. Corpulence. In cases, 1*s.* each.

*Plunkett (Major G. T.) Primer of Orthographic Projection.* Elementary Practical Solid Geometry clearly explained. With Problems and Exercises. Specially adapted for Science and Art Classes, and for Students who have not the aid of a Teacher. 2*s.*

*Poe (E. A.) The Raven.* Illustr. by DORÉ. Imperial folio, 63*s.*

*Poems of the Inner Life.* Chiefly from Modern Authors. Small 8vo, 5*s.*

*Polar Expeditions.* See GILDER, MARKHAM, MCCORMICK.

*Porter (Noah) Elements of Moral Science.* 10*s.* 6*d.*

*Portraits of Celebrated Race-horses of the Past and Present* Centuries, with Pedigrees and Performances. 31*s.* 6*d.* per vol.

*Powell (W.) Wanderings in a Wild Country; or, Three Years* among the Cannibals of New Britain. Illustr., 8vo, 18*s.*; cr. 8vo, 5*s.*

*Poynter (Edward J., R.A.).* See "Illustrated Text-books."

*Pritt (T. E.) North Country Flies.* Illustrated from the Author's Drawings. 10*s.* 6*d.*

*Publishers' Circular (The), and General Record of British and* Foreign Literature. Published on the 1st and 15th of every Month, 3*d.*

*REBER (F.) History of Ancient Art.* 8vo, 18*s.*

*Redford (G.) Ancient Sculpture.* New edition. Crown 8vo, 10*s.* 6*d.*

*Richter (Dr. Jean Paul) Italian Art in the National Gallery.* 4to. Illustrated. Cloth gilt, 2*l.* 2*s.*; half-morocco, uncut, 2*l.* 12*s.* 6*d.*

—— See also LEONARDO DA VINCI.

*Riddell (Mrs. J. H.)* See LOW'S STANDARD NOVELS.

*Robin Hood; Merry Adventures of.* Written and illustrated by HOWARD PYLE. Imperial 8vo, 15*s.*

*Robinson (Phil.) In my Indian Garden.* Crown 8vo, limp cloth, 3*s.* 6*d.*

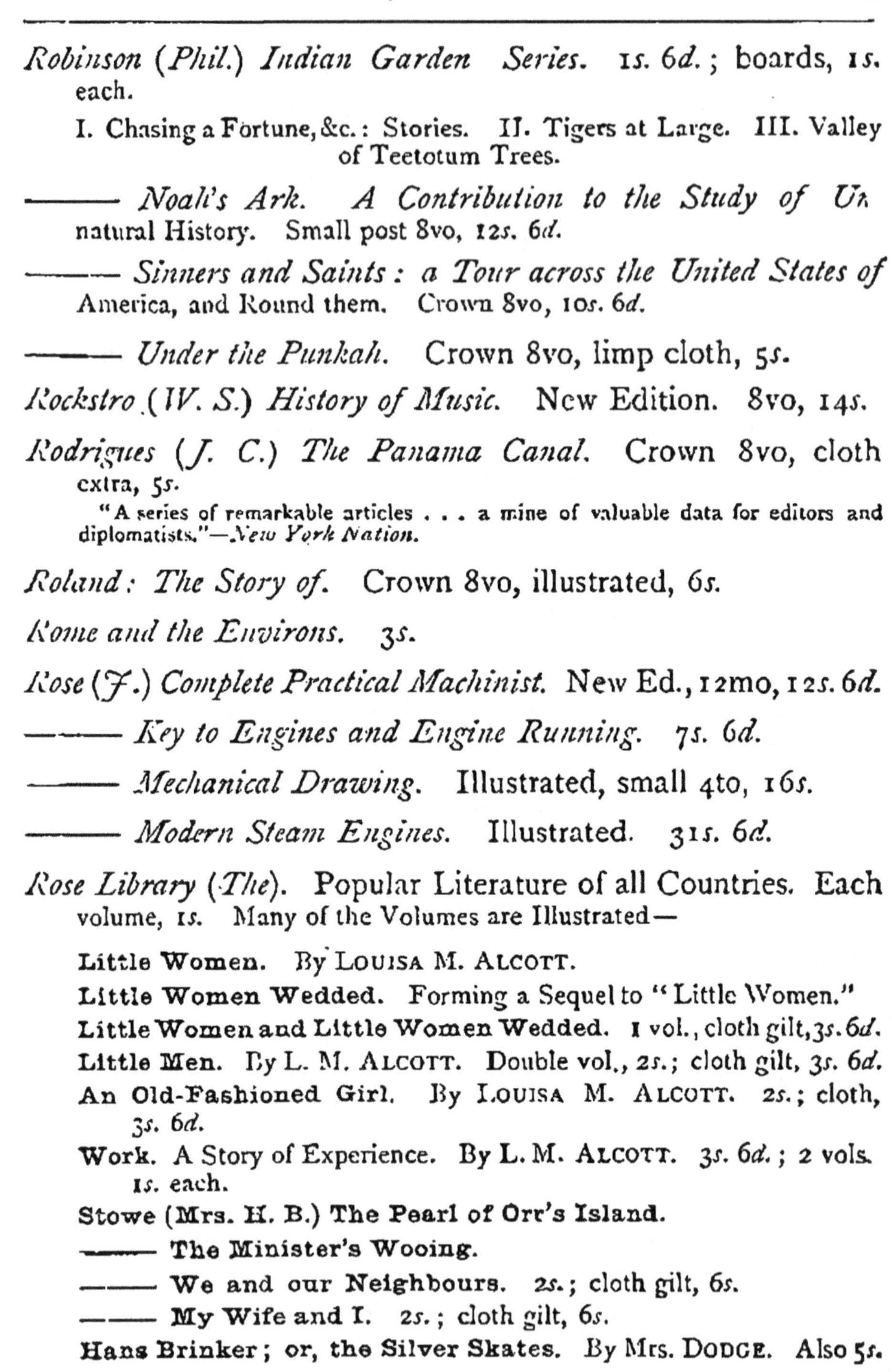

*Robinson* (*Phil.*) *Indian Garden Series.* 1*s.* 6*d.*; boards, 1*s.* each.

I. Chasing a Fortune, &c.: Stories. II. Tigers at Large. III. Valley of Teetotum Trees.

—— *Noah's Ark. A Contribution to the Study of Unnatural History.* Small post 8vo, 12*s.* 6*d.*

—— *Sinners and Saints: a Tour across the United States of America, and Round them.* Crown 8vo, 10*s.* 6*d.*

—— *Under the Punkah.* Crown 8vo, limp cloth, 5*s.*

*Rockstro* (*W. S.*) *History of Music.* New Edition. 8vo, 14*s.*

*Rodrigues* (*J. C.*) *The Panama Canal.* Crown 8vo, cloth extra, 5*s.*

"A series of remarkable articles . . . a mine of valuable data for editors and diplomatists."—*New York Nation.*

*Roland: The Story of.* Crown 8vo, illustrated, 6*s.*

*Rome and the Environs.* 3*s.*

*Rose* (*J.*) *Complete Practical Machinist.* New Ed., 12mo, 12*s.* 6*d.*

—— *Key to Engines and Engine Running.* 7*s.* 6*d.*

—— *Mechanical Drawing.* Illustrated, small 4to, 16*s.*

—— *Modern Steam Engines.* Illustrated. 31*s.* 6*d.*

*Rose Library* (*The*). Popular Literature of all Countries. Each volume, 1*s.* Many of the Volumes are Illustrated—

**Little Women.** By LOUISA M. ALCOTT.
**Little Women Wedded.** Forming a Sequel to "Little Women."
**Little Women and Little Women Wedded.** 1 vol., cloth gilt, 3*s.* 6*d.*
**Little Men.** By L. M. ALCOTT. Double vol., 2*s.*; cloth gilt, 3*s.* 6*d.*
**An Old-Fashioned Girl.** By LOUISA M. ALCOTT. 2*s.*; cloth, 3*s.* 6*d.*
**Work.** A Story of Experience. By L. M. ALCOTT. 3*s.* 6*d.*; 2 vols. 1*s.* each.
**Stowe (Mrs. H. B.) The Pearl of Orr's Island.**
—— **The Minister's Wooing.**
—— **We and our Neighbours.** 2*s.*; cloth gilt, 6*s.*
—— **My Wife and I.** 2*s.*; cloth gilt, 6*s.*
**Hans Brinker; or, the Silver Skates.** By Mrs. DODGE. Also 5*s.*

*Rose Library (The)—continued.*

**My Study Windows.** By J. R. LOWELL.

**The Guardian Angel.** By OLIVER WENDELL HOLMES.

**My Summer in a Garden.** By C. D. WARNER.

**Dred.** By Mrs. BEECHER STOWE. 2*s.*; cloth gilt, 3*s.* 6*d.*

**Farm Ballads.** By WILL CARLETON.

**Farm Festivals.** By WILL CARLETON.

**Farm Legends.** By WILL CARLETON.

**Farm Ballads: Festivals and Legends.** One vol., cloth, 3*s.* 6*d.*

**The Clients of Dr. Bernagius.** 3*s.* 6*d.*; 2 parts, 1*s.* each.

**The Undiscovered Country.** By W. D. HOWELLS. 3*s.* 6*d.* and 1*s.*

**Baby Rue.** By C. M. CLAY. 3*s.* 6*d.* and 1*s.*

**The Rose in Bloom.** By L. M. ALCOTT. 2*s.*; cloth gilt, 3*s.* 6*d.*

**Eight Cousins.** By L. M. ALCOTT. 2*s.*; cloth gilt, 3*s.* 6*d.*

**Under the Lilacs.** By L. M. ALCOTT. 2*s.*; also 3*s.* 6*d.*

**Silver Pitchers.** By LOUISA M. ALCOTT. Cloth, 3*s.* 6*d.*

**Jemmy's Cruise in the "Pinafore,"** and other Tales. By LOUISA M. ALCOTT. 2*s.*; cloth gilt, 3*s.* 6*d.*

**Jack and Jill.** By LOUISA M. ALCOTT. 2*s.*; Illustrated, 5*s.*

**Hitherto.** By the Author of the "Gayworthys." 2 vols., 1*s.* each; 1 vol., cloth gilt, 3*s.* 6*d.*

**A Gentleman of Leisure.** A Novel. By EDGAR FAWCETT. 1*s.*

**The Story of Helen Troy.** 1*s.*

*Ross (Mars) and Stonehewer Cooper. Highlands of Cantabria;* or, Three Days from England. Illustrations and Map, 8vo, 21*s.*

*Round the Yule Log: Norwegian Folk and Fairy Tales.* Translated from the Norwegian of P. CHR. ASBJÖRNSEN. With 100 Illustrations after drawings by Norwegian Artists, and an Introduction by E. W. Gosse. Impl. 16mo, cloth extra, gilt edges, 7*s.* 6*d.* and 5*s.*

*Rousselet (Louis) Son of the Constable of France.* Small post 8vo, numerous Illustrations, 5*s.*

——— *King of the Tigers: a Story of Central India.* Illustrated. Small post 8vo, gilt, 6*s.*; plainer, 5*s.*

——— *Drummer Boy.* Illustrated. Small post 8vo, 5*s.*

*Rowbotham (F.) Trip to Prairie Land.* The Shady Side of Emigration. 5*s.*

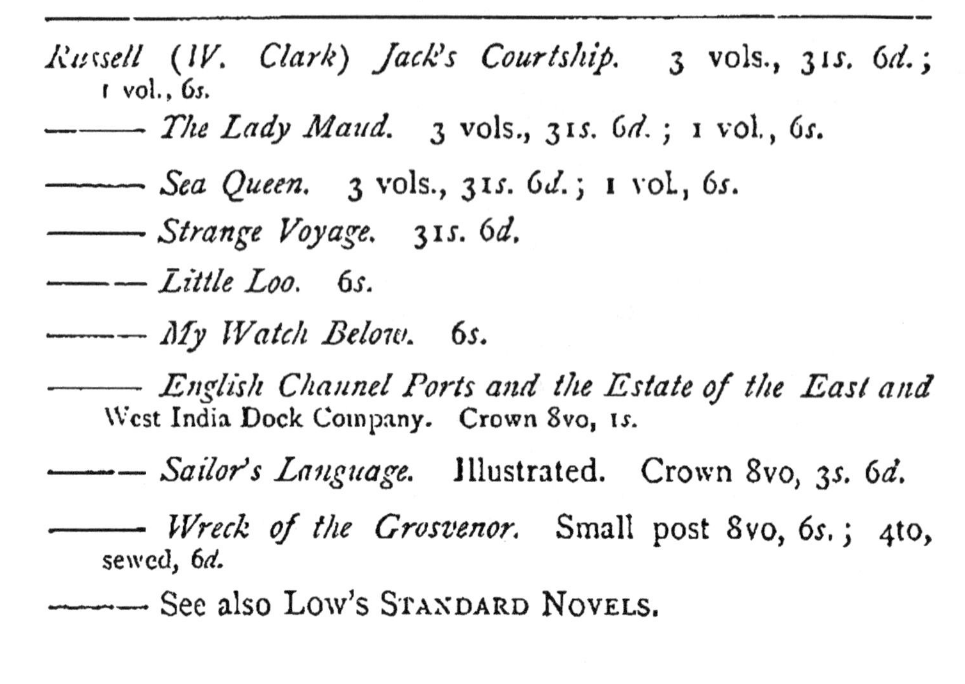

*Russell (W. Clark) Jack's Courtship.* 3 vols., 31*s.* 6*d.*; 1 vol., 6*s.*

—— *The Lady Maud.* 3 vols., 31*s.* 6*d.*; 1 vol., 6*s.*

—— *Sea Queen.* 3 vols., 31*s.* 6*d.*; 1 vol., 6*s.*

—— *Strange Voyage.* 31*s.* 6*d.*

—— *Little Loo.* 6*s.*

—— *My Watch Below.* 6*s.*

—— *English Channel Ports and the Estate of the East and* West India Dock Company. Crown 8vo, 1*s.*

—— *Sailor's Language.* Illustrated. Crown 8vo, 3*s.* 6*d.*

—— *Wreck of the Grosvenor.* Small post 8vo, 6*s.*; 4to, sewed, 6*d.*

—— See also Low's STANDARD NOVELS.

*SAINTS and their Symbols: A Companion in the Churches* and Picture Galleries of Europe. Illustrated. Royal 16mo, 3*s.* 6*d.*

*Salisbury (Lord) Life and Speeches.* By F. S. PULLING, M.A. With Photogravure Portrait of Lord Salisbury. 2 vols., cr. 8vo, 21*s.*

*Sandilands (J. P.) How to Develop Vocal Power.* 1*s.*

*Saunders (A.) Our Domestic Birds: Poultry in England and* New Zealand. Crown 8vo, 6*s.*

—— *Our Horses: the Best Muscles controlled by the Best* Brains. 6*s.*

*Scherr (Prof. J.) History of English Literature.* Cr. 8vo, 8*s.* 6*d.*

*Schley. Rescue of Greely.* Maps and Illustrations, 8vo, 12*s.* 6*d.*

*Schuyler (Eugène) American Diplomacy and the Furtherance of* Commerce. 12*s.* 6*d.*

—— *The Life of Peter the Great.* 2 vols., 8vo, 32*s.*

*Schweinfurth (Georg) Heart of Africa.* Three Years' Travels and Adventures in Unexplored Regions. 2 vols., crown 8vo, 15*s*.

*Scott (Leader) Renaissance of Art in Italy.* 4to, 31*s*. 6*d*.

——— *Sculpture, Renaissance and Modern.* 5*s*.

*Senior (W.) Waterside Sketches.* Imp. 32mo, 1*s*.6*d*., boards, 1*s*.

*Shadbolt (S. H.) Afghan Campaigns of* 1878—1880. By SYDNEY SHADBOLT. 2 vols., royal quarto, cloth extra, 3*l*.

*Shakespeare.* Edited by R. GRANT WHITE. 3 vols., crown 8vo, gilt top, 36*s*.; *édition de luxe*, 6 vols., 8vo, cloth extra, 63*s*.

*Shakespeare.* See also WHITE (R. GRANT).

*Sidney (Sir Philip) Arcadia.* New Edition, 6*s*.

*Siegfried: The Story of.* Illustrated, crown 8vo, cloth, 6*s*.

*Simson (A.) Wilds of Ecuador and the Putumayor River.* Crown 8vo.

*Sinclair (Mrs.) Indigenous Flowers of the Hawaiian Islands.* 44 Plates in Colour. Imp. folio, extra binding, gilt edges, 31*s*. 6*d*.

*Sir Roger de Coverley.* Re-imprinted from the "Spectator." With 125 Woodcuts and special steel Frontispiece. Small fcap. 4to, 6*s*.

*Smith (G.) Assyrian Explorations and Discoveries.* Illustrated by Photographs and Woodcuts. New Edition, demy 8vo, 18*s*.

——— *The Chaldean Account of Genesis.* With many Illustrations. 16*s*. New Ed. By PROFESSOR SAYCE. 8vo, 18*s*.

*Smith (J. Moyr) Ancient Greek Female Costume.* 112 full-page Plates and other Illustrations. Crown 8vo, 7*s*. 6*d*.

——— *Hades of Ardenne: The Caves of Han.* Crown 8vo, Illust., 5*s*.

——— *Legendary Studies, and other Sketches for Decorative* Figure Panels. 7*s*. 6*d*.

——— *Wooing of Æthra.* Illustrated. 32mo, 1*s*.

*Smith (Sydney) Life and Times.* By STUART J. REID. Illustrated. 8vo, 21*s*.

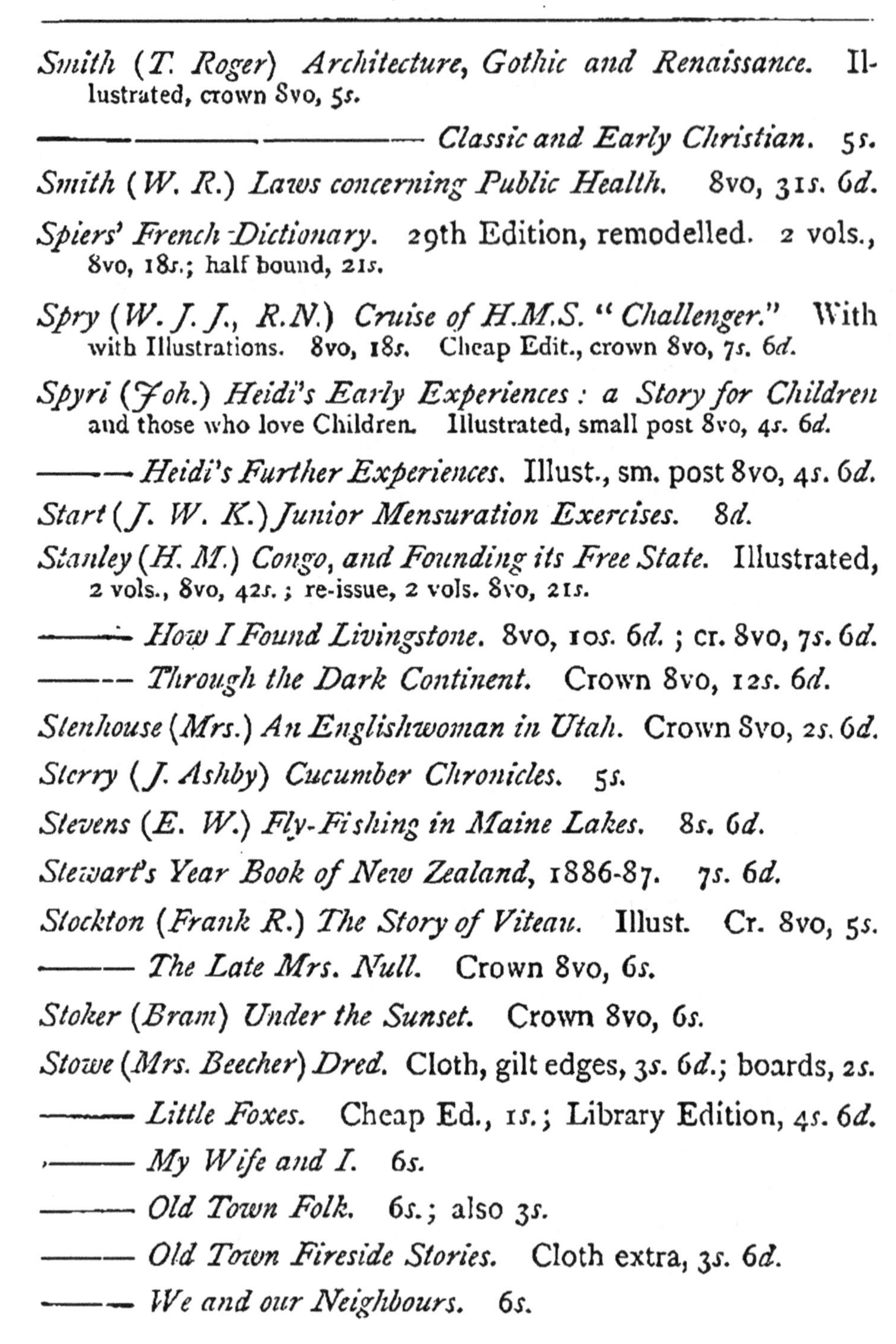

*Smith (T. Roger) Architecture, Gothic and Renaissance.* Illustrated, crown 8vo, 5*s*.

——— ——— ——— *Classic and Early Christian.* 5*s*.

*Smith (W. R.) Laws concerning Public Health.* 8vo, 31*s*. 6*d*.

*Spiers' French-Dictionary.* 29th Edition, remodelled. 2 vols., 8vo, 18*s*.; half bound, 21*s*.

*Spry (W. J. J., R.N.) Cruise of H.M.S. "Challenger."* With with Illustrations. 8vo, 18*s*. Cheap Edit., crown 8vo, 7*s*. 6*d*.

*Spyri (Joh.) Heidi's Early Experiences: a Story for Children* and those who love Children. Illustrated, small post 8vo, 4*s*. 6*d*.

——— *Heidi's Further Experiences.* Illust., sm. post 8vo, 4*s*. 6*d*.

*Start (J. W. K.) Junior Mensuration Exercises.* 8*d*.

*Stanley (H. M.) Congo, and Founding its Free State.* Illustrated, 2 vols., 8vo, 42*s*.; re-issue, 2 vols. 8vo, 21*s*.

——— *How I Found Livingstone.* 8vo, 10*s*. 6*d*.; cr. 8vo, 7*s*. 6*d*.

——— *Through the Dark Continent.* Crown 8vo, 12*s*. 6*d*.

*Stenhouse (Mrs.) An Englishwoman in Utah.* Crown 8vo, 2*s*. 6*d*.

*Sterry (J. Ashby) Cucumber Chronicles.* 5*s*.

*Stevens (E. W.) Fly-Fishing in Maine Lakes.* 8*s*. 6*d*.

*Stewart's Year Book of New Zealand*, 1886-87. 7*s*. 6*d*.

*Stockton (Frank R.) The Story of Viteau.* Illust. Cr. 8vo, 5*s*.

——— *The Late Mrs. Null.* Crown 8vo, 6*s*.

*Stoker (Bram) Under the Sunset.* Crown 8vo, 6*s*.

*Stowe (Mrs. Beecher) Dred.* Cloth, gilt edges, 3*s*. 6*d*.; boards, 2*s*.

——— *Little Foxes.* Cheap Ed., 1*s*.; Library Edition, 4*s*. 6*d*.

——— *My Wife and I.* 6*s*.

——— *Old Town Folk.* 6*s*.; also 3*s*.

——— *Old Town Fireside Stories.* Cloth extra, 3*s*. 6*d*.

——— *We and our Neighbours.* 6*s*.

*Stowe* (*Mrs. Beecher*) *Poganuc People.* 6*s.*

—— *Chimney Corner.* 1*s.*; cloth, 1*s.* 6*d.*

—— See also ROSE LIBRARY.

*Stuttfield* (*Hugh E. M.*) *El Maghreb : 1200 Miles' Ride through Marocco.* 8*s.* 6*d.*

*Sullivan* (*A. M.*) *Nutshell History of Ireland.* Paper boards, 6*d.*

*Sutton* (*A. K.*) *A B C Digest of the Bankruptcy Law.* 8vo, 3*s.* and 2*s.* 6*d.*

*TAINE* (*H. A.*) "*Les Origines de la France Contemporaine.*" Translated by JOHN DURAND.

| | | | |
|---|---|---|---|
| I. | **The Ancient Regime.** | Demy 8vo, cloth, 16*s.* | |
| II. | **The French Revolution.** | Vol. 1. | do. |
| III. | **Do. do.** | Vol. 2. | do. |
| IV. | **Do. do.** | Vol. 3. | do. |

*Talbot* (*Hon. E.*) *A Letter on Emigration.* 1*s.*

*Tauchnitz's English Editions of German Authors.* Each volume, cloth flexible, 2*s.*; or sewed, 1*s.* 6*d.* (Catalogues post free.)

*Tauchnitz* (*B.*) *German Dictionary.* 2*s.*; paper, 1*s.* 6*d.*; roan, 2*s.* 6*d.*

—— *French Dictionary.* 2*s.*; paper, 1*s.* 6*d.*; roan, 2*s.* 6*d.*

—— *Italian Dictionary.* 2*s.*; paper, 1*s.* 6*d.*; roan, 2*s.* 6*d.*

—— *Latin Dictionary.* 2*s.*; paper, 1*s.* 6*d.*; roan, 2*s.* 6*d.*

—— *Spanish and English.* 2*s.*; paper, 1*s.* 6*d.*; roan, 2*s.* 6*d.*

—— *Spanish and French.* 2*s.*; paper, 1*s.* 6*d.*; roan, 2*s.* 6*d.*

*Taylor* (*R. L.*) *Chemical Analysis Tables.* 1*s.*

*Taylor* (*W. M.*) *Joseph the Prime Minister.* 6*s.*

—— *Paul the Missionary.* Crown 8vo, 7*s.* 6*d.*

*Techno-Chemical Receipt Book.* With additions by BRANNT and WAHL. 10*s.* 6*d.*

*Thausing* (*Prof.*) *Malt and the Fabrication of Beer.* 8vo, 45*s.*

*Theakston* (*M.*) *British Angling Flies.* Illustrated. Cr. 8vo, 5*s.*

*Thomson* (*Jos.*) *Through Masai Land.* Illust. and Maps. 21*s.*

*Thomson (W.) Algebra for Colleges and Schools.* With Answers, 5*s.*; without, 4*s.* 6*d.*; Answers separate, 1*s.* 6*d.*

*Thoreau. American Men of Letters.* Crown 8vo, 2*s.* 6*d.*

*Tissandier, Photography.* Edited by J. THOMSON, with Appendix by H. FOX TALBOT. Illustrated. 6*s.*

*Tolhausen. Supplément du Dictionnaire Technologique.* 3*s.* 6*d.*

*Tristram (Rev. Canon) Pathways of Palestine.* Series I., with Permanent Photographs. 2 vols., folio, cloth, gilt edges, 31*s.* 6*d.* each.

*Trollope (Anthony) Thompson Hall.* 1*s.*

*Tromholt (S.) Under the Rays of the Aurora Borealis.* By C. SIEWERS. Photographs and Portraits. 2 vols., 8vo, 30*s.*

*Tucker (W. J.) Life and Society in Eastern Europe.* 15*s.*

*Tupper (Martin Farquhar) My Life as an Author.* 14*s.*

*Turner (Edward) Studies in Russian Literature.* Cr. 8vo, 8*s.* 6*d.*

*UNION Jack (The). Every Boy's Paper.* Edited by G. A. HENTY. Profusely Illustrated with Coloured and other Plates. Vol. I., 6*s.* Vols. II., III., IV., 7*s.* 6*d.* each.

*VALLANCE (Lucy) Paul's Birthday.* 3*s.* 6*d.*

*Van Kampen (S. R.) Nicholas Godfried Van Kampen: a* Biographical Sketch By SAMUEL R. VAN CAMPEN. 14*s.*

*Vasili (Count) Berlin Society.* Translated. Cr. 8vo, 6*s.*

—— *World of London (La Société de Londres).* Cr. 8vo, 6*s.*

*Victoria (Queen) Life of.* By GRACE GREENWOOD. Illust. 6*s.*

*Vincent (Mrs. Howard) Forty Thousand Miles over Land and* Water. With Illustrations. New Edti., 3*s.* 6*d.*

*Viollet-le-Duc (E.) Lectures on Architecture.* Translated by BENJAMIN BUCKNALL, Architect. With 33 Steel Plates and 200 Wood Engravings. Super-royal 8vo, leather back, gilt top, 2 vols., 3*l.* 3*s.*

# BOOKS BY JULES VERNE.

| Large Crown 8vo. | Containing 350 to 600 pp. and from 50 to 100 full-page illustrations. | | Containing the whole of the text with some illustrations. | |
|---|---|---|---|---|
| WORKS. | In very handsome cloth binding, gilt edges. | In plainer binding, plain edges. | In cloth binding, gilt edges, smaller type. | Coloured boards. |
| | s. d. | s. d. | s. d. | |
| 20,000 Leagues under the Sea. Parts I. and II. . . . . . . . | 10 6 | 5 0 | 3 6 | 2 vols., 1s. each. |
| Hector Servadac . . . . . . . | 10 6 | 5 0 | 3 6 | 2 vols., 1s. each. |
| The Fur Country . . . . . . . | 10 6 | 5 0 | 3 6 | 2 vols., 1s. each. |
| The Earth to the Moon and a Trip round it . . . . . . . . . | 10 6 | 5 0 | 2 vols., 2s. ea. | 2 vols., 1s. each. |
| Michael Strogoff . . . . . . | 10 6 | 5 0 | 3 6 | 2 vols., 1s. each. |
| Dick Sands, the Boy Captain . . | 10 6 | 5 0 | 3 6 | 2 vols., 1s. each. |
| Five Weeks in a Balloon . . . | 7 6 | 3 6 | 2 0 | 1s. 0d. |
| Adventures of Three Englishmen and Three Russians . . . . | 7 6 | 3 6 | 2 0 | 1 0 |
| Round the World in Eighty Days | 7 6 | 3 6 | 2 0 | 1 0 |
| A Floating City . . . . . . . | 7 6 | 3 6 | 2 0 | 1 0 |
| The Blockade Runners . . . . | | | 2 0 | 1 0 |
| Dr. Ox's Experiment . . . . . | — | — | 2 0 | 1 0 |
| A Winter amid the Ice . . . . | — | — | 2 0 | 1 0 |
| Survivors of the "Chancellor" . | 7 6 | 3 6 | 3 6 | 2 vols., 1s. each. |
| Martin Paz . . . . . . . . | | | 2 0 | 1s. 0d. |
| The Mysterious Island, 3 vols.:— | 22 6 | 10 6 | 6 0 | 3 0 |
| I. Dropped from the Clouds . | 7 6 | 3 6 | 2 0 | 1 0 |
| II. Abandoned . . . . . . | 7 6 | 3 6 | 2 0 | 1 0 |
| III. Secret of the Island . . . | 7 6 | 3 6 | 2 0 | 1 0 |
| The Child of the Cavern . . . . | 7 6 | 3 6 | 2 0 | 1 0 |
| The Begum's Fortune . . . . | 7 6 | 3 6 | 2 0 | 1 0 |
| The Tribulations of a Chinaman . | 7 6 | 3 6 | 2 0 | 1 0 |
| The Steam House, 2 vols.:— | | | | |
| I. Demon of Cawnpore . . . | 7 6 | 3 6 | 2 0 | 1 0 |
| II. Tigers and Traitors . . . | 7 6 | 3 6 | 2 0 | 1 0 |
| The Giant Raft, 2 vols.:— | | | | |
| I. 800 Leagues on the Amazon | 7 6 | 3 6 | 2 0 | 1 0 |
| II. The Cryptogram . . . . | 7 6 | 3 6 | 2 0 | 1 0 |
| The Green Ray . . . . . . . . | 6 0 | 5 0 | — | 1 0 |
| Godfrey Morgan . . . . . . . | 7 6 | 3 6 | 2 0 | 1 0 |
| Kéraban the Inflexible:— | | | | |
| I. Captain of the "Guidara". | 7 6 | 3 6 | 2 0 | 1 0 |
| II. Scarpante the Spy. . . . | 7 6 | 3 6 | 2 0 | 1 0 |
| The Archipelago on Fire. . . . | 7 6 | | | |
| The Vanished Diamond . . . . | 7 6 | | | |
| Mathias Sandorf . . . . . . | 10 6 | | | |
| The Lottery Ticket . . . . . . | 7 6 | | | |

Celebrated Travels and Travellers. 3 vols. 8vo, 600 pp., 100 full-page illustrations, 12s. 6d. gilt edges, 14s. each:—(1) The Exploration of the World. (2) The Great Navigators of the Eighteenth Century. (3) The Great Explorers of the Nineteenth Century.

*WAHL (W. H.) Galvanoplastic Manipulation for the* Electro-Plater. 8vo, 35*s*.

*Wakefield. Aix-les-Bains: Bathing and Attractions.* 2*s*. 6*d*.

*Wallace (L.) Ben Hur: A Tale of the Christ.* Crown 8vo, 6*s*.

*Waller (Rev. C. H.) The Names on the Gates of Pearl,* and other Studies. New Edition. Crown 8vo, cloth extra, 3*s*. 6*d*.

—— *A Grammar and Analytical Vocabulary of the Words in* the Greek Testament. Compiled from Brüder's Concordance. Part I. Grammar. Small post 8vo, cloth, 2*s*. 6*d*. Part II. Vocabulary, 2*s*. 6*d*.

—— *Adoption and the Covenant.* On Confirmation. 2*s*. 6*d*.

—— *Silver Sockets; and other Shadows of Redemption.* Sermons at Christ Church, Hampstead. Small post 8vo, 6*s*.

*Walton (Iz.) Wallet Book,* CIↃIↃLXXXV. 21*s*.; l. p. 42*s*.

—— *(T. H.) Coal Mining.* With Illustrations. 4to, 25*s*.

*Warner (C. D.) My Summer in a Garden.* Boards, 1*s*.; leatherette, 1*s*. 6*d*.; cloth, 2*s*.

*Warren (W. F.) Paradise Found; the North Pole the Cradle* of the Human Race. Illustrated. Crown 8vo, 12*s*. 6*d*.

*Washington Irving's Little Britain.* Square crown 8vo, 6*s*.

*Watson (P. B.) Marcus Aurelius Antoninus.* 8vo, 15*s*.

*Webster.* ("American Men of Letters.") 18mo, 2*s*. 6*d*.

*Weir (Harrison) Animal Stories, Old and New, told in Pic*tures and Prose. Coloured, &c., Illustrations. 56 pp., 4to, 5*s*.

*Wells (H. P.) American Salmon Fisherman.* 6*s*.

—— *Fly Rods and Fly Tackle.* Illustrated. 10*s*. 6*d*.

—— *(J. W.) Three Thousand Miles through Brazil.* Illustrated from Original Sketches. 2 vols. 8vo, 32*s*.

*Wheatley (H. B.) and Delamotte (P. H.) Art Work in Porce*lain. Large 8vo, 2*s*. 6*d*.

—— *Art Work in Gold and Silver. Modern.* 2*s*. 6*d*.

—— *Handbook of Decorative Art.* 10*s*. 6*d*.

*Whisperings.* Poems. Small post 8vo, gilt edges, 3*s*. 6*d*.

*White (R. Grant) England Without and Within.* Crown 8vo, 10*s*. 6*d*.

—— *Every-day English.* 10*s*. 6*d*. Words, &c.

—— *Fate of Mansfield Humphreys, the Episode of Mr.* Washington Adams in England, an Apology, &c. Crown 8vo, 6*s*.

—— *Studies in Shakespeare.* 10*s*. 6*d*.

—— *Words and their Uses.* New Edit., crown 8vo, 5*s*.

*Whittier (J. G.) The King's Missive, and later Poems.* 18mo, choice parchment cover, 3*s*. 6*d*.

*Whittier (J. G.) The Whittier Birthday Book.* Uniform with the "Emerson Birthday Book." Square 16mo, very choice binding, 3*s.* 6*d.*

——— *Life of.* By R. A. UNDERWOOD. Cr. 8vo, cloth, 10*s.* 6*d.*

——— *St. Gregory's Guest, &c.* Recent Poems. 5*s.*

*Williams (C. F.) Tariff Laws of the United States.* 8vo, 10*s.* 6*d.*

——— *(H. W.) Diseases of the Eye.* 8vo, 21*s.*

*Wills, A Few Hints on Proving, without Professional Assistance.* By a PROBATE COURT OFFICIAL. 8th Edition, revised, with Forms of Wills, Residuary Accounts, &c. Fcap. 8vo, cloth limp, 1*s.*

*Wills (Dr. C. J.) Persia as it is.* Crown 8vo.

*Willis-Bund (J.) Salmon Problems.* 3*s.* 6*d.*; boards, 2*s.* 6*d.*

*Wilson (Dr. Andrew) Health for the People.*

*Wimbledon (Viscount) Life and Times,* 1628-38. By C. DALTON. 2 vols., 8vo, 30*s.*

*Winsor (Justin) Narrative and Critical History of America.* 8 vols., 30*s.* each; large paper, per vol., 63*s.*

*Witthaus (R. A.) Medical Student's Chemistry.* 8vo, 16*s.*

*Woodbury, History of Wood Engraving.* Illustrated. 8vo, 18*s.*

*Woolsey. Introduction to International Law.* 5th Ed., 18*s.*

*Woolson (Constance F.)* See "Low's Standard Novels."

*Wright (H.) Friendship of God.* Portrait, &c. Crown 8vo, 6*s.*

*Wright (T.) Town of Cowper, Olney, &c.* 6*s.*

*Written to Order; the Journeyings of an Irresponsible Egotist.* By the Author of "A Day of my Life at Eton." Crown 8vo, 6*s.*

YRIARTE *(Charles) Florence: its History.* Translated by C. B. PITMAN. Illustrated with 500 Engravings. Large imperial 4to, extra binding, gilt edges, 63*s.*; or 12 Parts, 5*s.* each.

History; the Medici; the Humanists; letters; arts; the Renaissance; illustrious Florentines; Etruscan art; monuments; sculpture; painting.

---

**London:**

SAMPSON LOW, MARSTON, SEARLE, & RIVINGTON,

CROWN BUILDINGS, 188, FLEET STREET, E.C.